**“I’ve thought abou[illegible]
said at last. “The only solution is for me
to quit. You can hire someone else.”**

“Who?” Caleb challenged. “Widows with infants aren’t all that plentiful in Wolf Creek, and if I hired someone else it would just spark the same gossip we’re dealing with.”

Abby chewed on her lower lip. “I could take Betsy to my place,” she offered.

He shook his head. “We’ve already discussed that. She belongs at home. Winter will be here before we know it, and getting back and forth will be a nightmare when the weather gets bad. Besides, I already know how hard it is for you to manage things at your place, and I don’t think you can make it through the winter alone with three children.”

She sat down in her chair and rested her elbows on the table, regarding him with tear-glazed eyes. “What other choice do we have, Caleb? I can’t think of any other way.”

The full force of his silvery gaze met hers. “The only way I can think of is for you to marry me.”

Books by Penny Richards

Love Inspired Historical

Wolf Creek Wedding

Love Inspired

Unanswered Prayers

PENNY RICHARDS

has been writing and selling contemporary romance since 1983. Confronted with burnout, she took several years off to pursue other things she loved, like editing a local oral history project, coauthoring a stage play about a dead man (known fondly as Old Mike) who was found in the city park in 1911, got a double dose of embalming and remained on display until the seventies. Really. She also spent ten years renovating her 1902 Queen Anne home and getting it onto the National Register of Historic Places. At the "big house" she ran and operated Garden Getaways, a bed-and-breakfast and catering business that did everything from receptions, bridal lunches, fancy private dinners and "tastings" to dress-up tea parties (with makeup and all the trimmings) for little girls who liked to pretend to be grand ladies while receiving manners lessons. What fun!

Though she had a wonderful time and hosted people from every walk of life, writing was still in her blood, and her love of all things historical led her to historical fiction, more specifically historical mystery and inspirational romances. She is thrilled to be back writing and, God willing, hopes to continue to do so for many years.

Wolf Creek Wedding

PENNY RICHARDS

HARLEQUIN® LOVE INSPIRED® HISTORICAL

ISBN-13: 978-0-373-82988-0

WOLF CREEK WEDDING

This edition published by arrangement with Love Inspired Books.

www.Harlequin.com

Printed in U.S.A.

For the unbelieving husband is sanctified by the wife.

—*1 Corinthians* 7:14

This book is for Mom, my biggest cheerleader.
I owe all my creativity—cooking, writing, art,
all of it—to you. You were a great example.
Wish you were here to help me in the garden. I miss you.

ACKNOWLEDGMENTS

As always, thanks to LaRee and Sandy
for your input and encouragement.

Chapter One

Wolf Creek, Arkansas
October 1885

The faintest sound of a baby's crying was carried on the brisk October breeze. Dr. Rachel Stone's buggy pulled to a stop in front of a large, rambling farmhouse, which was located west of town, three miles down the road that led to Pisgah.

Forest-green shutters framed the front windows and contrasted with pristine white clapboards. A porch, complete with a green swing, spanned the front of the house. Autumn's chill was slow to arrive in southwest Arkansas. Blue morning glory climbed up posts toward the roof, and blankets of native clematis rambled onto the lawn, hundreds of tiny white flowers bobbing in the gentle breeze.

Abby Carter made a sound of disbelief, and her wide-eyed gaze found her friend's. On some level she'd known the Gentry family was one of the most affluent in Wolf Creek, but until now, she had never given it much thought.

Smiling at Abby's astonishment, Rachel climbed down and looped the reins over the hitching post. Rounding the carriage, she reached up to take baby Laura from Abby's arms.

"Mind your manners," Abby reminded six-year-old Ben as he scrambled down. Still wearing an expression of amazement, she jumped to the ground, and they all started up the broad steps of the porch.

They had barely reached the top when the front door crashed open. Abby's startled gaze flew to the face of the man who would be her new employer. Caleb Gentry. Wealthy gentleman farmer. Father of newly born Betsy. Widower, as of a few hours ago. He was a big man—tall, broad-shouldered and narrow-hipped, his features too chiseled and angular to be considered handsome. His clothes looked as if he'd slept in them—which he no doubt had, if he'd managed any sleep the previous night—and he was in dire need of a shave. His thick, coffee-brown hair stood on end, and there was a wild look in his steel-gray eyes.

He looked angry and unapproachable. Difficult. Abby's heart sank. What had she gotten into?

At the first sight of the quartet coming up the steps, Caleb flung open the door, relief sweeping through him. Their arrival offered welcome respite from the sickening churning of his stomach that had plagued him since Rachel emerged from his wife's room and informed him that Emily was dead. Stunning news to a man who had only recently come to terms with the idea of being a father.

Accustomed to dealing with the many unexpected problems that cropped up with the running of a successful farming operation and his most recent enterprise, a gravel business, Caleb felt that in general he handled his life with a certain competence. In the blink of an eye, though, he discovered things were going to be very different. When Rachel left him in charge of the baby while she went to talk to Abby Carter about becoming a wet nurse and to inform Emily's parents of her death, he'd known that he was not prepared to bear sole responsibility for every aspect of his daughter's welfare.

In fact, thus far, he'd done a miserable job of things.

The baby, whom he had named Betsy according to Emily's wishes, had spent more time crying than sleeping. Scared witless to hold her, he had nonetheless picked her up and patted, bounced and even tried singing to her. "Old Dan Tucker" vocalized in a gravelly baritone hadn't done a thing to still her wailing. He had drawn the line at diapering—she was just too little and it was too scary to handle her any more than necessary. No doubt she was wet as well as hungry, which is why he was so relieved to see the approaching foursome.

Rachel Stone led the way, carrying a baby who looked just under a year old. A boy of five or six followed her, and a slight blond-haired woman who must be Abby Carter brought up the rear.

"What the devil took you so long?" he growled, raking long fingers through hair that already stood on end.

"We got here as soon as we could," Rachel said in a conciliatory tone, ushering Ben ahead of her.

Betsy gave another ear-piercing wail. Without waiting for introductions, Caleb turned his wild-eyed gaze to the newcomer, grabbed her arm and hauled her through the doorway. "She's been screaming for hours," he snapped. "Do something."

Instead of answering, Abby Carter looked from the fingers gripping her upper arm into his eyes. Hers were calm, though he thought he detected a hint of reproach and maybe even irritation in their blue depths. He snatched his hand away, as if she were hot to the touch.

Without a word, Mrs. Carter crossed to the cradle sitting near the fireplace, where a small blaze kept the chill at bay. She took a diaper from a nearby stack and set about changing Betsy while murmuring whatever nonsensical things women say to children in need of comfort. Things that were missing from male vocabularies. Finished, she wrapped a flannel blanket around Betsy and looked at Rachel, a question in her eyes.

"The kitchen is through there," Rachel said, pointing. Without a word, Mrs. Carter disappeared through the doorway, bestowing the briefest glance on him as she passed.

Caleb planted his hands on his hips and dropped his head, silently berating himself for his impatience with the woman who had only come to help. From the kitchen, Betsy's crying stopped. Quiet, the first in hours, filled the room, bringing with it a calming peace that Caleb had sense enough to know was bound to be short-lived. He scrubbed a trembling hand down his face.

"I know it's nerve-racking," Rachel said. "You'll get used to it." Seeing the expression of panic return, she offered him a weary smile. "Abby can't fix everything, Caleb. Babies cry for lots of reasons, but everything is going to be fine. She's a good mother."

Caleb was not so sure about anything being fine ever again.

"Did the Emersons come while I was gone?" Rachel asked.

He nodded. "Your dad sent someone…for Emily. They're coming back later to see Betsy."

"Well, then," Rachel said, setting Mrs. Carter's baby on the floor, "I'll just take care of the birthing room, help get Abby settled and get back to town."

She gave Ben instructions to keep an eye on his sister, and disappeared into the room Emily had moved to early in her pregnancy because his "tossing and turning" kept her awake.

With silence reigning in the kitchen and the knowledge that Abby Carter was there to help smooth out this new wrinkle in his life, a sudden weariness overtook Caleb. Huffing out a deep sigh, he sank into a corner of the camelback sofa and revisited the events that had changed his life forever.

More than four hours ago, the crying and pleading and screaming had stopped, replaced by the sudden, angry wail of a baby. The reprieve lasted only until Rachel stepped into the room carrying a small bundle in her arms and told him that he had a daughter and that Emily was dead. He was trying to assimilate that fact when Rachel informed him the baby would require a wet nurse and suggested recently widowed Abigail Carter. His head spinning with the gravity and magnitude of the events unfolding in his life, Caleb acquiesced and sent Rachel on her way.

A log fell in the fireplace, bringing him out of his drowsy trance. His glance wandered toward the kitchen. Thank goodness Rachel had been right about Mrs. Carter's willingness to help.

In the kitchen, Abby's tender gaze lingered on the face of the baby in her arms while her fingertips skimmed the incomparable softness of Betsy's dark hair. Was there anything more precious than a new life or anything sadder than a child growing up without the love and guidance of a parent? She was struck with a sudden pang of loss. Even now, eight months after William's death, she often experienced a stark reminder that he would not be there to share or to help with the joys and trials that cropped up daily with Ben and Laura. As difficult as it had been for her since he died, she knew life would be just as trying for Caleb Gentry, though in an entirely different way, something that she'd understood full well when Rachel had arrived earlier and told her the news of Emily Gentry's death.

"How awful!" Abby had said. "I can certainly sympathize with Mr. Gentry's loss." She'd never met Caleb Gentry, but she knew who he was, as did everyone in Pike County.

"Of everyone I know, I knew you'd understand," Rachel told her.

"You look worn out," Abby noted, ushering her friend inside. "Come on into the kitchen and rest a bit. I just took some cookies from the oven and I'm rewarming the breakfast coffee."

"Thanks, but I can't stay," Rachel told her. "Too many things to do. Before I drove out here, I had to go and tell the Emersons about Emily so that they could make arrangements for her body to be moved."

"They must be devastated," Abby said, unable to imagine losing either of her children. "What can I do to help? Make Mr. Gentry a meal?"

"Under different circumstances, I'm sure that would be appreciated, but that isn't why I'm here. To be blunt, little Betsy Gentry is in need of a wet nurse." Rachel hurried on before Abby could object. "I know things have been tight for you since William died, and I thought you might be glad of the extra money."

Abby stared into Rachel's dark eyes, her mind whirling with implications of the unexpected offer. For months now, she had systematically, often tearfully, sold almost everything she owned of value, consoling herself with the maxim that her father's pocket watch and her mother's silver coffee service were just *things*. Things she did not *need*. She had juggled the meager funds and prayed for some sort of miracle to provide for her children. She'd even considered trying to teach again, but Wolf Creek was no different from other towns, which wanted only men or unmarried women instructing their young ones. Even if that were not the case, she wasn't sure how she'd manage a full-time job with two children of her own.

God will provide...He never shuts a door that He doesn't open a window...all things work for good.

Abby was familiar with all the platitudes, had even heard them coming from her own lips when the trials and losses were someone else's. She believed what the Bible said, and blamed the weakness of her faith that allowed worry to creep in, even though the Lord always came through.

Like now. Here was Rachel with the answer to her prayers, though the answer she offered in no way resembled anything Abby had considered during the long, worrisome nights. *Wet nurse!*

There was no one left to ask for help. Nathan Haversham at the bank had been more than understanding, but when she'd last spoken to him, he'd explained that he couldn't let his sympathy get in the way of the bank's business much longer, and just last week, she'd received a letter giving her a month to come up with the necessary funds or she would receive a notice of foreclosure.

She lifted a brimming blue gaze to Rachel's. When she spoke, her voice was as unsteady as her smile. "In truth, it's the answer to my prayers. When do I start?"

Rachel flipped open the cover of the gold watch that hung from a chain around her neck. "How about we gather up enough to tide you and the children over for a few days? I'll drive you to Caleb's, clean things up and help you get settled."

"Now?" Abby had asked, stunned.

Rachel had offered her a wan smile. "I imagine Miss

Betsy Gentry is getting mighty hungry about now, and I'm sure her daddy is pacing the floor and tearing at his hair, wondering what in the world he's supposed to do about it."

Abby had gone about gathering up as much from her kitchen as she could on such short notice, and grabbing the clothes she and the children would need for the next couple of days.

Now, remembering the conversation, a smile claimed Abby's lips. Rachel's description of Caleb Gentry had been right on the mark. When she'd seen him framed in his doorway, he'd looked exactly as if he'd been tearing at his too-long hair.

She smiled down at the sleeping baby. Wealthy or not, Betsy Gentry's daddy could still get as ruffled as the next man. Somehow the thought made him a bit less intimidating.

The sound of something crashing to the floor sent Abby's gaze flying to the kitchen door, her smile of contentment changing into a frown. She couldn't imagine what had happened, but suspected it had something to do with her children. There was nothing to do but go and see.

The sound of something breaking sent Caleb bolting up from the sofa. Realizing that he must have dozed, he rubbed at his gritty eyes and looked around to see what had caused the noise. It didn't take long to spot the shepherdess figurine that had belonged to his mother. Caleb had found it tucked away in one of his father's drawers after his death. Now the keepsake lay in dozens of broken fragments on the heart-pine floor. Abby Carter's son stood looking at him, guilt and fear stamped on his freckled face.

Caleb's lips tightened. The boy shouldn't have been snooping! He should have been sitting down minding his own business the way well-brought-up children should. So much for Abby Carter's mothering skills. Still, as furious, frustrated and exhausted as he was, he realized that he could not afford to fly off the handle, as he was prone to do. Not now. Instead, he stifled the words hovering on his lips, took a deep, calming breath and struggled to assess the situation with some sort of objectivity.

If he had to hazard a guess, he would say that the baby—a girl it seemed, from the lace adorning her smock—had been crawling around, doing some sort of infant reconnaissance while her brother followed her—though to what purpose Caleb could not fathom. Most likely the baby had bumped into the spindly legged table Emily had brought back from St. Louis when she'd gone to visit her sister, sending the porcelain shepherdess to her demise.

Caleb's gaze moved back to the boy, who regarded him with unconcealed apprehension. The baby had pushed to a sitting position amid the broken shards, poked two fingers into her mouth and regarded him with the same intensity as her brother. Then, in the span of a heartbeat, she plopped her plump palms to the floor and headed for a colorful, gilt-edged piece that snagged her interest.

Scowling with amazement at how fast she switched

her focus, Caleb strode across the room and swung her up just as she was about to grab the jagged shard. To his surprise, she gave a gurgle of laughter. Marveling again at the quicksilver shifting of her attention, he turned her to face him, holding her out at arm's length. She rewarded his frown with a wide grin. Something about that sweet and innocent smile with its four gleaming teeth took the edge from his anger. Arms straight out, he carried the baby to the sofa and plunked her smack-dab in the middle of the cushions.

Sensitive to the situation he found himself in, and as uncertain how to deal with Abby Carter's offspring as he was his infant daughter, he wondered what to do next. Other than him and his brother *being* children many years ago, he had never been around the peculiar little creatures, and what he knew about how to deal with them could be put in a thimble with lots of room left over. From what he'd observed around town, many of them were meddlesome and troublesome, which the recent incident proved. His tired, troubled gaze returned to the child who stood gaping at him in fearful anxiety. He had to do *something.*

Caleb raked a hand through his tousled hair and pointed from the boy to the couch. "You," he said in a too-quiet tone. "Sit."

Wearing an anxious frown, Abby emerged from the kitchen holding a sleeping Betsy close. Just inside the doorway of the parlor, she stopped. Rachel was nowhere to be seen. Ben sat immobile on the sofa, looking as if he were afraid to even breathe. Laura, unaffected by the tension in the room, leaned against him, happily chewing on the hem of her dress. Caleb sat on the hearth, elbows on his knees, his chin resting on his folded hands, daring him to move. Abby's lingering gratification at having helped Betsy Gentry and her father vanished.

"Can we go home now?" Ben asked, both his voice and his lower lip trembling. "I don't like it here."

Abby's gaze swung from the fear on his face to Caleb Gentry, who sat watching the boy with the intensity of "a hawk watching a chicken," as her grandmother might have said. Her heart sank. Ben had done something wrong. Her frantic gaze raked the room for confirmation, lighting on the pieces of what looked like a broken figurine that lay scattered on the polished floorboards.

Rachel chose that moment to exit the bedroom, an armful of bedding clutched to her chest. "I'll just take these to the laundry in town and bring them back in a few d—" She stopped in her tracks and looked from Abby to Caleb and back again.

Sensing the tension in the room, Rachel said, "I'm sure the two of you have a lot to talk about. Just let me take these out to the carriage, and the children and I will go into the kitchen for some of those cookies you baked. You did bring them along, didn't you, Abby? Ben, take Laura into the kitchen. I'll be there in a minute."

It didn't escape either Caleb or Abby that even though Rachel spoke in her most professional tone, she was almost babbling, something the no-nonsense doctor just didn't do.

Abby nodded, watching as Ben hefted his baby sister onto his hip and left the room, his relief almost palpable. Caleb's frown grew even darker. When the children were gone, he made no move to address the disaster, other than to get up and begin picking up the bits of pottery. Watching him, Abby found herself torn between demanding to know what had happened and the urge to tell him that she would not be taking the job, after all. The memory of the bank's letter stopped her. She could not afford to reject this lifeline out of hand.

Why did you have to die on me, William? she thought angrily. Realizing how silly it was to berate her dead husband and knowing that even if he'd lived, she would still be in a pickle at the bank, she gave a deep sigh, placed the sleeping baby in her cradle and went to help clean up.

She and Caleb worked together side by side, neither speaking as they picked up pieces of his past. Finally, he stood, held out his hands and said, "It was my mother's."

Having been forced to part with several things that had once belonged to her own mother, Abby could imagine how he felt losing something dear to his heart just hours after losing his beloved wife. She straightened and placed the pieces she'd gathered into his big hands. The backs of her fingers brushed against his. Caleb stiffened. Abby stifled a small gasp and plunged her hands into the pockets of her skirt. Her confused gaze met his. The anger was gone, replaced by something akin to bewilderment.

"I'm sorry," she said.

"Yes, well, so am I." The strange moment passed, and once more his voice held a note of annoyance. "If the children had been seated as they should have been, it would never have happened."

Abby gasped, thoughts of foreclosure forgotten. Anger rose inside her like Wolf Creek floodwaters in the spring. How *dare* he say anything about her children! How *dare* he? From across the room, Betsy snuffled in her sleep. The slight sound was enough to remind Abby of the sorrow and strain the man standing before her must be feeling. Fearing that her eyes still held the remnants of irritation, she lifted her gaze no higher than the second button of his shirt.

"You're right," she said with a nod. "They should have been seated." Then, feeling that her babies had been unfairly judged, she couldn't help adding, "But if you will recall, you were so anxious to see Betsy calmed when I arrived, that we weren't even properly introduced."

Her meaning could not be clearer. Caleb had *demanded* that she do something to calm his daughter, and in her hurry to do so, Ben and Laura had been left in his and Rachel's charge. Abby gave a small sigh. She probably shouldn't have mentioned that. Being correct did not give one the right to say so.

Her cautious gaze climbed up the tanned column of his throat to his rugged face. The red of either embarrassment or anger tinged his sun-darkened features. She stifled a groan and wished—as was often the case—that she could call back her rash statement. *Dear Lord, I try to bridle my tongue; You know I do.*

Yes, He knew she fought a constant battle with her stubbornness and her temper, which flared hotly and died just as fast. Always had, and, she thought with another sorrow-filled sigh, probably always would. Her quick tongue had often landed her in trouble as she'd grown up, but when she'd met William, she met a man who valued her opinions, one who insisted that anyone as intelligent as she was should speak her mind. Though the final decision was always his, he had listened to her thoughts and ideas—an advantage she was aware that few wives were granted. As for her temper, more often than not, he just grabbed her in a big bear hug and held her until she quit struggling, laughing at her all the while, which quickly defused her ire and had her laughing with him.

But Caleb Gentry was nothing like her husband, she thought, staring up at features that might have been carved from unyielding Arkansas stone. How could they ever deal with each other in a practical way when, aside from her brief, annoyed outburst, the thought of just *speaking* to him turned her legs to jelly?

Before Caleb could say the words she knew were hovering on his lips, Rachel, the basket of cookies hooked over her wrist, returned, slanting Abby an uneasy look before disappearing into the kitchen. Abby stood, her chin high, all thought of retaliatory criticism dissolving as she realized that her brief spurt of provocation had probably jeopardized the job he offered.

Without speaking, Caleb tossed the breakage into the ash bucket that sat near the fireplace. Swiping his hands on the legs of his denim pants, he turned to face her with his arms crossed over his chest and an unreadable expression in his unusual gray eyes.

She was still trying to formulate an acceptable apology when he heaved a great sigh and asked, “Is Betsy all right, then?”

Surprised, both at the evenness of his voice and the turn of the conversation, Abby stammered, “Y-Yes. Fine. She was just hungry.”

That basic problem, indeed *the* problem, cleared up to his satisfaction—at least for the moment—they stood there, their mutual strain growing with every indrawn breath. Finally, she took her courage in hand. Knowing that even if she had messed up her chance to provide for her children, she could not leave without offering him what comfort she could for the days to come; she cleared her throat.

“Mr. Gentry,” she said, lacing her hands together at her waist to still their trembling. “I want you to know that I am very sorry for your loss, and while I cannot know your exact feelings, I do know what it’s like to lose a mate. My husband died eight months ago, shortly after Laura was born.”

The expression in his eyes could only be described as bleak. “I had heard that.” He cocked his head to the side, regarding her with a curious expression. “Tell me, Mrs. Carter, did you love your husband?”

Abby’s eyes widened with surprise at the personal nature of the question. “Of course.”

“Well, let me assure you that in no way could your feelings be compared to mine.”

Her breath caught at the strength of his statement, and her twisting hands stilled. He must have loved Emily very much, though it was hard to imagine such a fierce, hard man ever feeling any emotion as tender as love.

Deciding to clear the air before she lost her courage, she said, "There are some things that we should talk about before we make the decision as to whether or not I accept the position you're offering."

Surprise flickered in his eyes. He was not used to a woman taking the lead in the dialogue.

"I agree."

"First, I would like to apologize again for the destruction of the figurine. Since I wasn't here, I can't say for certain how it happened, but please believe me when I say that Ben is seldom meddlesome, though he is quite curious, as most children are. I will be glad to repay you for it." Nerves made her speech stilted and formal, and she had no idea how on earth she would make good on her promise if she did not land this job.

"I didn't see it happen, either, Mrs. Carter, and I concede that you were right in stating that I was anxious when you arrived and did not give you time to see that the children were properly settled. Most likely your baby—"

"Laura," she supplied.

"Laura. Laura probably bumped into the table and toppled the figurine. We can certainly ask, uh—"

"Ben."

"Yes, Ben." He cleared his throat, and his next words seemed to come only with the greatest effort. "I would venture to guess that it was just an unfortunate accident."

She nodded, sensing how hard the admission must

have been. "You should know about all our warts," she said, determined to lay out possible problems beforehand. "Ben is very much a boy, and is often loud and rowdy, and Laura is just beginning to venture about and explore things. . . ." Her voice trailed away on a sigh, and she lifted her shoulders in a slight shrug. Surely he could see where she was leading.

"They are good children, Mr. Gentry," she said, an earnest expression on her face, "and they are easily set to rights, but they are children, nonetheless."

Sensing that he was about to speak, she rushed on. "Another thing. Ben still misses his father very much, and that grief manifests itself in different ways—sometimes tears, sometimes misplaced mischief and even anger. If I were to take this position, I would appreciate your showing us as much patience as possible as we try to find our way in our new roles. Of course, knowing the suddenness and depth of your loss, we will extend you the same courtesy."

She was surprised that Caleb did not interrupt as many men would have. Again, she chided herself for speaking with such boldness and ruining all chance of employment, but as much as she needed the position, it was more important that her family be happy.

"I appreciate your honesty, Mrs. Carter," he said in a tone whose mocking edge caused her to doubt the sincerity of the statement. "And you should understand that I'm unfamiliar with children as well as being rather set in my ways. It will take some time for us all to adjust. As you say, there will have to be compromises on both sides."

Abby swallowed hard. "I would like to apologize for my rude outburst. My husband was a man who felt women are intelligent individuals and should voice their opinions, even when those attitudes may cause discord." She released a soft sigh of contrition and met his gaze with a stubborn determination. "I fear I have become used to doing just that. I realize that his attitude is not shared by other men and will do my best to bridle my tongue."

She couldn't read the expression in his eyes, but he nodded. "I'll keep that in mind."

He shifted his weight from one foot to the other. "One more thing."

Abby looked at him, wondering what else was on his mind.

"Since this will be your home for the next several months, I would appreciate it if you took on the responsibilities of cooking and cleaning. I will, of course, pay you extra for that."

Abby felt her mouth drop open in surprise. She snapped it shut, as her fair eyebrows puckered. "My home? I'm not sure I understand."

Another of those frowns drew his dark eyebrows together in an expression of surprise that mimicked hers. "Surely Rachel explained that you and the children would have to stay here for the next few months. At least until Betsy is of weaning age."

Chapter Two

Abby's eyes widened. "Do you mean *live* here?"

Caleb resisted the urge to sigh. Without a word, he went to the kitchen door and summoned Rachel, who left Ben and Laura eating cookies. She came into the parlor, a troubled expression in the dark eyes that moved from one friend to the other.

"I think you'd do a far better job than I in explaining to Mrs. Carter why it's necessary for her and the children to make this their home for the next few months."

Rachel nodded and turned to Abby. "I can't see any other way, can you?"

When Rachel suggested Abby become Betsy's wet nurse and told her to gather up enough things for a few days, Abby had been so eager to help and so thankful to see some ease from her financial problems that she hadn't given much thought as to *how* seeing to Betsy's needs would be accomplished or what it might entail.

"Couldn't I keep the baby at my place?"

Rachel looked to Caleb with raised eyebrows. After

he'd vetoed the idea of Abby and her children moving in with him because they would be "disrupting his life, poking through his things, tracking in dirt and whining," Rachel had suggested that he allow Abby to take Betsy to her place until she was old enough to drink from a cup, at which time he could hire someone to care for her through the day, while he took the nights.

Caleb had nixed the notion outright, proving the inflexibility he was known for. "Betsy belongs here," he'd said. "Why can't Mrs. Carter come over a few times a day and uh…feed…Betsy and then go home, or maybe she could stay all day and go home at night?"

Clearly near the end of her rope with his stubbornness, Rachel had given him her most stern "doctor" look. "I understand how you feel, Caleb, but Abby lives almost two miles on the *other* side of town going toward Antoine. Around six miles from here. It would be impossible for her to traipse back and forth with two children in tow, especially with winter coming on. Besides, babies get hungry through the night, too, at least for a while. Caring for Betsy would be a full-time job. Still, she is your child, and it's your decision."

Setting his jaw, Caleb had stared down at the baby. Neither scenario suited him, but he felt his resolve eroding in the face of necessity. As usual, he'd been given little choice in what happened in his life. With a sigh of acquiescence, he had set aside his feelings and agreed to what was required.

"Betsy belongs here," he said now, repeating his earlier answer while staring implacably into Abby Carter's anxious eyes.

Abby chewed on her bottom lip, her practical side battling her tender heart, weighing the facts as if they were on scales. On one side was the letter from the bank; on the other was a baby who needed her. She sighed. It all boiled down to one thing. Did she believe what she professed? Did she really trust that God was in control and that He answered prayers?

She thought of her house situated a half mile off the road between Wolf Creek and Antoine, with its small, homey kitchen she'd made cheerful by the addition of yellow-print feed-sack curtains and the copper pots that once belonged to her mother—one of the few things she hadn't sold. Leaving the home she'd shared with William held little appeal, but with no other way to catch up on her missed note payments, there was no doubt in her mind that she would be leaving it sooner or later. One way or the other.

"How much are you willing to pay?" she asked, and gasped in surprise when she heard Caleb's generous offer.

"That would include your taking on the household chores and cooking that I mentioned earlier."

"I would be happy to take care of your household chores, since I'm not accustomed to idleness," she told him. A sudden thought struck her. She looked from Rachel to Caleb. "What about my animals? Who would take care of them?"

"I can make arrangements to move them here for the time being," her prospective employer offered.

Abby gave a helpless shrug. "It seems that between the two of you, you've thought of everything."

"Not everything, I'm sure," Rachel said. "The biggest obstacles, perhaps."

At long last, Caleb unfolded his arms and extended his hand. "It seems, Mrs. Carter, that we find ourselves in positions of mutual need. I will do my best to be patient with your children if you will take good care of my daughter. Do we have a deal?"

Weighing her children's requirements against the troublesome voice that whispered that she must be mad, she held out her own hand. Caleb Gentry's was warm and strong and rough with calluses. When he released his hold on her, she took a step back. It was too late to renege now.

"I hear Laura," Rachel said. "I'll go tend to her and Ben while you two work out a few details."

"Thank you."

Once Rachel disappeared into the kitchen, Abby and Caleb spent the next several moments discussing how she would pay for the things she needed to run the household, and she explained the number and kinds of animals he would be taking responsibility for. He specified what times he liked his meals, and Abby explained that she spent a portion of each morning in lessons with the children, and had Bible time before bedtime, assuring him that she would not let it get in the way of her care of Betsy.

"There is one more thing," she said, when it seemed they had most of the obvious wrinkles worked out.

"Yes?"

"Weather permitting, the children and I attend Wolf Creek Church every Sunday. I hope that won't be a problem. Of course, it's impossible to take Betsy out now, but I'll be glad to take her when she's old enough."

"I have no problem with that, but I will not be accompanying you." He excused himself, saying that he needed to unload her things from Rachel's buggy and speak to his hands about moving her animals.

When he left the room, Abby drew in a shaky breath. She and Caleb Gentry would do their best to deal equitably with each other the next few months, since each had something the other needed. Simply put, neither of them had much choice. No matter what happened in the coming weeks and months, they would grin and bear it.

More likely they would grit their teeth and bear it, she thought, recalling the look on his face when she'd entered the parlor after the figurine had been smashed. She remembered the expression on Ben's face when he'd said he didn't like it there. Well, life had a way of throwing a lot of things at you that you might not like, a lesson Ben ought to learn sooner than later.

Putting on a determined face, Abby headed to the kitchen to relieve Rachel of the children and see if she could get to the bottom of what had happened to the shattered shepherdess. She prayed she could find the words to tell Ben they wouldn't be going home for a while.

"Well?" Rachel said, when Abby entered the warmth of the kitchen.

Abby's gaze found her son, who was helping Laura drink from a cup, holding a dish towel beneath her chin to catch the drips. At the moment, he was not paying any attention to the adults in the room. "It seems I have a job. Thank you."

Abby leaned down and gave her friend a hug, then helped herself to a cookie and sat down across the table.

"I won't sugarcoat things," Rachel said with a grim smile and her customary honesty. "Caleb is a decent man, and I think folks who have business dealings with him would call him a fair man, but make no mistake, he is also a hard man and he doesn't suffer fools gladly. I'd be less than a friend if I told you the next few months will be easy…for either of you."

Abby broke off a piece of cookie, her lips curving in a wry smile. "Believe me, I know that."

She popped the piece of cookie into her mouth and Rachel sighed. "Somehow I feel guilty for putting you in this position, even though my intentions were the best."

Abby smiled. "I know that, too."

Once Rachel had gone back to town, Abby sat down on the bench next to her son, took Laura on her lap and handed Ben another cookie to help soften him up for the news she was about to impart. She decided to begin with the lesser of the two concerns. "The figurine that got broken belonged to Mr. Gentry's mother," she said. "It was very special to him. What happened, Ben?"

"It was an accident," he told her, his blue eyes earnest. "You told me to be good and mind my manners, and I was trying. Dr. Rachel put Laura on the floor and told me to keep an eye on her. I was afraid Laura would get into something she shouldn't, so I was trying to watch her." He took a huge bite of cookie, as if he needed to fortify himself.

Good intentions, then, Abby thought with a feeling of relief.

"She was crawling around, and then she sat up real fast, and when she did, she bumped the table and the next thing I knew we were in trouble."

"What did Mr. Gentry say?"

Ben shrugged. "Nothing much. He told me to sit down and then sat there just looking at me. I don't like him," Ben said. "I want to go home."

Abby uttered a silent prayer for guidance. "We need to talk about that, Ben." How did she explain the direness of their situation in a way he could understand without getting into past-due notes and bank foreclosures?

Loosing another sigh, she said, "I know you realize how hard it has been for us since your father died, and how I try to do not only my work but what I can of his, too. And you know how tired and cranky I've been sometimes."

Ben gave a solemn nod and finished off the last of his cookie.

"Before we came, I told you that Mr. Gentry's wife died today."

Another nod of understanding. "Well, Mr. Gentry is in the same position that I am in—needing to be both mother and father." How to explain in more detail? "Husbands and wives are partners."

"Partners are people who work together toward the same goal," Ben said.

"Yes." Abby smiled her approval. Every day, she tried to give him a new word definition and encouraged him to use the word as often as possible to build his vocabulary. *Partners* had been the word several weeks ago.

"In the case of marriage, that goal is to be a happy, healthy family who believes in truth and honesty and responsibility and hard work, one that puts God first. In most circumstances, the father is responsible for the hard, outside work like plowing and putting up hay and chopping firewood, as well as handling the money and seeing to the bills. The mother is responsible for taking care of the home and the children, the cooking and cleaning…that sort of thing. Though," she added, "in some cases, like ours and Mr. Gentry's, it becomes necessary for one parent to take on the duties of both parents, the way I've been trying to do."

Her faltering smile was sorrow-filled. How could she tell him that her present circumstance was due in part to William's inexperience, which had forced him to borrow from the bank? Or how she had sold almost everything she owned of value to try to satisfy the loan? She couldn't. Not now or ever. Ben had adored his father, and she would not be the one to say anything to lessen that feeling.

Her voice was thick with unshed tears when she spoke. "I've been having a hard time dealing with your father's responsibilities, Ben, and I'll be frank, I'm not doing a very good job."

"I think you're doing fine," he said. "I'll bet Mr. Gentry won't do nearly as good a job of being both parents as you do."

"Thank you, Ben. And that's the thing. Mr. Gentry already knows he can't do a good job as Betsy's mother." *Dear Lord, help me find the words.* "Men just aren't…equipped with the right…trappings…to be a mother. That's why Dr. Rachel came to me. Mr. Gentry would like for me—us—to stay here for a while so I can take care of Betsy."

Abby watched Ben's lower lip jut out and his eyes take on a familiar belligerence.

"It won't be forever," she hastened to say. "Just until Betsy gets a bit older, or until Mr. Gentry finds someone else. Until springtime, maybe. He and I will be partners, in a way. He will take care of our place and our animals, and I will take care of him and Betsy and the household chores. He will pay me a wage, just as if I had a job in town at the mercantile or the restaurant, and that money will help me take care of our obligations. That can be our word for the day.

"Obligations are things that are our responsibilities. Like what I was talking about when I described the duties of fathers and mothers. Parents have the obligation to bring up children to be good, God-fearing citizens. You are responsible for keeping your room clean and setting the table and feeding the animals and milking Nana. When I tell you to keep an eye on Laura, it is your obligation to see that she's safe. Sometimes, obligations involve money. Things we must pay for."

There! She had prepared him as best she could, though she felt she had done a poor job of it. To his credit, Ben did not spout off or throw a fit. Only the downward turn of his mouth and his refusal to meet her gaze spoke of his misery. Finally, he looked up at her.

"Like buying eggs when the hens stop laying and sugar and flour and coffee?" he asked.

"Yes." And shoes and shirts and medicine when your children get sick, Abby thought as she pulled him close to her side. "I have always been as truthful with you as I have felt you could understand, so I will not lie to you now. This will be hard on all of us."

Ben pulled away and regarded her with a solemn expression. "It won't be hard on Mr. Gentry. He doesn't have to live somewhere different."

"Actually, he does," Abby said with a gentle smile. "He won't be staying in his house while we're here. He'll be moving into the bunkhouse with his hired men. He will just take his meals here and use his office when necessary. That's quite a sacrifice for him, as well as having people he doesn't even know taking over his home. And we mustn't forget that his wife just died. I want you to think about how you felt when your father passed away. You were sad and angry with him and God for at least a month, and you took it out on your sister. Remember?"

Ben nodded.

Abby smiled and brushed back a lock of his fine blond hair. "Just remember that Mr. Gentry may be feeling the same way for a while, and try to be patient and forgiving. Can you do that?"

"I'll try."

"That's all I ask," Abby said.

She gave him a final hug and stood. As they were about to leave the kitchen, Caleb came through the door, looking rugged and unyielding, his arms laden with things she'd brought from her own kitchen. He set a loaf of bread wrapped in a clean dish towel onto the table next to the basket of cookies, and put a heavy cast-iron kettle of squirrel and dumplings on the stove.

"I've put your things in your room."

"Thank you," Abby said.

"Would you mind if Ben and Laura sleep with you for a day or two? I'll have to move some things from Emily's room into the attic for Ben to have his own room."

"That will be fine."

"I thought I'd put Betsy's cradle in your room, too, so you can be near both girls."

"Perfect."

"Let me show you around," he said, relieved that there were no objections.

He led the small procession down the hallway. The bedroom was furnished simply with a bed, an oak armoire and a highboy. Abby noted that he had built a small fire to combat the autumn chill, and warmth was already starting to spread throughout the area, which was far larger than any room at her home. As spacious as it was and even though she knew the furnishings were of good quality, the house seemed sterile somehow, as untouched as Caleb Gentry's heart. Shifting Laura on her hip, she ran her fingertip through the dust that had gathered on top of a chest of drawers. And it could use a thorough cleaning.

"I guess it needs a good cleaning," he said, echoing her thoughts.

The sound of his voice sent Abby's gaze winging

to his, and she saw that the dull red of embarrassment had crept into the harsh sweep of his cheekbones. Too late, she realized what she had done. Oh, dear! Could she and the children do nothing right?

"Emily didn't have much energy the past few months, and I—"

"There's no need to apologize, Mr. Gentry," she rushed to assure him. "Any woman who has carried a child to term understands." She offered him a non-judgmental smile. "It's a lovely home and it won't take much to get things in order."

"I suppose not." Clearly eager to be away from the house and all the turmoil and unhappiness in it, he said, "I need to get one of my hands to go over to your place and see to your animals tonight. We'll move them tomorrow."

"Thank you. I'm sorry to put you to the trouble."

"It's not a problem." She told him how to find her house and he gave a sharp nod. He looked as tense as she felt. It seemed as if they were both trying to outdo the other in civility.

She offered him a thin smile. "I'll just get our things put away and check on Betsy again."

"I have to go into town and make arrangements at the, uh—" he cleared his throat "—funeral home, so I can't stay to see that you get settled in. Feel free to just…look around if you need something. I'll be back by dusk for supper. Just fix whatever you want."

Laura muttered something that sounded remarkably like "supper" and offered Caleb one of her incredible smiles. Just as incredibly, the bleakness in his storm-gray eyes dimmed the tiniest bit. Though it in no way could be called a smile and was so fleeting that Abby was certain it must be a trick of the light, it seemed that just for a second, the unyielding firmness of his mouth softened somewhat.

She gave her daughter a squeeze. It seemed that at least one of the Carters was not intimidated by the overwhelming presence of the man, and even seemed to be taken with him! Much to her own mortification considering the circumstances, Abby realized that in his own rough, brooding sort of way, Caleb Gentry was an attractive man.

Caleb rode his gelding into town, his body past weariness, sporadic images flitting through his weary mind like flashes of lighting against a sullen sky. Rachel coming from the room where a baby's crying was the only sound after Emily had gone suddenly quiet. His gaze straying to the bed, where a sheet covered Emily's face. His heart stumbling in his chest, and the resolute, relentless ticking of the clock, while his exhausted brain struggled to assimilate what his eyes were seeing. Rachel's voice, filled with weariness and regret. Emily was dead and his baby daughter needed someone to take care of her, to feed her. An overwhelming certainty that there must be something terribly wrong with him for his inability to feel anything over his wife's death but panic and fear....

The random images faded, and reason—of sorts—returned along with memories of the past couple of hours. He conceded that he had jumped to conclusions with Mrs. Carter's boy. It wasn't his fault his sister had broken the shepherdess, but with Caleb's own emotions so raw, and his feelings of inadequacy at the surface, he had been eager to place blame. The truth was that his whole world was turned upside down. Nothing would ever be the same, so he might as well get used to the idea of Mrs. Carter and her children being around, at least for the foreseeable future.

Whether he liked it or not.

With a grunt of disgust, he guided the horse down Antioch Street, and took a right toward the railroad tracks. The house Rachel Stone shared with her father, which also housed her medical office, sat on a corner beyond the tracks that ran a block down from and parallel to Antioch. The funeral home was situated at the rear of the house, added a few years before, when Rachel's father, Dr. Edward Stone, had suffered a stroke that left him partially paralyzed.

Caleb rode around back, tied his horse to the hitching post and stepped through the doorway of the funeral parlor. Edward, who sat behind a gleaming desk, looked up when he heard the bell on the door ring, a solemn expression on his lined face. He rolled his wheelchair around to greet Caleb with his hand extended.

"I'm sorry, Caleb."

Caleb only nodded.

"Bart and Mary picked out a casket and brought her a dress. I didn't think you'd mind." When Caleb shook his head, the older man said, "She's ready, if you want to go on in."

Caleb nodded, though it was the last thing he wanted

to do. He entered the viewing room, where Emily lay dressed in a frilly gown of pale pink, her favorite color. Her dark lashes lay against the delicate paleness of her cheeks. If he didn't know better, he might think she was sleeping.

Dry-eyed, he stared down at the woman who had been a part of his life the past six years, waiting for the grief to overtake him and wondering if he should pray. But grief for losing a beloved wife did not come, and he had no idea what he could—or should—say to a God with whom he'd had so few dealings. The only sorrow he could define was sadness that Emily had been taken in her prime and would not be there for Betsy.

There was guilt aplenty.

Guilt aggravated by the nagging memory of the jolt that had passed through him when his fingers had touched those of Abby Carter. What kind of man was he to feel *anything* for any woman so soon after his wife's death?

The answer was clear. He was, perhaps, a man who hadn't tried hard enough to make his marriage a good one. A man who'd let someone else plan his marriage and shape his life…which might explain that unexpected awareness of Mrs. Carter but certainly did not excuse it.

He and Emily were both twenty-four when they married. Pretty enough, but thought to be a bit uppity, she was considered to be the town spinster. Caleb's father had instigated the notion of his marrying her. His father stated that since Gabe, whom Lucas Gentry bitterly referred to as the "prodigal," had shown no signs of abandoning his wayward lifestyle to come home and share the burden of labor, it was past time for his elder son to choose a wife and sire a son to inherit the Gentry fortune.

Emily's parents had encouraged her to accept Caleb's offer—most probably her last. So they married and lived with Lucas in the house he had built for his own wife, Caleb and Gabe's mother, Libby.

Unfortunately, Lucas had died of a stroke three years ago, without seeing the birth of his grandchild. More regrettable perhaps was the fact that despite the tales Caleb had heard about love often following marriage, for him and Emily it had not.

Until now, he had never questioned why. They'd both been content to let the days slip by…sharing a house but not their lives, treating each other with respect but not love, neither of them caring enough to look for a spark of something that might be fanned into the flames of love. In retrospect, he found that troubling, but then, what did he know of love? He and Gabe had lost their mother to another man at a young age, and love was a sentiment foreign to their embittered father.

Father. *He* was a father now, and he hoped to be a better one than Lucas Gentry had been. He *would* be better. He might not know anything about loving his daughter, but he knew how to take care of her. Duty and obligation were things Caleb Gentry understood very well. And he would let her choose her husband when the time came.

Chapter Three

With a few free moments before starting the evening meal, Abby poured herself a cup of coffee and sank into a kitchen chair. Emily's funeral service had been held that morning, and Caleb had yet to return from town. Laura and Betsy were down for their afternoon naps, and Ben was taking advantage of the sunny afternoon, playing on the back porch with the wooden train set William had made him last Christmas.

The two days since she and the children had arrived at the Gentry farm had been somewhat stressful as they tried to adjust to their new home and responsibilities, but with the absence of any further mishaps or misunderstandings, Abby felt she was beginning to find her stride.

She took a sip of her coffee and contemplated what to fix for supper, which turned her thoughts to Caleb. In an effort to please her new employer, she had asked what he did and didn't like to eat, and he had informed her that not liking something was a luxury he and his brother had not been allowed. He ate everything, and she soon learned he ate a lot of it, tucking into a meal as if it might be his last. So much food might have made another man overweight, but Caleb was as fit any male she'd ever seen.

She'd learned a bit about him the past couple of days. His work ethic could not be faulted. The care he took with his animals and the upkeep of the farm spoke of concern, dedication and pride in his accomplishments, which was reflected by his affluence. In fact, he worked from sunrise until sunset with an intensity she understood too well, readying the farm for winter wheat planting between visits from the few neighbors who came to offer food and condolences.

Abby was a bit surprised that there were not as many visitors as she might have imagined considering the Gentry family's long-standing presence in the community. She was also surprised at how uncomfortable he seemed with accepting their simple kindnesses.

She understood filling your days with work in an attempt to hold the pain of loss at bay, but she did not comprehend his awkwardness in accepting well-meaning compassion from people who wanted to show they cared. It was almost as if he didn't know how to deal with their kindness.

He seemed to be trying his best to make her job easier, always giving a polite answer to her questions about the workings of his household, and plenty of leeway to take care of Betsy in whatever way she thought was best. Still, in no way could his actions be interpreted as friendly. Sometimes she caught him looking at her with a strange expression that seemed to straddle the fence between skepticism and remorse.

She often caught him regarding the children with wary uncertainty, sometimes giving them looks that dared them to so much as breathe, but he also tried in a heavy-handed way to engage them in various ways. Despite how painful accepting their presence might be, Abby couldn't help feeling that he was doing his best, even though his best lacked enthusiasm or warmth and more often than not fell short.

There had been one sticky moment that first evening when he had started eating the squirrel and dumplings she had brought from home, only to be halted by Ben who regarded him in disbelief and said, "We didn't say the prayer."

Looking somewhat abashed, Caleb had stopped, bowed his head and listened while Ben gave thanks for the food. He had never forgotten after that. It was a small thing, but one for which Abby was grateful. She was also grateful that other than to show up for meals, she had seen little of him, which made everyone's life easier, especially the days she recalled the unexpected spark she'd felt when their fingers touched. Labeling it a figment of her imagination made it no less troubling.

The morning after her arrival, Caleb had taken Frank, one of his two hired men and a wagon to her place where they'd rounded up her few remaining chickens, the rabbits and their cages, and Nana, one in a long string of goats she and William had purchased because Ben had not tolerated cow's milk well. They had tethered Shaggy Bear, her milk cow, to the wagon, loaded what feed she had and brought the whole kit and caboodle back to his place. When Caleb had come in for supper, she thought she'd heard him mumbling something about "milking goats" under his breath, but she could not be sure.

She was doing a top-to-bottom cleaning of the house and admitted that caring for it was much easier than caring for hers. While not a fancy place per se, the Gentry home was more than a simple farmhouse, designed not only for the convenience of a farming family, but also with an eye toward rustic charm. The house was the product of Gentry money, yet nowhere was there a hint of ostentation. The oak floors had been planed smooth and waxed to a satin sheen, as had the bookcases flanking the massive rock fireplace that was the hub of the parlor. The plaster walls throughout were painted in various colors, most of them too dark for Abby's taste, but classic colors that somehow suited Caleb.

Though blessed with a fine house, Emily Gentry seemed to have taken little interest in putting her stamp on it. Abby understood being so dragged down by pregnancy that regular cleaning became a chore, but where were the little touches that showed care and love? Other than a quilt or two and the occasional pastel drawing Emily had done, there were few of the personal touches Abby felt transformed lumber and nails from a house into a sanctuary away from the cares of the world.

If it were her home, she would paint the rooms light colors and swap the heavy drapes framing the windows for white muslin curtains, perhaps with a crochet-and-tassel edging to brighten things up.

Shame on you, Abby Carter! How dare you presume to redecorate a dead woman's house or think it lacked love?

Why, Caleb himself had indicated that even though Abby had lost her husband, she could have no idea how he felt at his own loss. A sudden wave of melancholy for the simple, love-filled house she and William had once shared swept through Abby, but she pushed it aside. Indulging in nostalgia for the past served as little purpose as speculating on Emily Gentry's personality and her relationship with her husband.

Caleb never so much as mentioned her name, and though Abby saw the grimness in his eyes as he approached each day with stubborn determination, she knew only too well what he must be going through.

Though she and William had not seen eye to eye the last months of their marriage, she had loved him, and it was weeks before anyone could mention his name without her tearing up. But as her preacher had counseled her, God made our wondrous bodies not only to heal themselves when overtaken with physical problems—if given care and time—He had done the same with our emotions. Time, he had told her, was the cure for her sorrow. He'd been right. There were still moments when thoughts of William brought tightness to her throat and tears to her eyes, but for the most part he had been relegated to a special place in her memories and her heart.

So, when things became tense and stilted between her and Caleb, she reminded herself of his recent loss and prayed that the sharpest edges of his pain would be smoothed over by God's grace.

And you still haven't decided what to fix for supper.

She was debating on whether to cook a pot of beans or fry some salt pork and potatoes and cook up the turnip and mustard greens Leo had picked for her that morning, when she heard footsteps on the front porch. Caleb must be back. Then, hearing a woman's voice and what had to be more than one person's footsteps, Abby leaped to her feet. It must be someone coming to pay his respects. She had been so careful not to overstep the boundaries of the duties Caleb had outlined that she wasn't sure if she should answer the door or not.

Then again, he wasn't here. Deciding that she should welcome his guests, she hurried through the kitchen, smoothing both her hair and her apron as she went. She was halfway to the front door when it was pushed open, and Caleb, accompanied by a rush of cool air and carrying a pot of something, stepped through the opening. His in-laws followed, each holding a wooden tray covered by a tea towel. Their eyes were red-rimmed, but their wan faces wore resolute smiles.

Abby's questioning gaze flickered to Caleb. "The people from town fixed enough food for an army," he told her. "We brought what was left here."

"Indeed they did," Mary Emerson interjected, doing her best to summon a vestige of cheer. "There's no way Bart and I can eat it all before it goes bad, and I know Caleb eats like a horse, so we decided to share with you and the children this evening. I hope you haven't started supper."

"No. No, I haven't," Abby told her. "That's very kind of you."

"Besides," Mary added, with another smile, this one faint and sorrowful, "it seemed only right that we come spend some time with Betsy. Especially today."

Again, Abby's gaze sought Caleb's, hoping to gauge his reaction to the impromptu visit, but he had already disappeared through the kitchen door, and she could only nod.

"We'll just put it in the kitchen, then."

"That's fine," Abby said as the older woman followed her husband and Caleb through the house.

Not wanting her presence to remind the Emersons of their loss, Abby decided that she should stay out of sight and hopefully out of mind. She went to check on the babies and found them still sleeping. Letting herself out the front door, she rounded the house to the back porch to check on Ben. He was still playing with his train, the three open cars loaded down with green-and-black objects.

Abby's eyes widened when she recognized the cargo for what it was: onyx-and-jade chess pieces from the set displayed on the table next to the front window. A vivid recollection of the scene with Caleb and Ben she had interrupted mere days ago leaped into her mind. Her heart dropped to her toes and she sucked in a horrified breath. While she watched, he took the kings from their respective cars and began to have them "fight" each other. Her first instinct was to yell at him to put them down, but caution prevailed. If he dropped one of them and it broke, it would be total disaster!

Instead, she sauntered over to the steps. "Hi, sweetheart. Having fun?"

Ben's head snapped up and his wide eyes met hers. The guilt she saw there said without words that he knew he was in trouble. He swallowed and nodded.

"Aren't those Mr. Gentry's chessmen?"

He nodded again.

Abby sat down on the steps. "What are you doing with them?"

"Just playing sheriff and train robber," he said in a low voice.

"I see." She hoped her tone was reasonable. "Did Mr. Gentry give you permission to play with them?"

If possible, Ben's eyes grew even wider. "No, ma'am." His voice was the merest thread of sound.

"Hmm," she said with a nod. "You know full well you are not to bother other peoples' belongings, don't you, Benjamin?"

"Yes, ma'am."

"Then why did you?"

Ben stared at the now-abandoned chess pieces. "I just needed something to haul in my train. I was being careful."

"I'm sure you meant no harm, and I'm sure you were being careful, but accidents happen. Remember Laura breaking the figurine? What if you'd broken one of Mr. Gentry's chess pieces? What do you think he would say?"

Ben looked up, his freckle-splashed face draining of color.

Abby sighed. "Well, no harm done. I don't think

he knows they are missing yet. I'll put them back, and when Mr. and Mrs. Emerson leave, you will tell Mr. Gentry what you did and apologize."

Ben's face crumpled. "Do I have to?"

"You do." Abby reached out and took the chess pieces from the train, placing them in the pockets of her skirt. "Why don't you spend some time on your reading?"

"I'd rather go fishing," the boy said, a forlorn look in his eyes.

A sudden pain racked Abby's heart. Fishing was a venture Ben and his father had shared and something she knew Ben missed very much. She swallowed back the tightness in her throat and forced a smile. "It would be nice for you to get in one more good fishing session before it gets too cold," she agreed. "The next time we go into town, I'll ask Dr. Rachel if Danny can come out one day and fish. Frank says some mighty big crappie live in Wolf Creek."

"That would be fun," Ben said, his eyes brightening. Rachel's son, Daniel, was Ben's best friend. "Maybe we could take a picnic the way we used to when Dad..."

The sentence trailed away and his smile faded.

"A picnic is a definite possibility," Abby said, "if the wind isn't blowing too much for the baby. It's still pretty warm, and we could take a basket for her and a quilt for Laura, though I think she'll be walking before much longer."

Ben's wide grin made Abby's heart glad. "Yeah, she's pulling up to everything the past few days."

"If we had the picnic at midday, Mr. Gentry might like to join us," Abby suggested.

Ben's happy smile vanished. He looked up, his mouth already open to tell her that he didn't want Caleb to come along.

Abby tapped his mouth with a gentle finger "Matthew 7:12."

"Treat others the way you want to be treated," he said in a disgusted tone.

"Close enough," Abby said with a smile. "Now go find something to read for an hour or so. The Emersons have come to see Betsy and they brought supper, so there will be a lot of good things to choose from." She winked at him. "I even saw a chocolate cake."

Ben's blue eyes brightened at the mention of his favorite.

"This is a sad time for them, Ben, so be extra nice, all right?"

Ben nodded. Abby bent and pressed a kiss to his white-blond hair, then ushered him through the kitchen and into the parlor. To her surprise, he went straight to Mary Emerson and gave her a hug, following suit with Bart. Abby felt the sting of tears behind her eyelids. He *was* a sweet boy.

"Sorry," he mumbled, his gaze moving from one adult to the other and lingering on Caleb, whom he made no move to hug. Then without another word, he went to the room he shared with Abby.

She stifled a groan while fighting the conflicting urge to smile. The apology had not only been for Ben's sorrow about Emily. By snaring Caleb's eye, she somehow felt Ben had cleverly included his regret for playing with the chessmen without permission. Well, she might as well follow suit and take the coward's way out, too. There wasn't much Caleb could do or say with Emily's parents in the room. Straightening her shoulders, she crossed the room to the chess set, pulled the pieces from her pocket and placed them on the board. Heaven only knew if they belonged in a special spot. She was only thankful they were undamaged.

That done, she shot Caleb a quick glance. It was no surprise to see that his pewter-hued eyes had gone a stormy gray, like gloomy, rain-drenched clouds before a summer thunderstorm, one that would no doubt hit after the Emersons left.

Bart and Mary spent the remainder of the afternoon alternating between rocking Betsy and going through Emily's belongings, separating them into piles to keep, be given away or be tossed. Caleb had retreated to the fields, telling them to take whatever they wanted. Abby spent the afternoon taking care of the babies' needs, trying to be as unobtrusive as possible and biting her trembling bottom lip and blinking back her own tears when the sounds of sobbing escaped through the closed door.

By late afternoon, the chore was done, and everything was packed into two trunks and loaded onto Bart's wagon. Abby made sure that supper was warm when they finished, so that Mary, who must be emotionally exhausted, would not feel the need to offer her help.

The meal was over and they were almost finished washing the dishes when Mary said, "I understand from Rachel that you didn't bring much with you."

"No. We were in a bit of a hurry to get here."

"If you'd like, I can drive out early in the morning to watch the children while Caleb takes you to gather your things. I know you'd be more comfortable if Laura had her crib."

"I appreciate it, Mrs. Emerson, but I'm not sure that would be convenient for Caleb, and I don't want to make any more work on him than necessary."

"Please call me Mary," Emily's mother said. "I've already talked to him, and he's fine with it, as long as you don't mind my watching Ben and Laura."

"Of course I don't mind."

Mary's eyes filled with tears, and she reached out and clasped one of Abby's hands. "Bart and I are so very glad that you're here for Betsy and Caleb, and we want to do everything we can so that you'll feel more at home."

Abby was overwhelmed by the heartfelt declaration. "Thank you, but I'm sure you'd have found someone, and actually, I'm the grateful one."

Mary and Bart left soon after the dishes were washed and put away. Just before stepping onto the front porch, a tearful Mary pulled Abby into a close embrace. "If you or the children ever need anything, please let either me or Bart know."

Abby promised she would and watched the carriage disappear down the lane. She drew a relieved breath at the older woman's glad acceptance of the situation. If only she could somehow bring some of that acceptance and just a smidgen of joy into Caleb's life, perhaps the next few months would be worth it.

Abby and Ben were in the parlor later, having their evening devotional, when Caleb came into the room. Abby looked up from the verse she was reading and found his gaze on Ben. She held her breath, hoping against hope that he would not fly off the handle.

"Ben."

"Sir?"

Abby heard the quaver in his voice.

"That chess set was a gift to me from Doc Stone," Caleb said in an even voice that somehow managed to fall just short of angry. "It isn't a toy, son, and it isn't to be played with unless you're playing an actual game of chess. If you want to learn—"

"Don't call me son!" Ben shouted, lifting his belligerent blue gaze to Caleb's.

"Benjamin!" Abby cried, leaping to her feet. She was stunned by Ben's sudden outburst, when Caleb had been trying to discuss the matter in a conciliatory tone. "You will apologize to Mr. Gentry at once."

"I won't!" he yelled, scrambling off the sofa and running to the bedroom. "I'm not his son!" The door slammed with a jarring thud.

Abby lifted her horrified gaze to Caleb's, wondering if he would tell her to start packing "I—I'm so sorry," she said in a near whisper. "I don't know what got into him."

His silvery eyes held a weary sorrow. "I do. I understand exactly why he's upset. I've been where he is, remember?"

Abby recalled that he'd lost his mother when he was young. "You're being very decent about this."

"You told me yourself to expect that kind of outburst, and even though I may be short-tempered and stubborn, I like to think I am a decent man."

"I never meant to imply—"

A fleeting sorrowful smile lifted one corner of his mouth. "I know."

Abby regarded him thoughtfully and set out to try to make him understand. "Ben had no idea how expensive that chess set is, but that's neither here nor there. He knows better than to bother other people's things. I'm not trying to make excuses, but he just wanted something to haul in his train cars. He—"

"Leave it, Abby," Caleb said, but the weariness of his smile took the sting from the command. "I was going to offer to teach him how to play chess in the evenings, but I don't think he'd be very receptive to that just now."

Without another word, he crossed the room and began moving the chess pieces, presumably where they had been before Ben confiscated them. Caleb had made no mention of sending them packing, and she wasn't going to bring it up. She gave a rueful shake of her head, not fully understanding why he had not flown off the handle, but grateful that he had not. It was progress. Of sorts.

Bright and early the following morning, while dew still sparkled on the browning grass, Abby found herself seated in the wagon beside Caleb. Mary had arrived shortly after daybreak to take care of the children. She'd brought along a newfangled bottle from the mercantile so that she could give Betsy a little sugar water if she grew fussy before Abby returned. Frank, the older of Caleb's two hired hands, followed the wagon on a bay gelding.

Caleb leaned forward, his elbows resting on his denim-clad knees, his tanned, callused hands holding the reins in a loose grasp. Completely and easily in control. Again, she thought that even though he was not what one might call handsome, there was something striking about him. It was no wonder that he'd once been the catch of Pike County, or little doubt that once a decent time of mourning had passed, he would be again.

It was only when it came to expressing the more tender emotions that Caleb Gentry seemed to be wanting. That and the lack of a relationship with God. She wondered why he had left no place in his life for a God who had been so generous to him, but she was far too cautious to ask. In truth, she spoke to him as little as possible, since she had the impression that he did not want anyone getting too close to him and seemed disinclined to get close to anyone, which was rather sad, even though it made her life easier.

She glanced again at his hands. They were strong hands, hands whose callused palms and scarred fingers spoke of hard work. She'd seen those hands move in unerring swiftness to soothe a nervous horse and calmly remove an adventurous kitten from the branches of an oak tree, proving he was capable of tenderness. Yet for some reason that kindheartedness was not extended to people—at least not that she had seen.

Well, that was not exactly true. Even in the few days she had been at the farm, she'd seen his softening toward Laura, who made a habit of pulling up to his legs and demanding that he hold her, something he did without hesitation or complaint. He even allowed her to explore his face, poking her tiny fingers into his ears and eyes, and once offering him a wet, openmouthed kiss. When he'd swiped a palm down his cheek and made a soft growling sound of disgust, Laura had laughed in delight, which only made his scowl grow fiercer. It was all Abby could do to keep from laughing herself, but she managed to stifle the urge, knowing it would not do at all.

She saw him growing more confident with Betsy, too, as he made time for her after the evening meal and before going to his study to work on his account ledgers. Abby wondered if he saw Emily's face when he looked down at their daughter's delicate features. Once, he ran a strong finger over the curve of Betsy's cheek, and remembering the little shock that had run through her when their hands touched, Abby experienced a brief, sudden stab of longing. It seemed like aeons since she had felt the tenderness of a man's touch. Would she ever again bask in the certainty that she was so cherished?

"Are you all right?"

The sound of his voice brought her wandering thoughts back to the present. Her gaze flew to his, which held a curious gleam. "Y-yes. Why do you ask?"

"You made a strange sound, and I thought something might be bothering you."

"Just thinking."

"About what?"

She slid him a sideways glance and said the first thing that came to mind. "No offense, Mr. Gentry, but you don't pay me enough to be privy to my thoughts." As soon as the words left her lips, she wished she could call them back. They were something she might have said to William. Almost…flirty, somehow. And totally inappropriate.

He regarded her for a moment, and then something bearing close kinship to a smile lifted one corner of his mouth for a heartbeat. "No offense taken, Mrs. Carter, and you're right. It's just that it's seldom you're so quiet. You're always talking to the children about something—even Laura and Betsy, who have no idea what you're saying."

"I was just respecting your privacy. You don't seem like the kind of man who indulges in idle chitchat."

"You're right," he said with a slow nod. "I have little use for chitchat and gossip, but I enjoy an intelligent discussion now and again."

Abby wasn't surprised that he valued intelligence. Chess was not a game for dummies, and no man who handled the myriad business responsibilities he did could be lacking in intelligence. If his impressive book collection was any indication, he was well read. The shelves on either side of the parlor fireplace were filled with titles that ranged from F. H. Bradley's *The Principles of Logic* to treatises on successful farming. There were many poetry and art-related books, no doubt Emily's. Abby tried to envision the creative Emily sharing her views on art and literature with her husband.

"I suppose you miss those discussions with Emily," Abby said, partly to keep the conversation going and partly because she was curious about his relationship with his dead wife.

"Emily and I had few common interests," he told her in a tone that said that line of conversation had ended.

"So," she asked after a few uncomfortable moments, "what shall we talk about?"

"You."

"Me?" She choked back a laugh. "There isn't much to tell, I assure you. You'd be very bored."

"That remains to be seen. From what you said the other day, your husband valued your comments and opinions, so I admit that I'm curious to hear some of them." He slanted a wry look her way and added, "A bit taken aback by your forwardness, but curious nonetheless. I'm also interested as to why you agreed to help me with Betsy."

"That's simple," she said with her customary bluntness. "Money."

He shot her a shocked look. "Rachel never led me to believe you were the avaricious type."

Again, Abby berated herself for speaking without thinking. This man was *not* William, and should not be answered with flippancy. "Oh, I'm not. Not really. I have little use for money for its sake, but we were forced to borrow against the farm, and the wages you've agreed to pay me will help me get caught up at the bank."

Caleb frowned. "I thought you bought your place outright."

She arched an eyebrow. "Ah. Gossip?" she challenged.

This time there was no denying his dry smile or the hint of color that crept into his lean cheeks. "The good old Wolf Creek grapevine," he acknowledged with a nod.

"The good old Wolf Creek grapevine had it right," she told him. "When my parents died, William and I used the money from the sale of their home to buy the farm and the equipment we'd need to farm it. And if you've heard that much gossip, you also know that he was a teacher, not a farmer. He had to borrow against the land."

"I know he took a job with the Southwestern Arkansas and Indian Territory Railroad Company."

"Yes," Abby said quietly. Neither mentioned that William Carter had been killed a short time after his daughter's birth while trying to connect two lumber-loaded railcars headed for an out-of-state market. Neither did Abby mention to Caleb that a few days before the accident, he had confided with an air of excitement that he had a potential buyer for the farm and he was thinking of taking the offer and moving them back to Springfield, Missouri, to be near his brother and his family.

Unfortunately, William was killed before anything could come of the deal, and Abby had no idea who the prospective buyer was.

"He should never have borrowed against the land," Caleb said into the gathering silence.

"That's an easy thing for someone like you to say,"

she told him, the memories bringing past heartache to the surface.

"Someone like me? What does that mean?" he asked, his tone mirroring his irritation.

"Someone who has money, has always had money and who never has to worry about how to buy feed for their livestock, or put food on the table or buy shoes for their children. Someone who has options."

Caleb didn't comment for long moments. When he turned his head to look at her, there was genuine concern in his eyes, but Abby, who was looking out over the dew-drenched fields, didn't see it. "So you did decide to take the job because of the money...because you had no other option."

Her gaze flew to his. "Oh! You make it sound so mercenary. Yes, I needed the money, but I wanted to help, too. Believe it or not, I do not pull wings off butterflies, nor am I greedy and avaricious."

Confusion filled his eyes. "I never thought you were. How have you managed these past months?"

Sensing that he was not angry, she gave a little shake of her head. "Though I hate to admit it, I've sold nearly everything I had that would bring a decent price." When he made no comment, she added, "Your offer was the answer to my prayers."

"Really?" he asked with an arched eyebrow of his own. "What took Him so long?"

"I beg your pardon," Abby said, not following or understanding the sarcasm in his voice.

"God. What took Him so long to answer your

prayers? Why didn't He provide some sort of help sooner? Where was He when your husband died?"

Abby looked at him, taken aback. "It isn't for us to question His plan for us," she told him in an even tone. "Through faith, we believe that all will work out the way He wants it to, and for our benefit. And as for where He was when William died, I would imagine God was where He was when *His* son died."

Caleb had the grace to look bowled over by that answer. Though he wanted to ask if she dealt with William's loss by trusting that everything would come out all right and that something better was around the corner, he was silent.

"Surely you believe in God." The statement was simple and to the point.

"I suppose so," he said with a negligent lift of broad shoulders. "It's just that my brother and I were taught to rely on ourselves, so I haven't had many dealings with God."

"On the contrary," she argued, wondering how he'd lost his mother. "You deal with Him many times a day. Every day. Just look around you! It's beautiful!" Abby spread her arms wide, encouraging him to look at the world around him, to see and acknowledge the glory of it all.

But Caleb wasn't looking at the fallow fields or the red and gold of the changing leaves. He was looking at Abby. Bonnet-free, she had thrown back her head and lifted her face to the soft shine of the sun. A capricious breeze had tugged tendrils of blond hair from the coil at the nape of her neck and whipped delicate rose color into her cheeks. For the first time, he realized that Abigail Carter was a very pretty woman.

Caleb forced his eyes back to the road. "Yes. It is beautiful," he said in a husky voice.

Abby glanced at him, saw the set of his jaw and decided that she'd said enough on the subject for the moment. She knew from past experience that the best way to teach was by example. There would be plenty of time to show him in small ways that God was present and working in his life.

Almost a week had gone by since she and Caleb had made the trip to her place. The intervening days had passed quickly, and things had been going as well as could be expected. Abby's new routine had taken on a familiar rhythm as she grew accustomed to her new station in life and her new home. So far, neither Ben nor Laura had done anything else to antagonize the prickly Mr. Gentry.

As was her custom, Abby spent thirty minutes each night with Ben in Bible study. On two separate occasions, she had looked up and seen Caleb leaning against the doorjamb of his study, arms folded across his chest, listening as she read or questioned Ben about certain verses. He never commented, and on both occasions, he had quickly shut the door, bade them good-night and headed for the bunkhouse.

Today he was going into town for some feed and to pick up some pantry items Abby needed. When he came into the kitchen to tell her he was leaving, she said, "If you have time, I was wondering if you'd deliver a message for me."

His eyebrows lifted in surprise, but he only nodded. "I'd be glad to."

"I'm not used to dealing with this sort of thing, but I can. It's just that William always did, and you're familiar with business, so I thought..." She drew in another breath and rushed on. "I know it's an imposition, certainly beyond what most employers would do, but it will be so hard for me to get away with the babies, and—"

"Stop dithering, woman, and spit it out," Caleb said, scowling at her.

Abby's eyes widened and she bit back a sharp retort. *Dithering? Woman?* She lowered her gaze to his shirtfront and struggled to keep her tone pleasant. "It's just that... would you mind stopping at the bank to let Mr. Haversham know that I'm working for you now, and that I'll start making up the back payments as soon as possible?"

Some emotion she couldn't place flickered in Caleb's gray eyes. "I'd be glad to," he told her. "Anything else?"

"No. And thank you."

"You're welcome."

She watched the wagon disappear down the lane with a sigh of relief. He had agreed readily enough, and didn't seem to mind any inconvenience it might cause. But it *was* business, after all, and business was something he understood well.

"How are things, Caleb?" Emily's mother asked as he glanced over the list Abby had given him after making a thorough check of his pantry shelves.

What could he say to his dead wife's mother? He suspected that neither Mary nor Bart suspected the true circumstances of his marriage and how even though he had more money but was self-educated, he had always felt intellectually inferior to Emily, who had received her education at a fancy girls' school in St. Louis. He doubted they knew that Emily had taken far more joy from her drawing, reading and poetry writing than in making a home, or trying to build a marriage, so that when she had announced she was expecting a baby, it had come as a bit of a shock to them both.

Throughout the following months, her inability to come to terms with the whole idea of motherhood had left Caleb feeling as if he were solely to blame for her miserable pregnancy…and now her death. Thus the daily guilt he suffered.

Her dying had ended the steady ebb and flow of his life. Though Abby had a hot meal waiting for him when he returned to the house each evening, it was difficult for a man who liked the status quo to walk into the house and find strangers there. Being unable to enjoy the quiet peace and comfort of his home in the evenings made him nostalgic for the uncomplicated life he'd grown accustomed to during his marriage. Being with someone for six years forged habits and rituals that, when they ceased to exist, were missed nonetheless.

"I miss having her around," he told them truthfully.

The smile on Mary Emerson's face told him that his answer had pleased her, and that was all the thanks he needed.

Consulting Abby's list, Mary helped him select some just-picked apples and a small tin of cinnamon. He had a hankering for an apple pie, and so far, Abby hadn't balked at anything he'd suggested she fix, which, he had to admit, was a pleasant change.

"How is the arrangement with Abby Carter working out?" Bart Emerson asked, as if he could read his thoughts.

The troubled expression in the older man's eyes warned Caleb that something was wrong. "As well as can be expected, I suppose," he said, eyeing the older man thoughtfully. "What is it? I can tell something's wrong."

Bart cleared his throat. "I hate to mention it with everything you've been through lately, but you'll find out soon enough, I reckon."

"Spit it out," Caleb said, leaning against the counter.

"Well, uh, there are some folks in town making a terrible fuss about Mrs. Carter staying at your place."

Caleb's dark eyes narrowed. "What do you mean, fuss?"

"They don't think it's right, both of you being single and living under one roof."

Caleb swore beneath his breath. Though he was far from perfect and couldn't claim to be religious, the maliciousness of some so-called Christians never failed to astound him.

"Don't they know I just lost my wife, and I have a baby who needs to be fed every few hours?" he demanded. "Besides, Abby is newly widowed. And just for the record, I'm staying in the bunkhouse."

"I know, I know," Bart soothed. "You'd think they'd be more understanding what with Emily—" he cleared his throat "—and all. I'm thinking the problem is that Abby Carter is young and pretty. Maybe it would be different if she was old and ugly."

"And if she was old, I wouldn't need her, would I?" Caleb countered. He pinned Bart with a hard look. "Who exactly is 'they'?"

"Several in town," Bart hedged. "But the main one is Sarah VanSickle."

"The biggest gossip in three counties," Caleb muttered. He slapped his list onto the counter. "When I leave here, I have some business to see about for Abby, and then I'll go have a talk with Sarah."

"It won't do any good," Mary said. "She'd just make something of that. She's like a spoon, Caleb. She likes keeping things stirred up. The best thing to do is ignore it."

"Ignore it? That's easier said than done. I don't fancy being grist for the town's gossip mill, and I suspect Abby won't like it, either."

"I suppose not," Mary said, frowning. "Will you tell her?"

"No!" Caleb said in near panic. "She might decide to leave, and there's no way I could manage without her just now."

"I see your predicament, son, but you really ought to tell her before she finds out from someone else," Bart reasoned. "It's just a matter of time before Sarah's poison makes its way through the whole county."

Caleb hadn't thought of that, but knew Bart was

right. He couldn't let Abby come to town and face the gossips without even preparing her, but how would he tell her? What would her reaction be? Furious and fearing he already knew the answer to that, he ground his teeth. Was anything in life ever easy?

It was almost dark when Caleb pulled the wagon to the rear of the house. The temperature was dropping since the sun had gone down, and he shivered, dreading the conversation to come. The feeling of trepidation vanished somewhat the moment he opened the back door and felt the tide of warm, cooking-scented air rush out to meet him. Breathing in the delicious aromas, he shifted the heavy sack of flour from his shoulder to the floor. Venison. Purple hull peas. Cornbread. Every night since Abby had come to stay he'd come in at suppertime to find something simmering on the back the stove.

Never much of a cook, Emily had stopped all attempts to do so when she'd announced her pregnancy, complaining of nausea, backaches and a general malaise. Soon she declared she was unable to do anything but knit and read, and in the subtle way she had, she made him feel like pond scum for putting her in her delicate condition. Rather than let the whole town know the situation, Caleb himself did what cooking and cleaning was to be done. Coming in and finding dinner waiting was nice, cooked by a stranger or not.

"How were the Emersons?" Abby said, setting the plates on the round oak table.

"Fine."

"Did you get the apples?"

He nodded. "Just picked."

"Wonderful." They sat down to eat, Ben said the prayer and after a few more questions that received short answers, Abby deduced that Caleb was not in the mood for any type of conversation and stopped talking except to ask if she could pass him any more food.

When the awkward meal was finished, she put Laura in the square, quilt-lined "pen" William had made for her and gave Ben a piece of butterscotch Mary had thoughtfully sent. Abby told him to eat it on the porch and to get ready for bed as soon as he was finished. Caleb helped clear the table, something he'd gotten used to doing while fending for himself and continued to do for Abby.

He was setting a glass into the dishwater when she turned suddenly, a frown on her face. She was so close that he could see the almost-purple flecks in her blue eyes. So close he could smell the faint scent of the gardenia-scented soap she used for bathing. The sudden rush of awareness that jolted through him caught him off guard. Bart was right. Abby Carter was pretty. Very pretty. The revelation was swept away on another tidal wave of guilt. He took a sudden step back. What was the matter with him? His wife dead not two weeks, and he already found himself responding to the nearness of another woman!

"You seem distracted, Caleb. Is something wrong? Did Mr. Haversham refuse to discuss the farm?"

"No," Caleb said, thankful to turn his thoughts to something else. "As a matter of fact, he said he'd drop by on Sunday afternoon on his way back from his daughter's."

"Good," she said, but the worry stayed in her eyes. "Do you think he'll be open to what I have to say?"

Careful not to look at her, he wrapped the leftover cornbread in a flour-sack dish towel and lifted his wide shoulders in a shrug. "I didn't get into things with him, but Nate's a fair man, so I'm inclined to think he'll listen with an open mind."

"That's a relief." Neither spoke for several seconds.

"Abby, I—"

"Caleb, what—"

They both started to speak at once.

"Ladies first."

"It's just that something's wrong," she said, her blue eyes worry-filled. "I can tell. Did Ben—"

Caleb's first thought was that it was amazing that she could read his mood after less than two weeks, something Emily had never been able to do. "Ben's done nothing that I know about."

"Then what?"

He drew a deep breath, crossed his arms over his chest and plunged. "There's gossip in town."

"Gossip? About what?"

"Us. It seems Sarah VanSickle and some of the others in town think it's morally indecent for us to be living in the same house."

"But I go to church with Sarah," Abby said, as if the statement would negate the whole affair.

"If that old battle-ax is a Christian, I want no part of it."

"None of us is perfect, Caleb, and you'd do well to think twice about throwing out the baby with the bath-water."

Though she said the right thing, in her heart, she wanted to go to Sarah, confront her about her vicious character attacks and demand an accounting. Had the spiteful woman given any serious thought to her actions? Did she have any idea of the harm she was causing two innocent people—even more if you considered the children? Abby blinked back the sting of tears. As much as she might want to confront her accuser, she knew she wouldn't.

A sudden thought occurred to her. "Caleb, we *aren't* living in the same house! If we make that clear, everyone will understand."

Caleb set the towel-wrapped bread in the pie safe, rested his elbow across its corner and regarded her with angry gray eyes. "Believe me, that was the first thing I pointed out to Mary and Bart, but they reminded me that a trifling thing like the truth does not matter one bit to Sarah. As a matter of fact, she's notorious about never letting facts get in the way of her maliciousness."

Abby cradled her hot cheeks in her palms. While the unwarranted accusations infuriated Caleb, the tears swimming in her eyes said she was more hurt and embarrassed than angry. He thrust his hands into his front pockets and stared out the window at the darkness, wondering what he could do to fix the mess they found themselves in.

"Do you think there are other people in town who feel the same way?" she asked.

He shot her a look that said he couldn't believe her naïveté. "Count on it."

"Well, then, I'll leave first thing in the morning," she said firmly, as if the decision would put an end to the whole matter.

"You will not!"

Shocked by his vehemence, she shook her head and said, "It's the only thing we can do. My reputation is at stake. So is yours."

"I'm not worried about my reputation," he said, a muscle in his lean jaw tightening. "People have been talking about the Gentrys for years. But I am concerned about you. And I'm very concerned about my daughter."

He took a breath and let it out slowly, as if he were trying to release the tension holding him. The fierce look in his eyes softened a bit as they met Abby's. "Look, we've already been through all this and decided this is the best way."

"But that was before Sarah's accusations."

"I understand, but we don't need to let her wreck a perfectly good partnership. Why don't we both sleep on it tonight. Things always look better in daylight. Maybe we'll dream up some way to resolve things that even Sarah VanSickle can't argue with."

Chapter Four

Abby lay quietly in her bed, the covers clutched in her fists, and tried to keep from flipping and flopping and waking Ben, who slept beside her. Though Sarah VanSickle's reputation as an inveterate gossip preceded her, the fact that Abby herself was now bearing the brunt of that hatefulness was a definite shock. The situation with Caleb was not what she would have chosen, but there was no denying that the opportunity to get her life in order had come along at a perfect time, and had seemed like the answer to her prayers. But if that were so, why was it being jeopardized by senseless gossip?

Dear God, what am I to do?

God was silent.

The faint fingers of dawn were poking through the window when she finally drifted off to sleep, tears of hopelessness drying on her cheeks as she faced the only moral decision possible. As much as Caleb might dislike her decision, as soon as she could gather her things, she was going back to her own farm.

With or without his daughter.

Being a man who preferred action, Caleb paced the path from the bunkhouse to the house over and over. He vacillated from self-pity over Emily's death and his current situation to fury at Sarah VanSickle for making an already bad situation worse. He wasn't sure why he was so surprised by the unexpected turn of events. Hadn't he always been the one saddled with the responsibility of doing the right thing?

As the older son of Lucas Gentry, it had fallen to Caleb to follow in his father's footsteps, while Gabe played the spoiled, pampered son. Though both boys were required to work the farm, more often than not, Gabe's contribution had been to keep everyone laughing at his jokes and antics, while Caleb was expected to toe the line and pick up the slack left by his younger brother. Caleb was the one who worked the longest hours and took the tongue-lashings and razor strap beatings, the one forced to learn farming from the ground up, including how to manage the soil and take care of the books. His father's demands left no time for fun, something Gabe enjoyed to the fullest.

Eight years ago, when Gabe was twenty and itching to experience more than Pike County had to offer, he'd gone to Lucas to ask for his inheritance, instead of waiting for his father to pass away.

To everyone's shock, Lucas had capitulated without argument, and Gabe had set out to see the world.

Though there had been a few letters along the way, as far as Caleb knew, no one in Wolf Creek had seen his brother since he'd boarded the train for points east.

Rumors ran rampant. Word filtered back from friends of friends and even the pages of the big-city newspapers that were regularly shipped to Wolf Creek for the enlightenment of the few folks in town who liked to keep up with national happenings. Gabe's name had been linked to those of actresses, wealthy men's daughters and scandalous divorcées. He had a reputation of being a drinker, a gambler and a womanizer as he traveled California, New York, New Orleans, St. Louis and even Paris, London and Austria.

Five years after Gabe left to live the high life, and three years after Lucas browbeat Caleb into marrying Emily Emerson, Lucas died. Edward Stone claimed it was his heart. Caleb didn't doubt it. Gabe hadn't come home for the funeral; no one knew where or how to reach him.

And what did I get? A lifetime of work and responsibility, a wife I didn't love as I should have and now this. A baby to bring up alone. It wasn't fair, Caleb thought, feeling the rise of the anger that often simmered just beneath his calm exterior. But then, as Lucas had always declared when Caleb voiced that sentiment, life was many things, but it wasn't always fair.

Dwelling on past injustices would solve nothing, he thought now, gazing up at the wispy clouds trailing over the face of the moon. All he could do was deal with it in the best way possible. But what was that?

If he were a betting man, which he wasn't—he didn't

work from dawn till dusk to fritter away his profits—he would say that Abby would once again suggest taking Betsy to her place, and if he didn't agree to that, she would quit. That meant that if he wanted to see his daughter, he would be running back and forth during the worst time of the year.

He wasn't sure just how the fatherhood thing worked, but he realized he was obligated to do his best by Betsy. His own upbringing had taught him the hard way that doing one's best involved being more than a tyrant who laid down the law and expected everyone to obey or suffer the consequences. He suspected that keeping a tight rein on his temper and being willing to listen to someone else's perspective was involved…the way Abby's husband had been willing to listen to her.

Caleb clenched his hands, and forced himself to consider every angle, something he did before making any major decisions. All right, beyond trips back and forth, what else would it mean if Abby left?

You'll come in from work to a cold, empty, unwelcoming house.

The notion held little appeal. He recalled the evening before when he'd stepped through the door and was greeted by the mouthwatering aromas of supper cooking on the big cast-iron woodstove. It had not escaped his notice that the dust and cobwebs that had collected the past several months had disappeared. The rugs had been taken out and whacked with a wire beater, and the wooden furniture gleamed with a combination of elbow grease, beeswax, turpentine and something that smelled of lemon.

If he refused to let Abby take the baby to her place and she quit, he would have to find a replacement, which, as he'd told Bart and Mary, would not alter his current situation one iota.

Which brought him back to the root of his quandary and kicked up his anger. Rumors and gossip. Why should he and Abby be concerned by the venomous ranting of a few small-minded, hypocritical folks? After all, they both knew there was nothing untoward going on between them.

He heaved a deep sigh. He also knew Abby was a decent, God-fearing woman who would never consent to remaining in a position that might damage her or her children—or him and Betsy, for that matter. Furthermore, what kind of cad would he be if he *let* her stay in a situation that would cause her reputation such damage? She'd have to leave the state to find another husband.

A terrifying thought slammed into his mind, stopping him dead in his tracks. A harsh, heartfelt "No!" shattered the silence of the moon-drenched night. Muttering about life's injustices, he stomped across the yard some more. Thought some more. Weighed the good against the bad. Just before dawn, he gave a sigh of acceptance and made his peace with the inevitable.

When, weary and haggard, Caleb entered the kitchen from the barn the following morning, he saw that Ben was already seated, waiting for him. Though they were rarely seated before Caleb came in from his early chores, he'd told Abby he had no problem with her feeding the children before he got to the table. Abby had replied that unless it was some sort of emergency, she considered it the height of impoliteness to start a meal without the man of the house at the table.

Caleb's gaze roamed the room. Betsy was in her cradle near the fire, and Laura sat in the high chair he'd brought over from Abby's place, squishing a glob of sorghum and pancake into her mouth with the heel of her hand. A platter of sausage sat warming near the back of the stove, and Abby was busy taking buckwheat pancakes from a large cast-iron skillet.

It might have been a scene from a happy marriage, until you noticed the frown on Ben's face and the dejected slump of Abby's shoulders. He felt the almost overwhelming need to do something to improve the mood, but all he could manage was a terse "Good morning."

Abby sent him a quick glance over her shoulder. "Good morning."

She looked as tired as he felt. Dark smudges lay beneath her red-rimmed blue eyes. Her nose was reddened, too, no doubt from crying. There was an unhappy droop to her lips, which some still-functioning part of his mind noted were very prettily shaped. From what he'd seen in the mirror when he'd shaved, he looked no better than she.

Caleb noticed the way Ben's gaze moved from his mother to Caleb, as if he somehow knew who was responsible for the unhappiness that seemed to roll from her in dark waves.

She set down the sausages, a platter of pancakes, a round of fresh-churned butter and a quart jar of sorghum molasses before returning to the stove for the coffeepot. After filling both their cups, she sat down to Caleb's right and Ben gave thanks for their food.

They ate in silence, much like other mornings, Caleb thought with unexpected depression. Much like the mornings he'd shared with his father. Even Gabe had known better than to cut up at the table, and Gentry meals had been reduced to cleaning their plates as fast as possible so they could escape to whatever backbreaking work Lucas had planned.

When they finished eating, Abby sent Ben out with the table scraps, and told him to milk the goat. When the door slammed shut behind him, Caleb picked up his coffee cup, wondering what to say. He'd fought with his decision and come to the only plausible conclusion, but he wasn't sure how to begin.

"I've thought about things all night," Abby said at last, saving him the trouble. "The only solution is for me to quit. You can hire someone else."

"Who?" Caleb challenged as she poured more coffee into his cup. "Widows with infants aren't all that plentiful in Wolf Creek, and if I hired someone else it would just spark the same gossip we're dealing with."

Abby chewed on her lower lip. "I could take Betsy to my place," she offered again, as he'd known she would.

He shook his head. "We've already discussed that. She belongs at home. Winter will be here before we know it, and getting back and forth will be a nightmare when the weather gets bad. Seeing her the way I should would be a hardship, if not an impossibility. Besides, I already know how hard it is for you to manage things at your place, and I don't think you can make it through the winter alone with three children."

She plopped down in her chair and rested her elbows on the table, regarding him with tear-glazed eyes. "Then what other choice do we have, Caleb? I can't think of any other way."

The full force of his silvery gaze met hers. "The only way I can think of is for you to marry me."

Abby's eyes widened and her mouth fell open in shock. "Have you taken leave of your senses?" she asked when at last she was able to speak.

"I don't think so," Caleb replied in what he hoped was a measured, sensible tone. "I was up the whole night, too, trying to figure out what to do, and of everything I came up with, marriage makes the most sense."

"It makes no sense!" Abby cried, jumping up and pacing to the back door. "Never mind that we aren't in love! We hardly know each other."

"I know that you're a good person and a good mother, and it seems to me that love is highly overrated."

Her eyes widened and she looked at him as if he'd grown another head. "That's a cynical attitude, especially since you told me you loved Emily very much."

"When?" he asked, frowning.

"You asked me if I loved William, and I said that I had—very much. Then you said that I could have no idea how you felt when Emily died."

"I'm afraid you misunderstood. My marriage to Emily was not a love match."

"All the more reason I would think you'd put love at

the top of the list when you look for another wife," she countered, taken aback by his admission.

"Actually, I had no clear idea whether or not I would ever marry again, and I confess that I haven't seen a whole lot of marriages that are based on love," he told her. "Besides, arranged marriages, mail-order brides—" he shrugged "—for the most part, those marriages work out just fine. Why wouldn't ours?"

His attitude went against everything Abby had been taught about love and marriage. His coldhearted approach to one of God's most special institutions infuriated and saddened her. Shoving aside the pang of sorrow, she snapped, "Because it wouldn't, that's why."

Seeing the beginning of a storm gathering in his gray eyes, she softened her tone. "Marriage is sacred, Caleb, and I hope to find someone someday who will love me and my children, and despite your doubts, I'm sure that in time you'll find someone to love, too."

In a gesture fast becoming familiar, he raked a hand through his already-mussed hair. "Believe me, I gave that a lot of thought last night, too, but there's no woman in town—married or single—that I can ever imagine loving." Seeing her skepticism, he pushed his advantage. "You know as well as I do that the chance for either of us to find love in Wolf Creek is slim to none."

"I don't know that!"

He admitted a grudging admiration for the spark of irritation in her eyes. He didn't think he'd ever known Emily feeling strongly enough about a subject to defend it.

"Will you at least listen before you—" he offered her

a brief, halfhearted smile and tossed her words back at her "—throw out the baby with the bathwater?"

She blinked, amazed by the change the wry quirking of his lips made in his craggy features. The notion that she found his smile fascinating triggered another stab of irritation. She did not want to find him attractive. She did not want to feel sorry for him, and she did *not* want to hear what he had to say. She crossed her arms over her chest. "Fine."

He looked at her, wondering again where to start. Telling her he was no happier about the idea than she was would not help his cause. He cleared his throat.

"First, I think we would both agree that fate and Sarah VanSickle's penchant for gossip have put us in a bad spot, and we have to figure out the best way to stop the rumors while still solving our mutual problems. After giving both sides careful consideration, I believe marriage is the best solution."

Abby pressed her lips together to keep from saying something inflammatory. She would hear him out.

He offered her another of those "almost" smiles. "I guess you've noticed that I'm not the most likable man in Wolf Creek, and the mirror tells me I'm not the most handsome."

Stunned at his brutal assessment of himself, she opened her mouth to offer a polite denial, but he held up a silencing palm. "Despite those drawbacks, I have it on the authority of several folks—including Emily's parents—that I am considered a good catch. If you consent to this marriage, I promise to take the best care I know how of you and your children. I realize that besides being your husband, I will be their father as well as Betsy's, which I confess frightens me more than I can say."

She couldn't picture Caleb Gentry being afraid of anything, yet his whole attitude was one of vulnerability.

"I have no idea how to be a father to my own child, much less someone else's. I know I'll need to work on being more patient and realize that there will be other incidents like the shepherdess and the chessmen, but I also know there would have been those same sorts of incidents between your children and their real father. I doubt anyone short of a saint could refrain from losing his temper on occasion."

Impressed by the thought he'd given to their predicament, Abby nodded.

His mouth twisted into another of those mocking smiles. "As troubling as this shortcoming is, I am somewhat consoled by the fact that you, too, have a temper."

Abby felt a blush heat her cheeks.

All trace of sardonic humor vanished. "Sit down, Abby. Please." When she did his bidding, he continued. "If you marry me, I promise I'll try to do better, but you must understand that I won't always succeed."

He had given this a lot of thought, and really was as concerned about her and her children as he was his daughter.

"I know you're an educated woman and that you'll want more instruction for your children than is available here. When they get older, I'll pay for their schooling wherever you like."

Abby's eyes widened. "You'd do that? Why?"

"Because I know that sort of thing is important to someone like you. Furthermore, I'll settle all your outstanding debts." He continued speaking over her indrawn breath. "If you're agreeable, I'll talk to Nathan Haversham about selling your farm. You can put the proceeds from the sale into a trust to secure your children's future—and yours, should anything happen to me."

Abby was surprised by the sudden sense of loss she felt at the thought of something happening to him. She sat, trying to absorb what he was saying. His offer was more than generous. And very tempting. To know she would never again have to worry about how to pay bills or feed her children. To feel secure in the knowledge that they would have every advantage the Gentry money could offer….

But things and advantages were no substitute for a father who would love them. Nor were they a suitable replacement for a husband who would care for her.

"You make it sound more like a business deal than a marriage."

"Maybe that's the best way to look at it. At least until we…come to know each other better." Abby blinked at the implication, and he cleared his throat. "There are some things you should know about me before you decide. I may not sit in a pew every Sunday, but I try to live a decent life."

Abby had never heard anything to the contrary.

"I don't gossip or stick my nose into anyone else's business, and while I drive a hard bargain, I believe anyone will tell you that I'm fair. To my knowledge I've never cheated anyone."

He sounded so perfect that Abby was beginning to wonder if she should offer him a laundry list of her own qualities—good and bad. With a breathless burst of self-conscious laughter, she said as much.

"I think I know the most important things about you, and it will be an adventure of sorts to uncover the others through the years. Just for the record, like you, I believe in the sanctity of marriage, and I take any commitment I make seriously, including marriage vows."

Abby regarded him, her brow furrowed in question. "Those vows speak of love, Caleb. What about that?" It seemed they had come full circle. She longed to experience that emotion again; he doubted its existence. How could a marriage between them ever work?

He spread his hands in a helpless gesture. "I don't know, Abby. But if love really exists, perhaps it will find us."

She wanted to ask what would happen if it didn't find them, but was unable to phrase the question for the thoughts swirling through her mind. She recalled one of William's favorite sayings: "An open heart will find love." Would he think her mad to contemplate such a thing, or would he think she was wise for doing what she must for the sake of the children? Was it possible that in time, if she kept an open mind, she would grow to love Caleb Gentry? And what of him? Would his heart open enough to let love in? Love not only for her and the children, but a love of God and His word?

The preposterous idea seemed unseemly, somehow,

and yet Caleb had a point. People did enter loveless marriages every day and for less pressing reasons than finding a mother for a child. Betsy would need a caring mother as she grew up.

And what about her own prayers? *Lord, is this the answer I prayed for? Is this what You would have me do?* She wished she had time to consider it more fully, but in the end, would it matter? The problems and choices would stay the same.

"I don't know what to say," she whispered in a tormented voice.

"Say yes, Abby," Caleb urged, his deep voice soft, pleading. "Say yes."

Abby still couldn't believe she'd agreed to Caleb's unexpected proposal. Once she yielded, they'd called Ben in to tell them the news. Abby settled him on the sofa and took the chair facing him.

"You know that Mr. Gentry's wife died," she began.

Ben gave a solemn nod.

"And you know how hard it has been for us since your father died." Another nod. "Well, since we're living here already, Caleb has asked me to marry him, so that we can make a new family, all of us. You and Laura and Betsy will be brother and sisters and Caleb will be your stepfather."

"Do you have to marry him, Mama?" Ben asked.

Abby sneaked a peek at Caleb, whose face had turned a dull red. "Yes, Ben, for the good of us all, it seems I do."

"Well, he's not my father," Ben shouted, jumping up and glaring at her. "And I won't call him that."

"Benjamin Aaron—" Abby began, only to be stopped by Caleb's hand on her shoulder.

"It's all right, Abby." To Ben, he said, "You don't have to call me Papa, Ben. Call me Caleb."

"But he can't!" Abby cried. "That's disrespectful."

"Not if I give him permission," Caleb countered. "I can't have him calling me Mr. Gentry for the rest of his life."

The rest of his life. The words sank into her mind, and a queasy feeling settled in her stomach as she faced head-on the seriousness of her bargain. "No," she whispered. "I suppose not."

"Ben," Caleb said, "I know I've been short with you sometimes, but you need to understand that I've never had children before Betsy, and I'm not used to them or the things they do."

Ben refused to lift his head and meet Caleb's gaze.

"I know it's been hard for you since your father died, and that it was hard for you to leave your home and come to a place that's unfamiliar and where there are new rules. It's hard for me and your mother, too. She says it will take time for us to get used to each other, and I think she's right."

Ben stared at the toes of his scuffed boots. When he didn't reply, Caleb asked, "Ben, did your father ever get angry with you?"

Ben nodded, still refusing to look up.

"And I imagine that sometimes you were mad at him, too. But you got over it, and you still cared for him, didn't you?" Without waiting for Ben to answer, Caleb added, "I suspect we will be no different. You're right. I'm not your father, but I hope the time will come when you will at least count me as a friend if you can't think of me as a father."

Leaving Ben with that to ponder, Caleb gave Abby's shoulder a gentle squeeze and left her alone with her son.

When he was gone, Abby went to Ben and drew him close. He buried his face against her as he seldom did since he'd turned six, and she thought she heard him snuffling. "I know this is hard for you, but it is necessary, Ben. I can't tell you all the reasons why, because they're grown-up reasons, and even if I did, you wouldn't understand. You must trust me when I tell you that the decision Caleb and I have made is for the good of us all."

Stepping back, she tilted up his freckled face and offered him a sorrowful smile. "I can't change the way you feel, Ben, but I need you to try to understand. We don't know what happened to Caleb that has made him—" *Harsh. Distant. Detached.* "—the way he is, but we need to try to get along. I know he wants things to be better. Rachel says he's a good man, and I don't think she would say that if it weren't the truth. We just have to give him a chance, the way he has to give us a chance. Will you try?"

Tears filled Ben's blue eyes and he nodded.

"We need to pray about it, too. We need to believe that we are where God wants us, even though we don't understand why. One day we will."

Ben nodded, swiped at his eyes and drew his shirt sleeve across his runny nose. *Snail trails.* She smiled.

Ben gave her a hard hug and left Abby wondering, despite their limited choices and her guarantees to her son, if she and Caleb really were doing the right thing for everyone involved.

Chapter Five

While Abby had her talk with Ben, Caleb went out to get his hands started on a final late hay-cutting. Then he and Abby spent the better part of an hour discussing their decision at length. If things went according to plan, the ceremony would be held in three days, on a Saturday afternoon at the house, since they both felt Betsy was too little to be taken out and about.

Shortly after the noon meal, Caleb headed to town to make the necessary arrangements for the wedding. He didn't relish the next couple of hours and kept the horse to a slow walk for most of the three-plus miles. He had agreed to take care of the legalities, including telling Emily's parents of the decision before doing anything else. He hoped they understood. At Abby's insistence that he take care of all the legalities, he would speak with Nathan Haversham at the bank about setting up a power of attorney and then selling Abby's farm and investing the proceeds for her children's future. Last,

Caleb would approach Abby's minister about performing the wedding ceremony.

He did not feel like a potential bridegroom.

Ever since she had agreed to his preposterous proposal, his feelings had vacillated between those of a shipwrecked sailor who spies land on the horizon and a man condemned to walk the plank. He was not happy about entering another marriage; contrarily, he was relieved that things would soon be resolved. There was even a small kernel of conviction that the decision was the best choice for everyone concerned.

Without a doubt there were those in town, such as Sarah VanSickle and her ilk, who would judge them as harshly for marrying so soon after Emily's death as they were for Abby staying at his house without a ring on her finger. His jaw tightened. There was just no pleasing some folks.

"Why so glum, young fella?" Frank asked, spying Ben sitting on an overturned bucket, his chin in his palms, his elbows resting on his patched, denim-clad knees.

"Nuthin'."

"Nuthin' doesn't make a fella look like he's lost his last friend. Come on, boy, tell me what's wrong, and maybe I can help."

Heaving a sigh, Ben looked up at the hired hand. "She's gonna marry him. He's gonna be my stepfather."

"Whoa, Nellie!" Franks said. "Are you sayin' your mama and Caleb are getting hitched?"

Ben nodded.

Frank took off his dirty felt hat, slapped it against his scrawny thigh, scratched his head and replaced the hat on his uncombed hair. “Well, if that don’t beat all!” he said, flipping over another bucket and plopping down. “I take it you ain’t too pleased about it.”

Defiance darkened Ben’s eyes. “I don’t like him.”

“Can’t imagine why not,” Frank said. “He’s a right good man once you get to know him. Course I been knowin’ him ever since he was a little guy like you, so maybe I’m a tad partial.”

Ben frowned. “You knew Caleb when he was a kid?”

“Yep.”

“What was he like?”

“A real hard worker. His daddy was a hard taskmaster. Seen to it that Caleb did more’n his share of chores around here.”

“I do chores.”

“I know you do, and it’s good for you. A man’s gotta work to be able to provide for his family.”

“My father worked for the railroad,” Ben said. “He got killed.”

“I heard that, and I’m real sorry.” They sat in silence for a moment and then Frank said, “Your mama lost her husband and Caleb lost his wife. Seems like a right smart thing to do to get hitched up so as they can help each other.”

Ben thought back to what his mother had said about both her and Caleb needing something the other had. Sighed.

“Don’t give up on Caleb before you ever get started,” Frank said, slanting a serious look at Ben. “He’s got his faults, but he's got a lotta good in him, too, and he can teach you things most boys don't know about."

"Like what?"

"Like runnin' a farm, and gravel business. Huntin'. He knows a lot about book learnin', too. He even taught me to read and write a bit. Smart man, Caleb Gentry."

A slight smile curved the old man's mouth. Smart enough to grab up a good woman when he had the chance, whether or not he realized yet that it was a good thing.

While Betsy slept in her cradle and Ben went to "help" Frank and Leo, Laura sat in Abby's lap gnawing on a hard crust of bread while she stared at a page of her mama's handwritten recipe book. With the wheels set into motion by Caleb's trip to town, her doubts had once again begun to creep in. She was trying hard to make herself believe the things she'd told her son, especially about trusting God that this marriage was the best solution for all involved—indeed the only solution.

Even though she'd only been at the Gentry farm a few days, she knew that one thing she'd said was true: Caleb was a decent and good man, as his generosity proved. If he was also a hard man, well, no one was perfect, as he had pointed out by reminding her of her own quick temper and the conjecture that things had not always been idyllic between William and the children—or her and William for that matter. Though it chafed to hear it, it was true.

At Caleb's suggestion, she'd spent the morning handwriting invitations to a few of her closest friends from church, asking them to come and witness the ceremony and to stay for some refreshment afterward. He'd promised to deliver the requests when he went to town. He also told her to make up a list of whatever she might need from the mercantile for the occasion, and he would go back for it the following day.

His unexpected thoughtfulness had come as a bit of a surprise. She knew his offer meant more time away from the farm, and she appreciated his wanting to make the wedding something more than a quick, secretive affair done solely to satisfy the gossipmongers. With the town rife with rumor and a few of the people in her own church in the middle of it, Abby wasn't sure how her invitations would be received. She was so hurt by the unexpected scandal that she was no longer sure who her friends were, or which ones were nothing more than pew warmers.

Well, there was no sense fretting over it, she thought, putting Laura in her playpen. In a demonstration of rare wastefulness, telling herself she deserved a treat, Abby dumped out the bit of leftover breakfast coffee and set a fresh pot on the stovetop to brew.

Resolutely, and with a deep sigh, she turned her mind back to the recipes. There was much to do and only a short time to do it. Since apples were in abundance, she would bake a fresh apple cake. She'd have Ben pick up some of the pecans from beneath the tree that grew out near the edge of the woods. Frank and Leo could shell them. She'd be making goat cheese tomorrow, which would go well with some of her muscadine jelly on fresh crackers she'd have Caleb pick up at the mercantile. She could make some small venison pastries....

The sound of someone knocking on the door disrupted her thoughts. Getting to her feet, she headed for the parlor and opened the door to see Rachel framed in the doorway, the wide smile on her face mirroring the one in her dark eyes.

"What can I do?"

Abby stared at her friend in disbelief. "About what?"

Rachel laughed. "The wedding, goose!" she said, stepping inside.

"How on earth did you hear about it so quickly?" Abby asked, closing the door behind her friend.

Rachel went straight to the fireplace. Though it was a glorious autumn day, there was a nip in the air. "I was on my way to the Donnellys' and passed Caleb on the road. He gave me the highlights, so when I finished there, I came on over."

Still stunned by how fast news traveled, Abby gave a weak smile. "Did he tell you why we're doing this?"

"Of course he did. I've been hearing rumblings the past few days, and if it's any consolation, I've been doing my best to stamp out the lies whenever I get a chance."

"Thank you. And thank you for coming. I'm feeling a bit overwhelmed."

"I'm sure you are."

"Come on into the kitchen. I just put on some fresh coffee, and I've been trying to figure out what sort of refreshments to fix. I don't have much time, so it can't be anything too elaborate—not that it should be too fancy considering the circumstances. I just felt I should offer something for those who accept my invitation… assuming anyone does."

"What do you mean? Of course they will," Rachel said, following Abby into the kitchen.

Abby set the coffeepot to a cooler part of the stove and turned toward her friend. "Thank you, Rachel, but even though they aren't true, and you're trying to stop them, it doesn't change the fact that gossips are bandying lies all over town, and plenty of people will judge me and Caleb because of it."

She turned away to fetch the cups and saucers to hide a sudden rush of tears, but she could not hide the tremor in her voice. "It's beyond me how something that started out as a mission of mercy and a way for me to provide for my children wound up as fodder for the gossip mill and a marriage between two people who'd rather be snakebit!"

"Trust me, marriage—even to Caleb Gentry—is a much better fate than being snakebit," the always-serious doctor said.

The fact that the words were spoken without an iota of humor struck Abby as comical, no doubt because her nerves were shaky. A reluctant smile tugged at her mouth. "Maybe you're right."

She filled the cups, set the sugar bowl on the table, punched a couple of holes in a can of condensed milk and set it next to the sugar. "Sorry," she said. "I don't have anything sweet. Caleb inhales anything and everything I bake."

Rachel groaned. "I don't need a thing! I had a slice

of pie at Millie's." She picked up the can of milk. "My, aren't we uptown?" she said with a lift of her dark eyebrows. "I'm not sure when I last had this in my coffee. It's a little pricy for a mere physician."

Abby knew that Rachel often went without pay or traded for her services. "Then by all means, enjoy. Compliments of Caleb Gentry." She sighed. "I'm pretty sure he has no problem paying for it."

"Probably not," Rachel said, stirring some of the thick, sweet milk into the fragrant coffee. She swallowed a healthy swig and shoved the sugar bowl away.

"What?" Abby teased. "No two spoons full of sugar today?"

Rachel's gaze met Abby's. "If I added sugar, it would be so sweet that even I couldn't stand it," she said with a dry solemnity that brought a burst of laughter to Abby's lips. Rachel's love of anything sweet was well known.

"Thanks, Rachel, I needed to laugh."

Rachel smiled back. "I aim to please." She took another sip of coffee. "So tell me how it all came about."

Abby spent the next few moments relating the gist of her conversations with Caleb. "So, here we are. As you know, he's on his way to see if the preacher can come out Saturday afternoon, and I sent invitations to a few people I thought might come. I was just looking through some recipes when you knocked."

"Tell me what you're planning. I'll be glad to bring something."

They spent the next half hour discussing things to serve. After decisions were made and Rachel volunteered to bring some serving pieces of her mother's for the event, the hint of animation in Abby's eyes dimmed.

"Why the frown?"

Abby cut a wry glance at her friend. "Oh, I don't know. Maybe the fact that I'm marrying a stranger, or maybe because both our reputations are in ruins."

"'This too shall pass,'" Rachel said. "Look, this will be the prime topic of conversation until something juicier comes along. Trust me, Abby, I know. Besides, Caleb's family is no stranger to controversy."

"What do you mean?"

"Evidently when he and his brother were small, Libby Gentry left them for another man."

Abby couldn't hide her shock. "B-But I thought she died. There's a marker under the magnolia tree out back. I assumed her remains were buried there."

"I've heard that Lucas forbade either of them to ever mention her name again," Rachel said. "He emptied the house of everything that was hers, set fire to it and buried what wouldn't burn. I guess in a way it *is* her remains."

Abby thought of the broken shepherdess and wondered how it had escaped Lucas Gentry's cruel hand.

"And then there's Gabe," Rachel said, averting her gaze.

The animosity in her voice drew Abby's attention back to the conversation. There was a grim expression on Rachel's face that was totally foreign to the woman Abby had grown so fond of.

"His younger brother," she said, remembering Caleb

mentioning him as he'd tried to explain the lack of love in his life.

"Yes, Gabe. Gabriel. Though he bears absolutely no resemblance to anything angelic. More like Wolf Creek's very own black sheep." She gave a little shiver, as if shaking off a chill or a bad memory, and offered Abby a forced smile.

"As for marrying a stranger, I wonder if we ever really know someone until we share their life."

It took Abby a few seconds to realize Rachel had switched topics. "I've thought of that, but I'm not sure I understand how strangers..." The words dried on her lips, the same way her mouth dried up when she thought of the deeper implications of the course she had willingly chosen for herself. She tried to imagine a future with Caleb as father to a child of hers and felt a blush spread over her face. "It's just...there should be...love."

Rachel nodded. "I know you loved William."

Abby nodded. "I did. He was a dreamer and a romantic and good to the bone. He was handsome and joyful and filled with ideas. Most of them were pie-in-the-sky aspirations, but he had a knack for getting so caught up in his dreams that he could light that same kind of fire in me—at least in the beginning. And I supported him because I loved him, and as his wife, that was part of my job."

"A wife's support is always important," Rachel said.

"I know, and I was glad to do so, at least in those early years." Abby gave a short little laugh and met her friend's troubled gaze. "In all honesty, I didn't want to leave Springfield and come here. My inheritance wasn't large, but it would have given us a more-than-comfortable lifestyle while we both taught. But he'd read an article in the *St. Louis Post Dispatch* touting the fulfillment of farming. He said he was tired of academia and wanted to work with his hands, so I agreed and we came to Wolf Creek."

She did not say that she had awakened one day to the bitter reality that not only was the money gone, but William's dreams and aspirations had vanished, as well. They'd been replaced by doubts and growing depression.

"Before he was killed, I often wished he were stronger-willed and a better manager. Looking back, it's scary how tight money has been the past couple of years."

"Yet you've always survived."

"Yes."

"And you didn't stop loving him."

Abby was thoughtful as she chewed on her thumbnail a moment before answering. "No."

She did not tell Rachel that even though she sometimes missed him so much she ached inside, she had come to realize that her feelings had always been those of a young girl caught up in the fantasy and romance of love, a love that sometimes faltered when tempered in the fires of reality.

"Even though you and Caleb don't love each other, you can still have a good life together. If you ask me, there may not be any better two things to build a relationship on than mutual respect and trust."

Abby noted that the cynicism was back. Was Rachel

referring to her relationship with her son Daniel's father? Abby knew there was no man in Rachel's life, and since she had offered no insight, and Abby was unwilling to ask someone and be guilty of being nosy herself, she had no idea what the situation was.

"I pray you're right." She lifted her head, met Rachel's concerned gaze and blurted, "Do you think I'm being mercenary for agreeing to marry a man who's promised to fix all my financial woes, feed and clothe me and my children, and be a husband and father to us for the rest of our lives?"

Rachel stared at her for a moment in stunned disbelief, and then burst out laughing. After a few seconds she grew serious and reached out to take Abby's hand.

"Oh, Abby! If you and Caleb *were* in love and he asked you to marry him, he would be doing the same thing. Besides, it isn't as if you're coming empty-handed into this marriage, you know. Besides working alongside him every day you're bringing warmth and love into the home and the life of a man who needs it desperately. Never, never feel as if Caleb is the one doing all the giving."

After Rachel left, Abby thought long about what she'd said. She had to admit that Rachel's perspective had taken the edge off her own anxiety. She *was* bringing something to the marriage. And, as hard and unapproachable as he might be, she did respect Caleb. More importantly, she trusted him. That trust engendered a feeling of safety she hadn't experienced in a long time.

Caleb would not be intimidated by what he confronted in life. He would look difficulties in the eye, size them up and proceed with determination and hard work to fix them, whatever they might be, just as he had when confronted with news of the scandal attached to both their names.

It gave her some consolation that he would do no less in their marriage. Whatever problems might arise between them, she felt he would somehow do his best to fix them.

The next morning, Abby was washing the breakfast dishes, and Caleb had once again gone to town to get the items she needed for the wedding refreshments. Though she still had doubts and fears, her heart had been somewhat lighter since Rachel's visit the day before. What concerns Abby could not banish, she managed to push aside with a flurry of housecleaning.

She had just set the cast-iron skillet on the back of the stove when she heard Ben yell, "It's Mr. Teasdale, Mama!"

There was no denying the excitement in his voice. Ben was always thrilled to see what new treasures the peddler might have tucked away in his satchels and crates.

Truth be told, Abby was glad to see him, too. A wee sprite of a man with a broad smile and false teeth far too big for his face, Simon Teasdale made a pass through the area every few months, bringing shoes, guns and knives for the menfolk; pots and pans, spices, perfumes, bolts of fabric and other frippery for the ladies.

Abby sneaked a peek at Betsy, who was asleep in her cradle, snatched up Laura and hurried to the door.

Maybe he would have something suitable for her wedding, since all her dresses—including her better ones—were not only out of style, but a bit worse for the wear.

She flung open the door. "Mr. Teasdale! It's good to see you. Come in!"

"Don't mind if I do," he said with a toothy smile. "Hello there, Ben. I believe you've grown a foot since I last saw you!" he said, hanging his hat on the coatrack and shrugging out of his coat. Ben grinned, anticipation glowing in his eyes. As expected, the peddler pulled two peppermint sticks from his coat pocket and handed one to Ben and one to Laura, who was still on her mother's hip.

With the children satisfied for the moment, Simon backed up to the small fire burning in the grate. "I didn't know what to think when I went by your place and it was shut up tighter'n a drum. Then I went on into town and heard what happened to Mrs. Gentry." He shook his balding head. "A pity. She always did seem such a frail sort. I always figured she was just here for a short time."

Abby didn't know how to respond to that. Simon brightened suddenly. "Well, now, there's no sense dwelling on sad things when I hear congratulations are in order."

Abby blushed.

"I saw Doc Rachel in town, and as soon as I heard the news I hightailed it out here to see if I might have some female trifle you might have need of for the big day. I didn't figure you could head off to town with two little ones in tow."

"It really isn't going to be a big day, Mr. Teasdale.

Just a few friends here at the house with a little refreshment afterward."

"Well, I have some nice cider that would be fine drinking with some cinnamon sticks and whole cloves simmered in it. The weather is perfect for something warm." He winked. "I even have some oranges and lemons you might add."

"That sounds wonderful, but what I could really use is a dress."

"A dress, hmm?" The little man cocked his head and looked her up and down. Coming from any other man, it might have been insulting, but Abby knew he was only trying to judge her size. "I'm sure we can find something that will be just the thing," he told her, heading back out to his wagon.

Abby passed on the gowns with bustles, declaring that they were too fancy for Wolf Creek and she'd get little use of them. Instead, she chose a simple dress of gold-hued velvet with a plain round neck, long sleeves and a fitted bodice with tiny abalone buttons marching down the front. The skirt flared gently toward the floor with no need for a multitude of petticoats. It was quietly elegant, and would be suitable for church.

She emerged from the bedroom fifteen minutes later and whirled around for Simon's inspection.

"You'll make a beautiful bride, my dear," he said. "Caleb will be as pleased as punch."

Abby didn't have the heart to contradict him. "I don't have much money right now," she said. "Will you take something in trade?"

"Please. Let it be my wedding gift to you," Simon said.

"Oh, I couldn't possibly!" Abby objected. "Wait here." She went back into her room and emerged in a moment with a lovely cameo brooch encircled with fine gold filigree. "This was my mother's. Would you take it in exchange for the gown?"

Simon looked as torn as Abby. "It's a lovely piece and worth far more than the dress. I hate to see you part with it. Perhaps—"

"Please," Abby coaxed, pressing the brooch into his bony hands even though she hated losing one of her last links to her mother. "I wouldn't feel right otherwise." Though neither of them was happy about the upcoming nuptials, she *was* marrying the wealthiest man in the county, and she would not have Caleb ashamed of her. "If it will make you feel better, you can throw in the cider, oranges and spices."

In the end, Simon added a shirt and some new Sunday trousers for Ben, who had taken a growth spurt the past couple of months, and a pair of dark gold shoes of the softest leather that matched Abby's dress. When he left, her heart was a bit lighter. Simon Teasdale was a good man who always brought a spot of sunshine when he came.

By Friday afternoon Abby wondered if she'd be able to get everything done in the next twenty-four hours. The children's clothes were ready and the house was spotless, but Betsy hadn't slept well the night before, and the usually sweet-tempered Laura was teething and whiny. Miserable, Ben slunk around like someone who'd lost his last friend, despite Abby giving him the piece of licorice Simon had left as a surprise.

Abby was weary from being up with Betsy, and Ben still needed a haircut and the cake needed to be baked. She would get up early in the morning to finish the last-minute details before the guests arrived.

Caleb must have sensed that she was feeling pressure, because he'd asked Ben to go with him to help Frank and Leo look for pine knots. Ben had declined at first, but Caleb had bent to whisper something in his ear, and Ben had given a reluctant nod.

Abby had just put both girls down for a nap and was mixing up the apple cake when she heard someone at the door. She opened it to find Rachel along with four other friends standing there, laden down with various items, their faces wreathed in wide smiles. Emily's mother stood at the rear of the group.

"Congratulations!" they chorused as one, breezing into the house.

"What's going on?"

"We've come to help with the wedding preparations," Allison Granger, a short, plump, redheaded schoolteacher, said. She swept past Abby and set a pair of silver candlesticks and two tall white tapers on the dining room table. Ellie Carpenter, who owned the café, uncovered three small cut-glass plates wrapped in dish towels. Rachel brought a tall cut-crystal vase that had belonged to her mother. Gracie Morrison offered a fine white damask tablecloth for the dining room table, and Lydia North's contribution was a silver charger piled high with delicate cookies laced with finely chopped pecans. Mary Emerson carried a large crystal punch bowl with matching cups that she announced had belonged to her grandmama. When she saw the tears in Abby's eyes, she took her hands and squeezed tightly. "Bless you, child," she whispered.

Then, amid a cacophony of chatter and laughter, Rachel shooed Abby back to the kitchen to finish the cake, while they finished "fixing things up." As Abby added the flour to the already blended sugar, butter, eggs and chopped apple, she could hear snippets of their conversations and their happy laughter. She wasn't aware of the smile that claimed her lips, but she was aware that her friends' appearance had restored her flagging faith in the goodness of the townsfolk.

When the cake was in the oven, she reentered the parlor. Her shocked gaze moved around the room and to the adjoining dining room in amazement. Both were transformed with English ivy and branches of French mulberry laden with clusters of fuchsia berries.

"What do you think?" Rachel asked.

Abby felt the sting of tears again. She did have friends who cared. "I think it's beautiful and that you are all wonderful, wonderful friends."

"Well, thanks. We love you, too," Allison said with a saucy grin. "We aren't finished yet. Rachel and I will be out in the morning to finish up."

"It couldn't look any better."

"Just wait until you see it tomorrow."

While Abby's friends were helping her with the wedding preparations, Caleb was sitting beside the boy who, come the following day, would be his stepson. Ben was stubborn, hardheaded and inquisitive, but thanks to his mother, he was mannerly. It hit Caleb like a freight train that he would be responsible, at least in part, for shaping Ben into the man he would one day be. It was a daunting realization. He hadn't the slightest notion of how to break through the child's animosity, much less make him a good man, but he had to do something, start somewhere. Bart Emerson had been adamant that Caleb try to get on a better footing with the boy.

"Thanks for coming with me, Ben," Caleb said, his mouth as dry as the desert. "Dr. Rachel and some of your mother's friends had a surprise for her, and I thought you might want to be with the men rather than a bunch of nattering women."

Ben's sullen expression vanished, and he slanted Caleb a questioning look. "What's nattering?"

"A lot of talking, which from what I've been told, is often about nothing in particular and everything in general, especially when ladies are involved. I understand the conversation usually centers around cooking and children and husbands and is accompanied by tea or coffee and a lot of laughter." Which didn't, he thought in amazement, sound too bad at all. "In this case, your mother's friends wanted to come help her with the last-minute preparations for tomorrow."

"A hen party," Ben said. "Danny says that's what he and his granddad call it when Doc Rachel's friends come over."

"Yes, I've heard it called that, too."

Ben didn't speak for a moment, and then said, almost conversationally, "I don't really want you to be my stepfather."

Caleb was taken aback by Ben's forthrightness, even while he admired his courage. It couldn't be easy for a child to speak his mind to an adult.

"I understand that," Caleb said, striving to make his tone calm and polite. "I'm sure your mother has told you that this...marriage is something that neither of us would have chosen, but sometimes circumstances force us to make difficult choices."

"Mama told me that you needed her for Betsy and she needed you to help with the farm and stuff. She said you were like partners."

He might have known Abby would do a far better job of explaining things than he could ever hope to do. "That's right. I know you had a very good father and that I can't hope to replace him in your life. I wouldn't want to, Ben."

A picture flashed in his mind, one of him and Abby and the three children around the dinner table, laughing. It was a pleasant image but pretty far-fetched. But was it? Surely they would find some closeness in the future.

"I do hope in time that we'll become a real family, even though our new family will be different from what we had before."

"Mama says different isn't bad, it's just a change."

"She's right. Are you looking forward to tomorrow?" Caleb asked as the wagon bounced down the rutted road.

"Not really," Ben said, his gaze focused on the trees in the distance.

"I thought you might be looking forward to all the good things to eat and seeing your friends."

Ben slanted him a glance. "What kind of good things?"

"Well, I know for a fact that someone brought some cookies, and your mother is making a cake with some apples and the nuts you picked up. I'm sure there will be lots of other good things."

Ben sat straighter and Caleb thought he saw a hint of a smile teasing the corner of his mouth.

"And your friends will be there."

"Really?" he said, showing the first animation since they'd left the house. "Daniel's coming?"

"Daniel and Toby and Sam are coming for sure. I'm not sure who else. And while the girls are having their hen party and nattering, we men will play horseshoes and sit out on the porch and chew the fat."

"I don't want to chew on any fat," Ben said, his eyebrows drawing together in a scowl. "I don't like fat."

Caleb couldn't help the laughter that erupted at Ben's lack of understanding. His eyes were still smiling they met Ben's narrowed gaze. "Chewing the fat is a bunch of men sitting around talking about fishing, or hunting or trapping, or their businesses."

"Sounds like a hen party to me," Ben said.

Caleb thought about that a moment, then smiled. "Exactly."

Chapter Six

Friends and well-wishers sat or stood around the large parlor whose wide aperture opened into the dining room, where the overflow crowd stood. All eyes were on the couple in front of the rock fireplace. A tall vase of wild grasses resembling horses' tails and turning a lovely autumn purple sat in the center of the mantel, which was laden with English ivy. More French mulberry was tucked among the feathery lengths along with stems of native sunflower. Deep burgundy grosgrain ribbon from the mercantile provided by Mary was wound cleverly throughout the ivy.

Mary cradled baby Betsy in her arms, and Laura sat on Rachel's lap, chewing on the yellow ribbon that graced the front of her smocked gingham dress. Rachel was flanked on either side by her seven-year-old son, Daniel, and Ben. Edward Stone sat in his wheelchair, and Bart Emerson stood sentinel next to him, ready to give assistance with the boys if it became necessary. The only guests representing Caleb were Frank and

Leo, Nathan Haversham and his wife, and a lawyer from town whom Abby recognized but had not met.

She clutched her trembling hands around a bouquet of ivy and the perky yellow flowers that grew in abundance along roadsides and fields, their yellow faces appearing to float on the autumn breeze, looking almost stemless. The past couple of days, Abby had felt as disconnected as the flowers looked. She'd done what was necessary, moving through the days without conscious thought or effort.

It seemed she had prayed nonstop since agreeing to Caleb's proposal. First she'd prayed that some other way to fix the muddle would come to mind, only to realize time and again that there was no other avenue that would work for everyone concerned. When she'd reached a tentative peace with that, she asked for courage and wisdom to be the wife and mother Caleb and Betsy needed. Still, doubts ambushed her fragile peace when she least expected them—like now. Was she doing the right thing?

Right or wrong, she stood beside Caleb, clad in her new wedding finery, uttering her vows in a soft, almost inaudible voice, while random memories of her first wedding stole through into her mind.

She and William had said their vows in a church in front of dozens of friends and family. Abby's parents had thrown a lavish garden party afterward. Sunshine poured through the lacy leaves of the trees, and birds sang sweet summer songs, promising more sunny days ahead. She and William had been so young, so inexperienced, so much in love. Never once did they consider all the things that could go wrong in a marriage, or in a life. Ignorance truly had been bliss.

She and Caleb were going into this union with no illusions of love or dreams of happily ever after. They knew exactly where they stood. They were two people with different needs, and this marriage was the best way for them to have those needs met.

Lost in her troubled thoughts, Abby's only link to the reality of the moment was the strong hand that clasped hers. Caleb's hand was as warm as hers was cold. She sneaked a glance upward from beneath her lashes. He had never seemed so tall, never looked so stern and unapproachable. Then, suddenly, the preacher reached the part of the ceremony where she promised to love and cherish Caleb for the rest of her life. She repeated the words because it was expected of her, feeling like the world's worst fraud.

Somehow she got through her part of the ceremony, and then it was Caleb's turn. Unlike her, he spoke his vows in a firm, almost determined voice, as if he were daring anyone to stop him. Finally, he placed a plain gold band on her finger, and seconds later, she felt the slightest tug on her hand and realized that he was pulling her closer and lowering his lips to hers in the traditional, expected, end-of-ceremony kiss. A brief gesture meant to seal the promises they'd just made.

Abby's eyelids drifted shut of their own accord. Though the touch of his lips was whisper-soft, she experienced an unexpected jolt of awareness, not unlike that she'd felt when their fingers brushed the first day they'd met. He raised his head suddenly, and her eyes flew open in surprise. That same expression was mirrored in his eyes. Awareness, and something else she couldn't put her finger on. Confusion? Thoughtfulness?

He released her hand and moved to her side while the minister prayed, asking for God's blessing on the new marriage and encouraging Caleb and Abby to put their trust in Him. After blessing the food they were about to enjoy, he announced that refreshments awaited everyone in the dining room.

The sound of Caleb clearing his throat once again made them the room's focus. "Abby and I would like to thank you all for your friendship and understanding, for your hard work in making everything look so special and for helping with the refreshments. We appreciate it." He followed the short speech with one of his rare smiles.

Abby's breath hung in her throat. She was always astounded at how the smile transformed his harsh features, bracketing his hard mouth with attractive grooves and deepening the network of tiny lines at the corners of his eyes, changing him from stern to handsome. Both the unexpected kindness and the smile caused her pulse to quicken in a way that was somehow both confusing and distressing. Then he took her hand, and together they preceded the guests into the dining room. Abby surveyed her friends' handiwork and her heart swelled with a feeling of love and gratitude.

True to their word, Rachel and Allison had driven out earlier to finalize the decorations. Vases of yellow flowers interspersed with branches of French mulberry were scattered throughout both rooms. Centered on the pristine whiteness of the borrowed tablecloth and encircled by more ivy sat Abby's cake on the silver platter, flanked by the silver candlesticks and white tapers.

Mary's punch bowl sat at one end of the table, surrounded by its matching cups. The cider had been heated to marry the flavor of the spices, and the faint scent of cinnamon, cloves and nutmeg wafted through the air. Flickering candle flames shimmered, reflecting the hue of the cider and flinging the amber glow from each crystal facet of the antique punch bowl.

There were two kinds of cookies beside the cake. A haunch of beef brought by Mary and Bart waited to be carved and placed on fresh-baked bread with freshly churned butter or soft herbed goat cheese. Abby's venison pastries, plump with meat and vegetables, were piled atop a footed plate. It was a lovely table, and she would be eternally thankful to the friends who had done so much to make her day memorable.

"You've done a fine job," Caleb said in a low voice, a look of appreciation in his eyes as he took in the room's simple elegance. It was his first comment to her as her husband, and his obvious satisfaction was a balm to her troubled heart.

"I had a lot of help from friends."

"It seems you have very good friends," he told her, almost as if the very notion was a foreign one.

"Yes," she replied, "I do."

He looked down at her, and something in his eyes told her he would like to say more, but just then Nathan Haversham came up and slapped him on the back before extending his hand in congratulations to them both. The next several minutes were spent accepting well wishes from those in attendance.

Since opportunities for fun were rare to the hard-working people in the community, the wedding guests used the next couple of hours to indulge in food and conversation. Thankfully, the autumn day was warm enough that those who wanted could sit outside. Caleb's chess set had been set up on the porch, and Edward Stone challenged Nathan Haversham to a game. The children were playing tag, and true to his word, Caleb had set up horseshoes for those who wanted to play. Inevitably, the men and women drifted into groups.

Finally, Rachel and the others began to clear away the dishes and the remaining food. Both babies were being taken care of, and Abby, who wasn't used to idleness, stood on the porch watching the guests and wondering, with a churning stomach, what would happen when they all left. It was something she and Caleb, who stood beneath the sheltering branches of a huge black gum tree talking to Emily's father, had not discussed.

"Abby?"

She recognized Mary Emerson's voice and turned with a tentative smile on her face, clasping her trembling hands together, her fingers coming into contact with the ring Caleb had placed on her finger. Though Mary and Bart Emerson had been very supportive, Abby wondered how they really felt about this marriage coming so soon on the heels of their daughter's death.

"I want to thank you for everything, Mrs. Emerson," she said, before the older woman could speak. "I truly appreciate all you and Mr. Emerson have done."

"We were glad to help," Mary said. "And please call me Mary."

Abby nodded. "I'm sorry all this happened," she said, her voice a thread of sound. "Neither Caleb nor I intended for things to end up this way."

"End up?" Mary said, reaching out and taking both of Abby's cold hands in hers. "My dear, things have not *ended up.* They are only beginning for you and Caleb, and I know full well that you both had only the best in mind for Betsy when Rachel brought you here."

Abby blinked back the sudden rush of tears. "It's hard to believe people can be so mean-spirited." She met Mary's gaze with customary directness. "I've never been anything but kind to Sarah VanSickle and her friends."

"I'm sure that's true, and I know how disheartening it can be when things like this happen, but I'm convinced there will always be people who love making others miserable. I've never been sure *why,* but I suspect it may be because they are so unhappy themselves."

Abby gave a short laugh. "What does Sarah VanSickle have to be miserable about? She's one of the most prominent women in Wolf Creek."

"Unfortunately, things and position don't guarantee happiness. I can't say for certain, but I do know that Sarah set her cap for Lucas Gentry back when she was just a girl, and when he chose Libby, she never really got over it. Or forgave him," Mary said in an attempt to explain the woman's mindset.

Abby did her best to dredge up some compassion

for Sarah's plight, but it was hard when she had tried so hard to wreck both Abby's and Caleb's reputations.

"We have no control over things that happen in our lives, but we can control how we react. Sarah chose to be miserable instead of embracing the man and the life she has now. Which is what I want you to do."

"I'm not sure I understand."

"Both you and Caleb have been put in a bad situation. You've both lost spouses and you both need something the other has." Seeing surprise on Abby's face, Mary offered her a gentle smile. "It's no secret in town that you've been struggling, Abby, or that you were struggling before your husband was killed. When Emily died, you and Caleb were brought together, and Sarah VanSickle's lies have more or less forced you into a marriage I'm sure neither of you wanted. I know that because Caleb wasn't too overjoyed when he and Emily married."

Though Caleb had told her as much, Abby was surprised to realize that Mary knew the truth. "And you knew it from the start?"

"Oh, yes. Actually, Emily wasn't too thrilled about marrying Caleb, either."

Abby shook her head in disbelief. "Yet they both agreed to a loveless marriage."

"Loveless?" Mary seemed to consider that as if it had never before occurred to her. "Yes, I suppose you're right." Wryness edged her voice. "Oh, Emily wanted to *get* married, but the eligible men in Wolf Creek were too rough around the edges to suit her. She'd gone to school in St. Louis to study art—though she never finished—

and she spoke of going back east to Boston or some such place, marrying some starving artist and living in genteel poverty on wine and cheese or something."

"Why didn't she?"

"She was very shy and not cut out for life in the big city," Mary said in a reminiscent tone. "Which is why she came home before finishing her studies. Also, I'm afraid Bart and I indulged her more than we should have. She was spoiled. There's no way she was going to strike out on her own. Time passed and before we realized it, she was twenty-four and considered a spinster."

"How did the marriage come about?" Abby asked.

"Lucas Gentry wanted grandchildren," she said bluntly, "and since it didn't look as if Gabe was ever going to come home and settle down, Caleb was the one expected to come up to scratch. He was always the one who tried to smooth things over when he and Gabe were children, and Lucas had come to expect it.

"If you think Caleb is hard, you should have met his father," Mary told Abby with a lift of her dark eyebrows. "Lucas Gentry was a despot if ever one breathed. He was always difficult, but when Libby went to Boston and he was left with the boys, he lost what little kindness he had. He always expected everything and more that Caleb could give him and the farm, and even more so after Gabe took off."

"Rachel told me a little about that. Has he ever been back?"

Mary shook her head. "Not to my knowledge, though we've heard plenty of rumors, none of them good."

"It's a wonder Caleb didn't grow up to be just like his father."

"In many ways he did, but thankfully, mostly the good ways. For all his bitterness and his toughness when it came to business dealings, no one can say Lucas Gentry was anything but honest. Sometimes ruthless, but honest. Caleb's just like him when it comes to that."

They didn't speak for a few moments, and finally Abby asked, "It didn't bother you that Caleb and Emily's marriage wasn't a love match, then?"

Mary laughed. "Oh, you young people and your romantic notions! The truth is that people marry for many reasons, but a scant few of them marry for love. Caleb and Emily had known each other all their lives, and they were fond enough of each other, and that was good enough for me and Bart. We knew Caleb possessed a strong sense of duty and that he would take good care of her, and I suppose we pressed her more than we should have. We wanted to see her settled in case something happened to us, and like Lucas, we wanted grandchildren nearby. Our other daughter and her family live in St. Louis, and it's too far to go unless you have more than a few days to stay. Unfortunately, Emily was never able to conceive until Betsy."

Abby was fascinated by Mary's willingness to share so much of her daughter's past, but still didn't know exactly *why* Mary was doing so. "What do Sarah's choices and Caleb and Emily's marriage have to do with me and Caleb?" Abby asked at last.

Mary offered her a sheepish smile. "I'm sorry. I do get to rambling, don't I? What I'm trying to say is that fate or circumstance or perhaps God has brought you and Caleb to this place in your life. You both took vows that bind you until death. You're both young and healthy, and God willing will have many years together and children of your own. I just don't want either of you to do what Sarah has done and dwell on the past, whether it's William's death or Emily's or what might have been. Do you see what I'm getting at?"

Abby gave a tentative nod. "I think you're saying to let go of the past and look to the future." Though Mary hinted that Emily had not made Caleb happy, Abby couldn't find the courage to have that confirmed. "So you and Mr. Emerson don't mind that Caleb and I have married so soon after Emily's death?"

Mary shook her head. "Not at all. In fact, we're thrilled that you'll be Betsy's mother, because we believe you'll be a good one." She squeezed Abby's h nds again and her eyes filled with tears. "We loved our daughter, but we were not ignorant of her faults and weaknesses. She wasn't the right woman for a man like Caleb. I pray you are. Embrace this marriage and this new life as best you can. Caleb needs someone who can see the man he truly is. He needs someone who can bring joy into his life, Abby. Believe me when I say he's had little enough of it."

With a brief hug, Mary left Abby standing there with much to think about. After hearing what she had about Caleb's past from Rachel and now more from Mary, Abby was beginning to have a clearer picture of the man she had married. She understood now why there was so little softness in him, so little tolerance. He'd been duty bound and forced to take responsibility since childhood. Under the circumstances, he was accepting the invasion of his house by three strangers better than she would have done. It was a miracle he'd turned out as well as he had. It would behoove her to remember that when things between them grew rough.

Mary and Bart left soon afterward, and shortly after that Rachel and the other women trooped out of the house, announcing that things were back in order and both weary babies were asleep. Ben was going home with Daniel for a couple of days so that they could go fishing with the father of one of Daniel's friends before the weather turned too cold.

After giving Ben a goodbye hug, Abby stood next to Caleb watching the buggy pull down the lane and disappear around a curve. An uncomfortable silence stretched between them. It wouldn't be long until sundown. A slight breeze and the shade beneath the porch hinted of colder weather that would soon descend. Abby gave an involuntary shiver.

Without a word, Caleb shrugged out of his suit jacket and draped it around her shoulders. The warmth from his body and the woodsy scent of his soap permeated the fabric. Abby tipped her head back to look up at him, suppressing another tremor, one she suspected had nothing to do with the chill of the late afternoon and everything to do with the nearness of the man standing so close to her.

"Everything went better than I expected," he said, taking a step back and running his fingers through his hair in a gesture that spoke volumes about his real state of mind. He needed a haircut, she thought again, making her first wifely observation. And his lean cheeks were already shadowed with end-of-day growth.

Focusing her attention on the tree with its shedding crimson leaves, she said, "I thought it was very nice considering the time we had to get things together," she agreed in a voice that held an unnatural primness.

Wearing a solemn expression, Caleb held out his hand and cocked his head toward two rocking chairs that sat in front of the parlor window. "Let's sit for a while if it isn't too cool for you. I'm so stuffed I don't need any dinner, and hopefully the girls will sleep for a bit."

With a bit of reluctance, Abby placed her hand in his and let him guide her to one of the chairs. As before, his touch produced that peculiar tingling that sizzled throughout her body. Grudgingly, almost fearfully, she accepted the significance of the feeling. Not only did she find the irascible man she was now married to attractive, she was attracted *to* him. Her husband. Her reaction was unnerving and unacceptable. She and Caleb had a business arrangement, nothing more.

He released his hold on her, and they sat, both of them beginning to rock as they gazed out over the front lawn. Still somewhat befuddled by her reaction to his touch, she could not think of a single intelligent topic of conversation.

"You look very pretty," he said at last, turning to look at her. "Like newly minted gold."

"Th-Thank you," she stammered, surprised to find

that her voice still worked. "You look very handsome yourself."

Though brief, his laughter was rich and throaty, and that unexpected, arresting smile was back. "Handsome? I don't think so," he said with a shake of his dark, shaggy head.

"You need a haircut," she said without thinking, She looked away, stifling a groan. No telling *how* he'd react to that! He had not married her to be inflicted with her wifely judgments. How long his hair grew was none of her business. She waited for his response, her spine straight, her body racked with tension.

"Yeah," he said, scraping back his hair again. "I know. But I wasn't around the afternoon you cut Ben's, and we've all been so busy the past few days I didn't want to put anything more on you. I'm sorry if I embarrassed you."

"I wasn't embarrassed!" she said, aghast at the thought. "I was just—" she gave a helpless shrug "—making conversation." Actually, she found his slightly unkempt look appealing.

For long moments, the only sounds to be heard were the sassy solo of a nearby mockingbird and the squeaking of the rocker runners on the porch.

"What is it, Abby?" he asked.

She stopped rocking and turned his direction, without actually meeting his gaze. "I guess I'm wondering what happens next."

Her meaning could not be clearer, and he considered her question with care. "Well, I'm going to get up from here—preferably before it gets dark—take off this suit and put on my everyday stuff. Since Ben's not here, I'm going to milk your cow and that blasted goat while Frank and Leo feed."

"Oh." She was unable to deny either the relief that swept through her, or the tiniest pang of regret.

"I'd planned on moving my things back into the house, if you have no objections, but it's getting a little late for that."

Her eyes met his. Abby couldn't breathe…or think. "You don't have to ask my permission," she said. "It's your house."

"No, Abby. It's our house. Our home. It would make things easier if I moved back in, and there's no reason not to now, but if you'd be more comfortable with my staying at the bunkhouse, that's what I'll do. I thought I'd take the room with all the junk in it. It was my dad's."

It went without saying that she would be more comfortable the less she saw him, the less she had to deal with him, but that was not the issue here. No matter what he said, it *was* his house and he had a right to live in it, especially since no one in the community could possibly object after today.

"That's fine," she said. "I'll put clean linens on the bed for you."

"I can do that. I'm used to it."

"Absolutely not!" Her mother would roll over in her grave at the idea of any daughter of hers allowing a man to do her chores.

He nodded, and she imagined she saw the corners of

his mouth turn up just a bit. The expression in his eyes looked very much like wry humor.

"As for what happens next…I think it's called getting on with our lives, whatever that involves. We just go on doing what we've been doing. A few words and a piece of paper haven't changed anything except that now we don't have to feel guilty about our arrangement."

"Can it really be that easy?" she asked, letting her eyes meet his at last.

"Easy?" He seemed to consider the situation. "Let's see. We have two people forced into a marriage, one of them a man who isn't used to kids and is suddenly accountable for three—one of whom can hardly tolerate him." His tone was pseudo-serious. "We also have a man and a woman who both have hair-trigger tempers living under the same roof." He shook his head. "Easy? Hardly. But I've never had too many things come easy in my life, and I think I'm up to the challenge."

Challenge? Yes, that's what it would be, just as her life the past few years had been a challenge. Only the kinds of trials this new life presented would be far different from those she shared with William.

"Reach into the left inside pocket of my coat," he said.

Abby gave him a questioning look and did as he asked, her fingers encountering a small package. She pulled out a small gift wrapped in a piece of crisp tissue paper and tied with a length of red ribbon.

"What's this?" she asked, turning it over in her hands. It felt like something metal.

"It's for you. Consider it a wedding gift."

The unexpected gesture caught her off guard. "It never occurred to me… I don't have anything for you. I'm sorry."

He waved aside her apology. "Go ahead. Open it."

Abby untied the ribbon, wondering if she imagined the expression of anticipation in his eyes. Sliding the thin strip of satin from around the package, she spread aside the paper. When she saw what was inside, her eyes filled with tears and she choked back a sob of disbelief. Lying in the nest of tissue paper lay the cameo brooch she'd traded for her wedding dress. She lifted her stunned, tear-filled gaze to his. "How…?"

"Simon waved me down when I went into town the other day. He knew I'd want you to have it back."

"I can never repay you," she said, rising and clasping the precious pin to her chest.

"You repay me every day," he told her, getting to his feet. "By cooking and making this house a pleasant place to come to at night. By taking good care of Betsy. I'm the one in your debt."

"But you've had to take on people and responsibilities that—" He reached out and placed his fingertips against her lips to silence her. His touch almost stopped her heart.

"As far as I'm concerned, the responsibilities are equal on both sides, and I'm perfectly happy with our deal. How about you?"

Her gaze, still blurry with tears, clung to his. "I think so, yes," she whispered.

"Good." Then, without a word, he strode past her and down the steps, leaving her emotions in more turmoil than they had been before he subjected her to his unexpected gentleness…or his touch.

Caleb went to the bunkhouse and changed into clean work clothes, then set about doing his evening chores, his mind filled with memories of the day.

He thought of how he had fumed for days before the wedding about the unfairness of being tied to a family he didn't want and needed less. He'd even let God know how unhappy he was about it, but Bart had assured him earlier that God knew what He was doing, even if Caleb and Abby didn't.

When she'd stepped through the bedroom door, looking like a ray of autumn sunshine in a dress of rich gold, his fury vanished. Her blond hair was caught up atop her head. Curly wisps teased the nape of her neck and small sprigs of ivy and yellow flowers were nestled in an artful jumble of curls.

His heart seemed to stumble, and he'd swallowed hard. Then she'd spied him from across the room and headed in his direction, pausing to speak to people she knew along the way. When she stopped in front of him, the sweet scent of gardenia made a soothing assault on his senses. Funny, he'd never realized that she barely came to his shoulder. She'd looked up and attempted a smile that fell far short.

He'd wished he knew what to do to erase the anxiety from her eyes, wished that haunted look was not working its way into his heart and causing it to ache for something he couldn't put a name to and understood less. He'd stared down into her eyes. Large, bewildered and no less blue than the brilliant autumn sky, they were surrounded by thick dark lashes, totally at odds with her fair hair. He'd had to fight the urge to pull her into his arms and promise her that everything would be all right, that they would work through their uncertain future. Together.

Then someone had called his name and he'd snapped out of his crazy imaginings. His gaze had roamed the room, settling on Betsy, asleep in her grandmother's arms, and then moved to Laura sitting in total contentment on Rachel's lap, and finally to Ben who, standing alongside Daniel Stone, was poking a little girl standing in front of them with a stick they'd smuggled inside. The girl gave a whimper of frustration. Ben looked toward Caleb, the expression in his eyes daring him to say anything in a room full of guests.

Reality had kicked in with a vengeance. So much for the progress he thought they'd made. Nothing had changed. Ben did not like him or the idea of Caleb becoming a father figure. Abby still loved her husband. She didn't want this marriage of convenience any more than he did. As consoling as it might be to imagine a happily ever after, common sense told him it would be folly to even contemplate such a future.

Chapter Seven

It wasn't working, Caleb thought, standing another piece of firewood in place and swinging the ax downward. The piece of oak split beneath the satisfying show of strength. He'd been married to Abby for three weeks now, and November was more than a week old, but the tactics he'd decided to utilize in his marriage weren't working out as planned, or as he'd expected.

After realizing there was no real future for him and Abby, he'd decided to go about his life as he always had and treat her and her children as he had Emily—with polite civility. He'd count on them to hold up their side of the bargain while he did the same. That was the plan, but somehow it wasn't working out as he'd imagined.

They'd fallen into a routine, and inevitably, as he should have known it would, he saw their lives meshing in dozens of ways that demanded personal interaction.

Abby kept the house clean and tidy. She cooked the meals and cared for the children, teaching Ben spelling and numbers and reading. Though he usually escaped to his study after dinner, more than once, Caleb had heard her reading to Ben from books on history and farming principles and then explaining what she read. She continued the word of the day and the nightly devotionals. Several times, he'd come to get a book from the shelf and caught himself listening with more interest than he would admit as she explained certain Bible verses to Ben. Caleb was amazed at her ability to reduce the most complicated passages into something a six-year-old could understand.

Her smile intrigued him, as did the lilting laughter in her voice as she played with Laura. Ah, Laura! He was finding it impossible to resist Abby's baby girl, who offered him a smile when he came through the door in the evenings, and tugged on his pants legs and jabbered until he reached down and picked her up.

He marveled at Abby's patience as she walked the floor with Betsy when she had a belly ache. A time or two, he'd even taken a turn himself, rocking and walking so that Abby could snatch a couple of hours' sleep. There was no denying that he was fascinated and amazed by his new bride, or that he found a certain enjoyment at seeing the fire in her eyes when she was angry. No doubt about it, the keep-them-at-arm's-length approach to marriage was far easier to assume than execute.

Except with Ben.

So far, nothing Caleb had done had made any real inroads with the obstinate boy who resisted any and all overtures of friendship. But he kept trying, giving Ben light chores to get him out of the house and also so that he could spend time with the men and his new stepfather. Though he'd missed a lot by not having a mother's influence, Caleb reasoned that no boy should spend all of every day with females. Still, Ben was proving to be a hard nut to crack. Caleb set up another log and gave it a satisfying *whack*. Like the other one, it split down the middle. It would take time, but he was determined to get on an easier footing with the boy.

That evening after their Bible study, Abby tucked Ben in and checked on the girls. When she closed the bedroom door behind her she found Caleb sitting in front of the fireplace, his long legs stretched out and crossed at the ankles. It was a purely masculine pose, one she'd seen often in the years of her marriage to William.

She was surprised to see Caleb sitting there, since he usually went to his office to do bookwork after helping her in the kitchen, something he still insisted on, though she'd told him it was not necessary. It had become a comfortable routine, one that seldom varied.

"No bookwork?" she asked, turning toward the veritable smorgasbord of literary offerings lining the floor-to-ceiling shelves on either side of the fireplace.

"Nothing that won't wait until tomorrow," he said. He held up a new volume. "I was anxious to get started on my new Henry James book."

"The American?" she asked.

"Yes. You've heard of it?"

"A bit. You have a wonderful collection," she said on a sigh.

"Necessity."

She shot him a questioning glance over her shoulder. "Necessity?"

Caleb shrugged. "Lucas expected me to learn how to run things, so there was no way I could go away to school. I had to educate myself the best way I could."

Abby didn't miss the tightening of his jaw when he mentioned his late father.

"Well, you have a very eclectic collection," she said. Besides *The Sketch-Book of Geoffrey Crayon* and *Narrative of the Life of Frederick Douglass, an American Slave,* there were books on gold mining, meteorology, manners and birding. The shelves also held dozens of novels as well as several issues of popular magazines, including sporting journals and ladies' publications.

He gave a negligent shrug. "Lots of things interest me, so I send for whatever books are available." His tone was desert-dry, and he lifted one eyebrow and a corner of his mouth in a sardonic expression. "It's one of the advantages of having a lot of money."

Abby chose to ignore both. Ignoring the utterly masculine picture he made sprawled in the chair was not so easy. "You have quite a collection of fiction, as well," she said, appalled at how breathless she sounded.

His mockery was replaced by a fleeting, guilty smile. "It's one of my many failings. I'm quite a fan of fiction, and I even admit to enjoying a rip-roaring dime novel, as well. I'm a huge Allan Pinkerton admirer."

"Really?" she said, wide-eyed. "I like him, too." Then with an arch look, she pulled a volume from the shelf and said in a pseudo-serious tone, "I particularly like Alcott, Brontë and Stowe, as it seems you do."

"Those are Emily's," he said with a wounded expression.

"You haven't read them, then?" she asked. "Not manly enough for you?"

"Hardly."

"Well, perhaps you should read some of them. I'm a firm believer that all men should read some women's fiction."

"And why is that?" he asked, his rare foray into lightheartedness giving way to sudden gravity.

"So that they might gain a better perspective into the ways and thoughts of women, of course."

"And you think it's important for a man to understand women?"

"Not only do I think it's important, I think it's imperative if the two sexes even hope to live together in a semblance of harmony."

He frowned.

She laughed. "If it will soothe your ruffled masculine feathers, I believe it's equally important for women to attempt to understand the men in their life."

"Attempt?"

"Well, you are strange creatures," she said with raised eyebrows and a slight shrug.

"And women aren't?"

"Why, no," she told him with artificial sincerity. "Women are the soul of kindness, thrift, honor and decency."

Coldness molded his rugged features. "Begging your

pardon, ma'am, but that has not always been my experience. I offer Sarah VanSickle as an example."

"Oh. Well, I think most people would agree that Sarah is in a class all her own. But don't you find that I exhibit those qualities?" she asked with mock-innocence.

"Well, you… I mean that… I didn't mean that you…"

"Yes?" she asked with another lift of her fair eyebrows, her eyes alight with suppressed laughter.

"You're—you're teasing me!" He leaped to his feet, his tone disbelieving, shocked, even.

"I am," she admitted, straight-faced.

Caleb didn't recall anyone teasing him since he was a youngster and the brunt of jokes about his height. "I've not been teased as an adult," he told her.

"You and Emily didn't joke with each other?"

"No."

Abby stared at him for a moment, trying to digest what he'd said and put it into perspective with what she knew about his past. Her heart broke a tiny bit.

"Well, that's just…sad."

She saw him stiffen, recognized the familiar chill in his eyes. "I don't need or want your pity," he snapped.

"And you don't have it!" she shot back, frustrated with his unyielding attitude. "What you have is genuine sorrow that you've been deprived of so much joy in your life."

"Which equates to pity," he retorted. "I won't have it, Abby. Especially not from you."

Annoyance and futility washed over her. Was there no reaching the man? "If you don't want my empathy, what do you want from me, Caleb? What will you have?" she cried, tilting her head back to look up at him.

They stood there staring at each other, both breathing heavily, both angry, both hurt and wondering how such an innocent conversation could have turned into something so painful.

Everything. I want everything from you that you have to give.

The realization slammed into him with the force of a kicking mule, robbing him of speech. What were these unsettling emotions he felt for her? He had no yardstick with which to measure these new feelings. He only knew he had never experienced anything like it before, nor had he expected to. What he did know was that he didn't like feeling vulnerable and not in control, and he liked less the fact that he didn't know what to do about it.

Close on the heels of admitting that he was feeling things for her—things he had no right to feel with Emily hardly cold in her grave—came a rush of that ever-present guilt. Never mind that Abby was legally his wife. He turned away and headed for the door, needing to put some space between him and this woman, this stranger who had come into his life and taken over his home. The woman who threatened to take over his heart.

His hand was on the doorknob when her voice stopped him. He didn't turn, but stood stiff and unyielding. He heard her footfalls on the floor and felt her hand on his back, warm through the fabric of his shirt.

"I'm sorry," she said, her voice an anguished murmur.

He imagined he felt her forehead lean against his

back, a whisper-soft touch that spoke of regret and thickened his throat with tears.

"I never meant to hurt you, and you're very wrong if you think what I feel for you is pity."

He wanted to ask her what she did feel for him, but was too afraid of her answer, just as he was too terrified to speak of how he felt and what he wanted from her.

Abby was a warm and caring woman who knew how to laugh, how to make a house into a home. A woman who knew how to make a man feel wanted and welcome when he stepped through the door at the end of the day. She was accustomed to a man loving her and being unafraid to show that love. A man who knew how and when to *tease* her.

She certainly wasn't used to someone who had no knowledge of how to care for another person, and even less idea how to show that caring. He told himself it wasn't fair to saddle her with his shortcomings, that it was best if he kept things on an impersonal level as he'd planned to from the first, yet for a brief, heart-stopping instant he toyed with the urge to beg her to help bring him out of the shadows of mere existence and into a world of life and love.

Common sense stopped him. She still loved her William, and Caleb was not handsome, not funny and he didn't know how to tease. He was a man who knew only duty and the weight of responsibility. He might be considered the best catch of the county, but he was not the sort of man a woman like Abby could ever love. Accepting their impasse, Caleb felt his anger melt away to be replaced with an aching, unfamiliar remorse.

Steeling himself against the gentleness he knew he

would see in her eyes, he turned to face her. Her hand dropped away. The loss of her touch left him feeling empty and alone. He stared down at her, fighting the urge to pull her into his arms and try to absorb her sweetness into his very soul, but he knew it was crucial that whatever it was he was feeling be nipped in the bud before it had a chance to grow into something he instinctively knew held the potential to hurt him far worse than his mother's leaving or Emily's death.

He took an involuntary step backward, needing to put some space between them before he lost his head and his control. Then, deliberately, like a scalpel-wielding surgeon excising something harmful, he clenched his jaw and closed his heart to the tender feelings threatening to overwhelm him.

"What I want is for you to take care of my house and my daughter."

He imagined he saw the sheen of tears in her eyes before she lowered her gaze and gave a single nod. Her voice was a mere thread of sound as she said simply, "I see."

Then without another word he turned, wrenched open the door and stalked onto the porch. The cold darkness enveloped him. He was at the bottom of the steps when he heard the door click quietly shut. He walked away, his masculine pride intact and an empty void where his heart had been.

Her mother was right, Abby thought as she set the table for the evening meal. Life did go on, even when your pride had been trampled in the dust, your heart had been torn to shreds and your only defense was to fortify that bruised heart with an all-consuming anger. She blinked back the hot sting of tears that had been her constant companion ever since her altercation with Caleb.

How had it come to this? Was it possible that she had fallen in love with her new husband in such a short span of time? Guilt surged through her. How could she betray everything she had felt for William—a man of goodness and kindness—by falling for a man whose heart was as hard as the rocks that were so prevalent throughout the pastureland at her old home? A man who hadn't the slightest notion how to love.

Ever since their argument three days ago, they had both maintained a polite stoicism that bordered on the ridiculous. There were times she would have laughed had she not been afraid her laughter would turn to tears. If possible, Caleb had grown more silent, more unapproachable, working from sunup until sundown, pushing Frank and Leo past any reasonable limits, and piling chores on Ben that she deemed far too heavy for a child his age.

Beyond starting all-out war, her only recourse was to do her housework and take care of Betsy with the same attention as before. She slammed down an ironstone plate and slapped down a handful of silverware next to it. It was not the innocent baby's fault her father was a stubborn, pigheaded, mulish…idiot!

Like Abby, Caleb not only embraced his anger, he looked for ways to fuel it. Determined to live up to his reputation, he doubled down on the outside work, which brought about a lot of muttering and cussing from Frank and Leo. When they finished with one chore, he found something else to keep them all busy. Anything to keep from going into the house until darkness and his growling stomach forced him inside. Anything to keep him away from a woman whose only transgression was kindness and two little girls who were working their way into his heart.

The morning following his altercation with Abby, Ben had cornered him in the barn, his fists clenched at his sides, his freckled face wearing a pugnacious expression that said without words that he wished he were ten years older and a hundred pounds heavier.

"You leave my mother alone," he ground out from between clenched teeth.

Caleb's first reaction was to give the boy a piece of his mind. He couldn't believe Ben had the audacity to talk to him like that—or any adult for that matter. Then he remembered wishing he had the guts to confront his own father when Lucas had jumped on Libby about something. He also realized he was dealing with Abby's son. Evidently she had passed down the impertinence gene to her son.

"Whatever is between me and your mother is our business, not yours."

"She's my *mother!*" Ben shouted.

"And she's my wife," Caleb said, struggling to maintain his authority without becoming argumentative. "Don't you remember how we talked about how it was going to take time for us to all learn to get along and how we would have times when things didn't go exactly right?"

Some of the anger left Ben's face at the reminder.

"This was one of those times. Now I want you to go milk Nana, and then I'll show you how to milk Shaggy Bear."

"It's cold."

At the plaintive note in the boy's voice Caleb surrendered his anger. "I know that, but you know they have to be milked twice a day, cold or not. Owning livestock means they have to be taken care of no matter what."

When Abby found out Caleb had turned over both the morning and evening milking to Ben, she cast her husband a look that would have made a lesser man quake in his boots. He heard her muttering under her breath about it being too hard.

When he had Ben stack the firewood as it was split and added keeping the fireplace boxes filled with wood and kindling to his list of chores, she adopted an overly polite demeanor that warned Caleb a storm was brewing. He bit back a grim smile. It was only a matter of time before her temper got the best of her, and with his own bad humor festering like a sore tooth, he relished the notion of their clashing of wills. Anything was preferable to their cold truce.

"It's too much," Abby said later that evening as she indicated for Caleb to take the chair that sat in the middle of the parlor. Furious with him or not, he was weeks past needing a haircut. He'd passed the attractive shaggy stage soon after the wedding and had now reached the point of embarrassment. She couldn't have him going to town looking like a hobo off a train. When she'd told him as much after putting the children to bed, he'd snapped, "Fine. Get the scissors."

So here he sat with a sheet draped around his shoulders while Abby combed and snipped and heaved deep sighs of annoyance. Caleb turned with a frown, almost causing her to cut out a chunk of hair over his ear.

"Spit it out," he said with his customary brusqueness.

"Hold still." She took hands full of his hair and jerked his head back where she wanted it.

A muscle in his jaw tightened.

"It's too much."

"What's too much?" he asked, noting the closeness of the scissors to his face from the corner of his eye.

"All the work you've given to Ben. He was already milking the goat and feeding the chickens and dogs, and now you've added milking the cow and carrying in big chunks of firewood."

"I don't hear Ben complaining."

"He's afraid to complain. You frighten him."

That bit of information set Caleb back on his heels. He didn't reply for a long time, and finally said, "I'm going to tell you what I told Ben when he jumped me about yelling at you."

Abby moved around to stand next to his jean-clad thighs. Her eyes held disbelief as she stared into his. "He heard us arguing?"

Caleb held her gaze. "Evidently. I told him that what happened between you and me was none of his business. Now I'm telling you that what happens between me and

Ben is none of *your* business. I've given you free rein with Betsy. You're the only mother she'll ever know. For all intents and purposes, I'm now Ben's father, and I deserve to bring him up as I see fit."

"I don't yell at Betsy," Abby said, sifting the front of his tobacco-brown hair through her fingers, looking for stray long strands. His hair was soft and thick and clean, and as he did, smelled like something woodsy and masculine.

A biting smile lifted one corner of Caleb's mouth. "Give it time. She's not grown yet."

Abby stared at him, her hands stilling in his hair.

"What?" he asked, seeing the look of wonder in her eyes.

"I…I think you were… Were you just teasing me?"

Caleb thought about it a moment but had no answer. Had he been teasing her? Was it really such a simple thing?

Abby felt some of her anger dissolve and heaved another sigh. Could he disarm her so easily? "I don't want Ben to grow up with nothing but rules and work and demands."

Caleb thought about his own raising and how his father's never ending orders had chafed. He would never be that unreasonable with Ben. There had to be a compromise. "He needs to learn a good work ethic and how to be responsible."

"He's just six years old," she reminded.

"Old enough to start learning. What he's doing won't hurt him."

She breathed another grudging sigh. "Probably not."

Reluctantly, she conceded that part of her anger was based on the knowledge that by Caleb taking more of a role in Ben's life, she was losing some of her own influence. She felt the sting of tears in her eyes. "I want him to know he's loved."

"He knows you love him."

"Yes, but fathers are to love their children, too, Caleb, and as you pointed out, you're the one who has taken over William's place. Being a father is more than laying down the law and doling out chores. The Bible says that fathers shouldn't provoke their children to wrath."

"And what does that mean, exactly?"

"I've always thought it meant to be consistent and fair in your treatment of all your children. To not be overly harsh with one or the other, and not to show favoritism. Like you do with the girls. You show them much more positive attention than you do Ben."

His lips tightened. "At everyone's insistence, I'm trying to get to know my daughter, and as for Laura…" He paused, then continued. "Much like her mother, she refuses to take no for an answer when I try to discourage her." Though heaven only knew why, the way he tried to keep her at arm's length.

"She likes you," Abby told him, combing his forelock back to blend into the rest of his newly cut hair. "She gets so excited when she hears your voice and your boots stomping on the back porch at night."

Abby did not notice the strange longing in her voice, and Caleb had no comeback.

"So you think I need to show Ben more positive attention."

"Yes. Balance work with fun things."

"Fun?" He said the word as if it were foreign to him.

"Yes, fun. What did you like to do for fun when you were a boy?"

"I didn't do anything for fun," he told her in all seriousness.

She stared down at him, wide-eyed. "Nothing? Surely you went fishing or hunting."

He shook his head. "Gabe was the one who had fun. I worked. If I hunted or fished it was to bring food home for the table."

"And laughter?"

He gave a snort of something that might have passed for a scornful laugh. "Not after my mother left. If we laughed about anything, we took a tongue-lashing for slacking off."

Abby tried to grasp what he was saying and failed. How could any child grow up without laughter? How could any child grow up the way Caleb had?

"Would William have listened to you if you two were having this conversation?" he asked, the change in conversation catching her off guard. "Would he have backed off on Ben if you begged him with tears in your eyes?"

She summoned a wobbly smile. "William would not have known how to instill a good work ethic—not that he was afraid of work," she hastened to clarify. "But he was too much inclined to let himself be sidetracked by other things that interested him more than daily chores. He was not as...disciplined as you are."

"And by so doing, put you in the bad financial position you found yourself in."

"Yes. God forgive me, but I pray Ben did not inherit an overabundance of that particular trait from his father."

"So it's possible that maybe I'm saving some other young woman that fate, if Ben listens and learns from me."

"Maybe," she admitted. "I've thought many times since coming here how wonderful it would be if Ben had a father with your work ethic and William's ability to find the fun in life."

"*Finding* the fun?"

"Oh, yes! Fun doesn't always just rush out and meet you. Sometimes you find it in something as simple as skipping rocks on the creek, or playing a game of pattycake or peekaboo. But it's there."

Another silenced stretched between them as they both mulled over their conversation. Abby realized with something of a start that somehow, when she'd finished cutting Caleb's hair, she had placed her hands on his shoulders. Embarrassment swept through her, and she began to brush at the hair lying there.

Filling her voice with lightness she did not feel, she took a step back. "All done. And mighty handsome you look, too, if I may say so."

He gave a derisive grunt of laughter.

Abby fought against tears and the rush of the empathy he wanted no part of. She ached to take away his pain, to see the harsh slash of his mouth curved in laughter, his eyes filled with contentment.... Silently, she vowed to never let her temper get the best of her again. She would not be the one to deal him any more grief. Heaven knew he'd suffered enough of that in his lifetime. But even as she made the promise to herself, she knew that somewhere, someday, probably sooner than later, she would fail to keep it.

She snuffled and brushed at his shoulders with more vigor. "You are a very attractive man," she told him. "I can't imagine why you think otherwise."

"Maybe because I look at my face in the mirror every morning when I shave," he suggested with a touch of that unexpected, infrequent irony.

"While no one would say you are a conventionally handsome man, I think almost every woman in Wolf Creek would admit that your face is very intriguing. Women are easy targets for a man with a dangerous look about him."

"Dangerous?" he mocked.

"Mmm," she said, nodding. "Especially with that end-of-day beard. I imagine it's safe to say I'm the most envied woman in Wolf Creek for landing you."

Reaching up, he manacled her wrists with his callused fingers. Though purely innocent, she was suddenly aware of leaning against his thigh. His gaze meshed with hers.

"And what about you, Abby? Are you a sucker for a dangerous-looking man?"

"I don't know." She looked and sounded thoughtful. "It depends, I suppose."

"On?"

"On the man, and whatever other qualities he might have."

Caleb exerted the slightest pressure on her wrists, forcing her to lean over until her face was mere inches from his. Drawing a decent breath became very, very tricky. Finally, she had to shut her eyes; the intensity in his was too much to understand…or to bear.

At that precise moment his lips touched hers. All sorts of alarms rang in her head, and a scorching heat swept through her while a tiny voice whispered that she must be out of her mind to let him….

He's your husband. He has every right.

Long before she was ready, he ended the kiss. Trembling the slightest bit, Abby straightened. Pulling her hands from his grasp, she pressed her fingertips to her throbbing lips. His eyes revealed a compelling thoughtfulness that set her heart to racing. In that moment, she knew she had done a very foolish thing. For better or worse, she had fallen in love with Caleb Gentry.

"Oh. My."

The two words were the height of inadequacy and in no way expressed the host of feelings coursing through her. Astonishment. Dismay. Guilt. Hopelessness. She wanted to cry. To hide somewhere and examine the amazing feelings bubbling up inside her. Wished she could tell someone about that kiss. Wondered how she could hide this tender, burgeoning feeling from a man who, so bereft of sentiment himself, seldom missed any nuance of emotional change in others.

"Careful there. You'll turn my head." The words were spoken in a low, husky voice.

Despite the emotional turbulence tumbling through her, she grasped his meaning. “You’re getting pretty good at that.”

“What?”

“Teasing.”

One corner of his mouth hiked in a sardonic smile. “I thought I was being sarcastic. Ironic.”

She sighed. “With you, it seems to be the same thing, which makes you even more dangerous.”

“The only thing dangerous in this room is you wielding those scissors. I’m surprised you haven’t used them on me.”

“Why would I do that?” she asked.

“For taking advantage.”

“But you didn’t. You have every right.”

For long moments the words and all their implications hung suspended in the quiet of the room. When he made no move to answer, she pulled free the sheet she’d draped over him and shook the hair onto the floor to be swept up. Hoping to ease the tension, she said briskly, “At any rate, you’re all respectable-looking again.”

He stood and turned to face her. “Thank you.”

“My pleasure.”

“Mine, too.”

Without another word, he turned and left her standing in the middle of the room, wondering what—if anything—she was to make of *that* comment.

Chapter Eight

I love him.

Lying in bed, the back of her wrist resting against her forehead, Abby stared into the room's darkness and pondered the disturbing revelation. Surely this couldn't have happened! *How* had it happened?

For weeks now she'd experienced a feeling of pleasure when he came through the door and a sense of satisfaction when she saw him growing closer to the children. She'd liked knowing he was there and that she could count on him. She had admitted long ago that he was an attractive man, if you liked the rugged, rough-hewn type…which she obviously did, but one did not fall in love with a person for that reason…especially when said person resembled a prickly cactus in most other respects!

Neither did one fall in love with someone because the mere touch of his lips on yours sent your senses head over heels! That feeling was a vital part of love—indeed was often mistaken for love—but alone it was a mere shadow of that precious emotion. No, what she felt for Caleb was much more complicated than what she felt when he kissed her.

Abby made a mental list of all the reasons this new state of affairs was impossible. First, he was very intelligent, but he had no idea what spontaneity was and she doubted he had ever done anything on the spur of the moment. He was impatient, stubborn and even ruthless in many ways. He was unyielding and measured in his approach to everything he did, and even in the short time she'd lived beneath his roof, she'd realized that once he set his mind on a course, he was not apt to deviate from it.

She liked impromptu events, whether it was carrying supper out onto the lawn in the spring or taking that extra loaf of bread to some housebound friend. Caleb's notion of impulsiveness was to decide there was still enough daylight to fell another tree or plow another field.

Second, she definitely had a mind of her own, as well as her own views on how things should—or could—be done. She was accustomed to voicing those opinions. From the expression on his face the few times she had spoken her mind, her new husband found the notion of women being outspoken outrageous at the very least. She doubted he could learn to tolerate that trait in a wife.

Third, she loved children and had chosen teaching because of that love. At best Caleb tolerated them. No, that wasn't exactly correct. It was not fair for her to fault him for not understanding how to deal with children when he had been shown so little love himself. In truth, he was beginning to be much more at ease both with Betsy and Laura, thanks in part to Laura's unflagging determination that Caleb pay attention to her whether he wanted to or not. Abby had even heard him laugh when Laura grabbed his ears and planted a sloppy kiss on his nose, and there had been many times in the past few weeks she had seen his eyes light up when Betsy gave him a sleepy smile.

He can learn to love, a small voice whispered. *He is learning to love.*

Even though she had been unable to attend church services since coming to live in Caleb's house, her relationship with her Lord was a vital part of her life. Caleb barely acknowledged His existence. Her and William's mutual love of God had been the cement that kept their love alive and gave her the strength to stand by him when he made bad decisions, lost both his smile and his self-worth, and sank deeper and deeper into debt and depression. Those were the times she clung to God's promise that they would not be brought to any ordeal that they could not overcome with His help.

Caleb knew little of the strength that came from God, and even less about the comfort to be found as a child of His. He was the sort of man more accustomed to relying on his own strengths than trusting in anything or anyone he could not see and did not understand.

She gave a deep sigh and felt tears trickle from the corners of her eyes. *Time to face the truth, Abby.* The truth was that even though Caleb might be drawn to her in some physical way—after all, he *had* kissed her—

and since they had little in common except hot tempers and a love of reading, there was scant chance of a marriage between them surviving.

Marriages between vastly different people survive all the time. True enough. Without love, they might not thrive and grow, but they could and did survive. The problem was that she wanted more. Even though her marriage to William had been less than perfect at the end, they had gone into it with a genuine love for each other, and though that love might have changed somewhat with their problems, it had never died.

What next?

She knew she had to change her attitude. It was not all about her, after all. Instead of taking refuge in anger and dwelling on their differences, she should consider all the good things that had come into her life because of her unexpected and inconvenient husband.

First and foremost, her future and the future of her children were secure. No one knew better than she that possessions were not the important things of life, yet she slept better knowing that Ben and Laura did not have to worry about a roof over their heads or food to eat through the coming winter. Because of Caleb, all her old debt was wiped clean.

Then there was Betsy, the reason for everything that had transpired the past few weeks. Abby was now mother to a precious baby girl who had already carved out a special place in Abby's heart.

She lived in a beautiful house that she would gradually make her own. She was married to a man any woman in the county would be proud to call husband.

Even though he had a reputation as a hard, unyielding man, Abby knew better. He was a man who, despite having a hard-as-nails father and a mother who had left him as a child, had somehow grown into a decent person. He was fair, worked hard and gave impeccable attention to anything left in his care, whether it was a field, a child or a wife.

So where did that leave her?

Whether or not she wanted it to be, it seemed she was in love with her husband. Though she felt a twinge of guilt for betraying what she and William had shared, she knew he would want her and the children to be happy and taken care of. God wanted that, too, and He had brought her to this place. So the question remained, did she really want things to change between her and Caleb? If so, what could she do to change them?

"When you don't know where to go or what to do, go to God." The words her mother had often spoken drifted through Abby's troubled mind, stilling the turbulence and settling like a balm on her heavy heart.

Realizing how wrong she had been to try to "do it herself" and knowing she did want theirs to be a real marriage, Abby prayed with a heart of thankfulness instead of one of bitterness and rebellion. She thanked God for bringing Caleb into her life and providing for her and her children. She prayed that somehow, someway, some little everyday thing would touch his heart and help him to see just how much he needed God in his life. And she prayed that one day theirs would be a marriage where love, not necessity, bound them.

By the time she whispered "amen," Abby knew without a doubt that what she'd told Ben was true. Nothing that had happened to her or Caleb was by chance. They were exactly where they were supposed to be, exactly where God wanted them. It was up to her to teach him about love—all kinds of love. It was up to her to guide him to the place God wanted him to be.

To be the man God wanted him to be.

Caleb stared at the mirror that reflected back bloodshot eyes and scraped off twenty-four hours' worth of whiskers. He'd tossed and turned much of the night, torn among a dozen uncertainties, and recriminations for giving in to impulse and kissing Abby. He had betrayed not only Emily's memory but his own planned course of action. After giving careful consideration to the dozens of reasons a deeper relationship between him and Abby wouldn't work, he had let the memory of her tear-drenched eyes and the heart-wrenching quaver in her voice penetrate the wall he'd erected around his heart after his mother left. Sad eyes and a soft smile and a single kiss.

The memory caused his razor to slip. He jerked at the sudden sting, and stared at the thin trail of blood trickling down his chin. Dabbing at the cut with the corner of a towel, he acknowledged that he was in big trouble and had no idea what to do about it.

His approach to dealing with her and her children was not working at all. Polite civility didn't stand a chance against Abby's inherent goodness or the dozens of ways she was insinuating herself and her traditions into his life. Overt acts and an attempt to penetrate

Ben's antagonism had not brought him and the boy any closer. Cool neutrality certainly hadn't put off Laura, who simply ran roughshod over his intentions to remain detached by simply granting him one of her radiant smiles. The child would be a heartbreaker in a few years, he thought, and felt a rush of panic when he realized that he would be the one responsible for keeping all prospective beaux at bay.

Muttering under his breath, he squeezed the excess hot water from a towel and pressed it to his face, knowing he had just about used up his excuses not to go in to breakfast.

He put off hurrying to the kitchen because it was what he wanted to do so badly.

Definitely in trouble.

He shuffled down the hallway in his stocking feet, both dreading and anticipating what the day might bring. Having no idea what to expect from one day to the next was itself something to look forward to.

He heard Betsy crying in the kitchen and figured right away that his morning was not off to the start he'd imagined. He pushed through the swinging door and surveyed Abby's usually peaceful domain. The unmistakable smell of bacon burning assailed his nostrils. Not only was Betsy crying, but Ben, who was usually waiting for his arrival, was nowhere to be seen. Abby, whose hair was twisted into a haphazard knot atop her head, put the baby down, then rushed from the cradle near the fireplace to the stove, grabbing up a meat fork and scooping the charred meat from the smoking grease.

The only semblance of normality was Laura. As

usual, she greeted him with a wide grin and an unintelligible but heartfelt greeting. The sight of her smile lifted his heart. She *did* like him! The pleasing notion settled over his heart like a benediction.

Without thinking of his actions, he crossed the room, bent down and pressed a kiss to her blond curls. She reciprocated by reaching up and patting his cheeks with oatmeal-coated hands, while bombarding him with more baby gibberish, some of which sounded very much like "Dada."

Caleb was in the process of wiping the mess from his face when he heard Abby give a cry of pain. He whirled toward the stove and saw her pressing her palm to her mouth. He also saw the dark circles beneath her eyes.

"What happened?" he asked over the sound of Betsy's continued wailing.

"I was trying to move the skillet to a cooler part of the stove and picked up the handle with a damp towel."

Caleb moved closer, grasped her hand and turned it palm-up. An angry red weal streaked her hand. "I'll go out to the barn and get the bag balm."

"It'll be fine," Abby assured him. "It's a long way from my heart."

One corner of his mouth hiked upward in a half smile. The statement was one his father had always quoted to him and Gabe when they got hurt as boys—Lucas Gentry's way of telling his sons to take it like a man. Coming from someone as decidedly feminine as Abby, the saying seemed out of place.

"But you *can* help."

He regarded her with lifted eyebrows.

"You can either fry your own eggs, or you can try to calm Betsy down, which is usually Ben's job."

"I always break the yolks," he said, going to the cradle and picking up his baby girl. He nestled her against his shoulder, splaying one big hand on her back and cupping the other beneath her bottom. He began to bounce and pat. "Where's Ben?"

"In the barn, and thank you. Choice number two. You can either have no bacon or burned bacon." Without giving him time to answer, she said, "He decided to take advantage of the break in the rain and get the milking over with before it started up again."

Caleb was impressed with the child's forethought. "No bacon. What's wrong with Betsy?" She was usually a contented baby.

Abby shot him a look he couldn't quite decipher and reached for a couple of large brown eggs. "I overslept, and got behind with breakfast. I imagine she's starving."

All his plans to stay emotionally detached faded as Caleb wondered if the memory of their kiss had kept her awake and led to her oversleeping, as it had him.

A particularly ear-splitting scream from Betsy brought him back to earth in a hurry. Bouncing and patting wasn't working. Betsy was hungry, and he had no idea what to do. "Hold up on the eggs," he said, as Abby was about to crack the first one into the skillet.

She looked up at him, frowning.

"It's a miserable day. There's nothing I can do outside right now, so there's no hurry for breakfast. I'll go out and help Ben with his chores while you feed Betsy. We can start over on breakfast later."

Usually unflappable, Abby looked as if she were about to burst into grateful tears. "That would be a tremendous help. Thank you."

She placed the eggs back into the crockery bowl and reached for the baby, cradling her in one arm. Without thinking, she reached out her free hand and pushed an unruly lock of damp hair off Caleb's forehead. Then, as if she realized what she was doing, she jerked away. "I really appreciate this, and I know Ben will."

Wearing a frown of his own, Caleb said, "Between us, we'll make short work of things."

He grabbed his coat from the hook just inside the kitchen door and stepped out onto the porch, wondering what had just transpired in his kitchen. Burned meat. Burned hand. Crying baby. Happy baby. Two parallel conversations going on at once and he had somehow, miraculously, managed to follow both. A far cry from breakfast when he was married to Emily and had done most of the cooking himself. An even further cry from life as he'd known it in the past.

For the first time in his life, he was beginning to understand that marriage was a partnership, and how that partnership worked. It was two people with vastly disparate jobs working together and helping each other as needed. It was sharing not only happiness but problems, large and small.

He slipped his arms into his coat and snatched up the milk bucket. It was an interesting concept, one that held infinite possibilities.

Caleb found Ben in the barn, milking Nana, who was happily munching on some hay. He was as surprised to see Caleb as Caleb had been to know that Ben had taken it on himself to start his chores before breakfast.

"How are you doing?"

"Fine." The milk hit the bucket with a hiss.

"Have you milked Shaggy Bear yet?"

"No, sir."

"I'll do it, and we can get back inside where it's warm faster," Caleb offered.

Ben cast him a questioning, sideways look.

Caleb cleared his throat. "I appreciate you getting started with this. It was a smart decision."

Ben frowned. "I don't know how smart it was, but I couldn't take any more of Betsy's crying. It gets pretty bad between her and Laura some days."

Ah, Caleb thought, smothering a grin behind a sudden bout of coughing. A man after his own heart.

"Why do you think I told your mom I'd come and help you?" he said, settling on the three-legged milking stool. "It was a madhouse in there. Abby burned the bacon, and her hand, and—"

"Is she okay?" Ben interrupted.

Ben's obvious concern for his mother's welfare was touching. He'd always heard boys had a special relationship with their mothers, but he and Gabe had been deprived of that. Suddenly Caleb wondered if he would have had a good relationship with his mother if she'd stayed, and he wondered if her leaving had somehow been at the root of all Gabe's problems.

"It'll be fine," he told Ben. "I'll take the bag balm in when we go back inside."

"I hate when she burns the bacon," Ben said on a sigh.

"Me, too." Caleb relaxed into the rhythm of milking. "I told her I'd come help you while she took care of the babies and then we'd start breakfast from scratch. Once we get the animals fed, there isn't much we can do, so it looks as if we'll be spending another day inside."

Ben heaved another sigh. "I'm tired of being inside."

"I know." As they milked, the barn was filled with the first companionable silence they'd shared. Civility hadn't worked; maybe companionship would ease the tensions between him and Ben. Caleb struggled to find another topic of conversation that might prolong the tentative peace.

Holidays! he thought at last. Kids loved holidays.

"Thanksgiving is coming up next week. Does your family do anything special?"

"We usually go to Doc Stone's and spend the day, so Mom and Doctor Rachel can drink coffee and have a hen party after we eat." He shot Caleb a quick, conspiratorial grin at mention of the hen party, obviously remembering their earlier conversation on the subject. "On Christmas, they come to our house. My dad and Doc Edward used to play pinochle and dominoes, and Danny and I play something outdoors if the weather is okay."

"Sounds like fun." Fun. As he'd told Abby, he had no idea what comprised fun, although Ben's description did sound like a pleasant way to spend the day. As he'd grown up, one day was pretty much like the other, holiday or not. He wondered if Abby would want to keep up with the tradition, and wondered what his reaction would be if she asked him about going. Whatever happened, Caleb knew Abby's family would celebrate all the good things of life in one way or the other.

"I thought I'd go turkey hunting when it gets closer to time and see if I can get one. Would you like to go?"

Ben looked at him, his eyes filled with cautious eagerness. "I'd like to, since I've never been hunting before, but I don't have a gun. My dad didn't hunt," he added as an afterthought.

Caleb, who'd grown up with a rifle and shotgun in his hands, couldn't hide his genuine shock. If William Carter had bought every bite of meat his family put in their mouths, no wonder he had financial woes.

"High time you went, then. I have a shotgun you can use." Caleb found the idea of passing down his first gun to his new stepson a pleasing one.

"I doubt Mom will let me. She says I'm too young."

Caleb offered what he hoped was a conspiratorial look. "Moms are too protective sometimes," he lamented with a shake of his head. "Most women are. I got my first shotgun when I was about your age. In fact, it's the one I'll let you borrow. I think she'll change her mind if she knows I'll teach you how to be really safe with it."

"You'd let me use your shotgun?"

"Sure. Why not?"

Ben turned back to his milking, but not before Caleb saw the wide smile that spread across his face.

"Absolutely not!" Abby raged when Caleb broached the subject over breakfast some thirty minutes later.

"He's too young for that sort of responsibility! Firearms are dangerous."

Ben looked from his mother to Caleb, his head swiveling from one adult to the other as he monitored the heated conversation.

"I disagree," Caleb said in a calm, rational tone. "Firearms aren't dangerous if you're taught to use them correctly and respect what they're capable of doing. Ben needs to learn to use a weapon, both for food and for protection. There are still a lot of nasty critters out there, both four- and two-legged. Shooting is an important skill for a man."

"Exactly. A man. Ben is six years old."

Abby, whose hair had come loose even more, paced the room in long, angry strides, waving her arms in agitation and pointing her finger at Caleb when she wanted to make a point.

Caleb set his napkin aside and leaned back in his chair, crossing his arms over his chest. He knew in the end he would win the battle, but for the moment, he was relishing the vision of his wife in the glory of her motherly protectiveness. Pretty enough, but in no way beautiful, Abby was magnificent when she was angry. Her creamy cheeks were flushed with the heat of battle; she tipped back her head and looked down her straight little nose at him as if she were a queen and he nothing but a lowly subject. Disapproval turned her blue gaze to ice, and her eyes glittered like sunshine splintering off the frozen surface of the pond in winter.

He could not recall a single argument between himself and Emily. They had been too disengaged to trouble themselves with forcing an opposing opinion on the other.

"Abby."

She stopped stalking around the room, put her fists on her hips and glared at him. "Yes?" she replied in an imperious tone.

"I've listened to your opinions and your arguments, since you've made it clear that you've been accustomed to expressing yourself in the past." His voice was calm, his demeanor unthreatening.

Wariness crept into her eyes.

"Now, as I also understand is customary, I, as your husband, will make the final decision."

Her mouth dropped open in surprise, then snapped shut when she had no ready comeback. Her eyes flashed, and polite civility aside, Caleb realized that he wanted very much to kiss her again.

"Ben will be going hunting with me. He will be carrying a gun. A shotgun, to be exact. He will be taught to use it responsibly and safely." He turned to Ben. "If you've finished your breakfast, come with me. We can have our first lesson right now."

Eagerness in every line of his body, Ben jumped up from the table—without pausing to ask permission—and followed Caleb to the kitchen door. An enraged breath hissed from Abby's lips, but she did not say another word.

He turned in the aperture. "By the way, I'll be teaching our girls how to shoot as soon as they're old enough."

He could have sworn he heard an actual growl of anger.

He offered her a benign smile that failed to reach his eyes. "As a matter of fact, wife, come spring, I'll be teaching you, as well."

He turned and left the room, but not before he saw her slam the dishrag she was using into the pan of hot soapy water, or before he saw that water splash up into her startled face. He didn't laugh, but the pleased smile on his face was every bit as broad as Ben's.

Halfway down the hall, he stopped in his tracks. In his own way, he'd been teasing Abby, knowing that she had talked herself into a corner—so to speak—by telling him that so long as she got to voice her opinion, William had made the final decision.

When she'd first gotten so riled about the hunting trip, Caleb had quickly seen the advantage of letting her use her own position on the husband-wife relationship to his advantage and had turned the tables on her to get the result he wanted. He did chuckle then, but not so loud that she'd hear him. He doubted she would see the humor in the situation.

Hoisted by her own petard!

Recalling how easily he had turned her sanctimonious speech about William listening to her views right back on her, Abby's face flushed with sudden heat. Caleb had entered the discussion knowing full well how she felt and with full intention of using her own position against her. If his smug attitude was anything to go by, he had enjoyed every minute of it!

Still seething, she set the clean cast-iron skillet on the stove with a satisfying clang, and then shot a look toward the playpen where Laura grasped the edge of the railing and stared at her with a serious expression on her usually smiling face.

"Mamamamama," she said, holding out her arms.

Her sweet entreaty dissolved the lingering traces of Abby's anger. "Hey there, little girl," she cooed. "Do you need a dry diaper?"

She did. Abby carried her into the bedroom, changed her and spent the next several minutes playing peekaboo and blowing air bubbles against Laura's bare tummy, which sent the little one into gales of giggles. Every time she stopped, Laura lifted the hem of her dress for Abby to do it again.

"What's Laura laughing about?" Ben said from the doorway.

"I'm blowing on her belly, and she loves it, and so did you when you were a baby."

"Let me try," Ben said with a wide grin. As soon as he took Abby's place, Laura began to fuss and try to get away from him, doing her best to roll over onto her stomach and crawl away.

"I guess she's tired of that game," Abby said. "Or she doesn't like you doing it."

Ben's bottom lip stuck out in a pout.

"No sulking, young man," she ordered, riffling his hair with her fingers. She set Laura on the floor, where she clung to the quilt hanging over the edge of the bed and took off around its corner.

"She's probably getting sleepy. It's about time for

her morning nap." Injecting what she hoped was non-chalance into her tone, she asked, "Where's Caleb?"

"In his office. He said he had some figures to go over, and then he might teach me how to play dominoes."

"Oh." Abby felt her eyebrows lift in surprise. First Caleb offered to help with the milking, and then insisted on teaching Ben how to hunt, and now he planned on giving her son a lesson in dominoes. What was going on? Could Caleb's sudden interest in Ben be God's way of answering her prayers?

"Did he teach you about the rifle?"

"It's a shotgun, Mom," Ben said in a self-important tone. "There is a difference."

"Oh. I wasn't aware of that."

"Well, there is. Shotguns are described by 'gauge' and rifles by 'caliber.' There's a lot of other stuff I don't understand yet about how many lead balls are in a shell—they're real small for birds—but Caleb says it won't take me long to learn. He showed me how to load it and everything, and he says I should always have it on 'safe,' never to point it at anyone and don't put my finger on the trigger until I'm ready to shoot."

Abby had to admit she was impressed with what Ben had learned in such a short time and the care Caleb was taking with his teaching.

"He said we'd practice when it dries up some."

"That sounds…nice," she said.

"I'm tired of all my toys," Ben said, leaning against her in an increasingly rare show of dependence.

"Well," she said, smoothing his hair, "I suppose you

could read *Swiss Family Robinson* until Caleb finishes, or you can come and scrape carrots for a stew I'm going to make."

"Do you mean you're actually going to let him use a sharp knife?"

The irony-laced question brought up Abby's head. Caleb stood in the doorway, hands braced over his head on either side, regarding her with the merest hint of a mockery lighting his eyes. He was so tall and his shoulders were so broad…and he looked so steady and safe somehow. *And you, Abigail Gentry, are in deep, deep trouble.*

She pressed her lips together in a prim line. Why, he was actually baiting her! She'd encouraged him to loosen up, but she hadn't meant for him to find his pleasure in mocking her. Or had she? Abby let out a slow breath and took a firm grasp on her temper.

"I believe he'll be fine with adult supervision," she said in her best schoolmarm voice.

"I believe you're right," he said with equal stuffiness.

"Dadadada!"

Laura had spied him in the doorway and let go of the quilt. To Abby's surprise, she reached out with her chubby hands and took two toddling steps toward him and stood there, swaying like a drunk on Saturday night. When she realized what she was doing, her smile faded.

More to Abby's surprise, Caleb squatted down, holding out his arms to her. "Come on, baby girl," he said, motioning for her to keep coming. "Come see Daddy."

The encouragement was all Laura needed. Abby

watched in stunned bemusement as, with her solemn expression mirroring the concentration of Caleb's, Laura took another tottering step and then two more before losing her balance a scant yard from him and plopping onto her bottom. She promptly burst into tears while Abby fought back tears of her own.

An instant later, Caleb had scooped her up into his arms and was planting quick, light kisses on her chubby, tear-streaked cheeks, crooning to her that it was all right, that she was a really big girl, and she'd done a good job. Laura stopped crying and nestled her face against his shoulder.

Caleb's wide-eyed gaze sought Abby's. "She's walking!" Then, seeing the shimmer of tears in her eyes, he said, "I'm sorry." The stiffness was back in his tone.

"You have nothing to be sorry for," she said, wiping her damp cheeks with her fingertips.

"But her first steps were to me, not you."

"No, it's fine. Really."

He seemed to be thinking over the past few moments to try to figure out what else might have caused her tears. "I'm sorry," he said again, his eyes dark with contrition. "I called myself Daddy."

"But you *are,*" Abby told him. "You are her father. For the rest of her life."

"Then what is it?" he demanded. "Why are you crying?"

She sniffed back more tears. "Because it is very clear to me that whether or not you know it, whether or not you like it, she loves you and you love her."

Caleb shifted from one foot to the other, uncomfortable with the thought of love. "She's an easy child to be with."

The answer wasn't what Abby hoped for, but she should have known better than for him to admit to loving anything or anyone, at least not so soon. She had never doubted that God would respond in some way to her prayer, but she had not known what form His answers would take. What she had just witnessed between her daughter and her new husband was an amazing step in the right direction.

Chapter Nine

As expected, the Stones issued their usual Thanksgiving invitation, this time via Caleb when he went into town for oats. There had been no major problems the past few days, and he and Abby went about each day much as they had the one before, which made the decision of when to approach her about the invitation much easier. He would wait until after their evening Bible study and the children were in bed, since he was uncertain how the conversation might go. Instead of spending Bible time in his office pouring over bookwork, he decided to read his new farming journal in the parlor.

They were studying the parable of the seeds. Caleb admired how Abby not only related the different soils with the conditions of peoples' hearts but also how she wove it into their own planting of crops in the upcoming spring. Caleb tried to focus on the pages of the magazine but couldn't keep his gaze from straying to her any more than he could keep from remembering the way her lips felt beneath his. Several times during the lesson, she looked up and caught him watching her. To his surprise, she looked uncomfortable with his presence, but was trying her best not to let it show.

He wondered at the new demeanor, one he'd seen more and more often lately. She'd seldom been this uneasy with him. In fact, he didn't think she had been since those early days, and it wasn't like her. He liked the fiery Abby who talked back, who challenged everything about him from his attitudes to how he expressed himself. He liked the gentle Abby, too. The one who patiently explained things to Ben, who sang to Betsy and Laura and smiled at him when he stepped through the kitchen door at night. He didn't like the wariness or the fact that ever since he'd kissed her, she'd seemed…

The kiss! She'd been acting funny ever since he'd kissed her. Caleb considered his own actions. If his goal was to hold Abby at arm's length as he had Emily, he'd done a bang-up job—except for the kiss.

A sudden thought held him stock-still. He and Emily had liked each other well enough when they married, but that relationship had deteriorated through the years until they might as well have been strangers living beneath the same roof. Was it possible that his detachment and cool behavior toward her lay at the root of their inability to connect in any meaningful way, or had his behavior come about because of her own standoffishness? He supposed he would never know.

What he did know was that he had no idea of how to be tender, how to accept or demonstrate simple acts of kindness, something that had hit home when his neighbors had come with condolences after Emily's death.

He had no idea how to love or be loved. Lucas had done a remarkable job of teaching him and Gabe that any show of gentleness made you less a man. For the first time in his life, Caleb wondered if his dad had always so inflexible, or if the high walls around Lucas's heart had been erected after his wife's desertion.

Another thing Caleb would never know.

Caleb faced the fact that despite his determination to keep his heart free from any entanglements, he was being inexorably drawn into Abby's web of goodness. *So what's wrong with that? What can it hurt to embrace all the good things she could bring to his life? Why not welcome and enjoy Laura's undeniable adoration? Why shouldn't I accept the challenge of becoming a real father figure to Ben?*

"Is everything all right?"

The sound of Abby's voice brought him back to the present with a jolt. Though he'd done nothing to clarify his thoughts, he was glad to leave his uncertainty behind for a while. He looked around the room and saw that Ben was nowhere in sight, the Bible was put away and Abby stood in the doorway of Ben's room, staring at him with concern in her blue eyes. She must have finished her lesson, checked on the babies and put Ben to bed while he was woolgathering.

"I'm fine. Why?"

"Well, you don't often sit out here in the evenings, and you seem distracted."

"I suppose I am," he said, laying the publication aside. "I need to talk to you about something."

"Is it life or death?" she quipped with a hint of her usual spunk.

"Of course not," he said. "Why?"

Her shoulders rose in a slight shrug. "You have a very grim expression on your face."

"Oh. Actually, it's nothing grim at all. I saw Rachel when I was in town and she asked us to join them for Thanksgiving."

She looked surprised. "Oh. We've joined them every Thanksgiving since we came from Missouri, but I wasn't sure she'd ask this year, with William…" Her voice trailed away.

"Ben told me that's how you usually spend the day," Caleb confessed.

"He did?"

He gave a slow nod. "The day we did the milking together, and I told him we'd go turkey hunting. Would you like to go?" He heard the wariness in his voice and sensed they were both feeling their way through the conversation…as if they were walking through a swamp with dangerous quicksand pits.

"What did you and Emily do?"

"After my dad died, we went to her family. Before that, I usually dropped her off and came home. It was just another day."

The flicker of shock that crossed her features was so fleeting he might have imagined it. "Eating with the Stones would certainly be a nice change of pace since I haven't been anywhere since Betsy was born," she said, a thoughtful expression on her face.

"Of course you should go, then."

She looked into his eyes for several uncomfortable seconds, as if she were trying to see into his very soul. Then she smiled, the simple action stealing Caleb's breath. "As much as I might like to get out, this will be the first holiday season for both of us without—" she paused "—without Emily and William. I'm thinking it might be a bit uncomfortable for us both. Besides, I think Betsy is too little to be taken out yet, especially with the weather so nasty. So if it's all the same to you, I'd like very much to stay at home and start our own Thanksgiving tradition."

Caleb slowly released a strangled breath. "That's fine. I'd like that," he said and realized as he spoke that it was the truth. "Ben and I will go out tomorrow and see if we can get a turkey."

"I have every confidence in you," Abby told him, her blue eyes alight with a teasing humor, "but just in case you come home empty-handed, we can have one of those beautiful hams you smoked."

"Great." Why did he sound so stiff? Why couldn't he show an enthusiasm to match hers?

"The Stones usually come to us for Christmas," Abby said, "but again, I'm not sure that would be a good idea. I think we both need some time to get accustomed to our new life and each other, don't you?"

"I do," he said. "But if you change your mind, if we're a bit more settled as a family in a month, we could rethink it."

"That sounds like a good plan," she said, attempting a smile that fell a bit short of the mark. "Will you let them know our decision the next time you go into town?"

"I'd be glad to. Is there anything I can bring you from the mercantile?"

"Bring me?"

"Whatever else you might need for the meal."

She narrowed her eyes in thought and tapped her forefinger against her lips, drawing Caleb's attention to their soft fullness. "Let me think on it a bit. I know you eat everything, but is there anything you'd especially like me to fix?"

"I don't expect you to cook anything special for me," he told her, actually taken aback by the offer.

She fisted her hands on her hips. "Of course I'll fix whatever you want. We're starting a new Gentry holiday tradition. Funds permitting, I always make some sort of fruit salad for me, and Ben wants sweet potatoes with lots of butter, brown sugar and pecans on top."

Caleb's mouth began to water. "I'd love some sweet potatoes," he confessed. "My dad hated them."

He offered no further information; the simple statement said it all. "Then you will have sweet potatoes. Anything else?"

"Do you know how to make pecan pie? My mother used to make it, but the only time I get it now is if I happen to stop by the café when Ellie's made one."

"Not only do I make the best pecan pie in town, I'll match my crust to anyone's in the state."

Caleb was unable to stop the quick smile that quirked his lips. "Pretty boastful, aren't you?"

"It isn't boasting if it's the truth, is it?"

"Well, we'll see, won't we?" Caleb wondered if the question was his way of teasing.

"We will," she said with a saucy lift of her chin. "If you think of anything else, let me know. This is the one holiday I go a little crazy in the kitchen. Christmas is a bit lower key so that we can enjoy the day, our gifts and each other."

Enjoy the day. The concept was foreign, as was the idea of just spending time enjoying gifts and each other. Gifts! Though he'd always picked up something for Emily at the mercantile, usually something her mother said she'd like, Caleb had never bought Christmas gifts for anyone before. This year he would need not only something for Abby, but Ben and Laura, as well. He raked his hand through his hair, a bit overwhelmed by the whole idea. Well, he had almost a whole month to deal with that!

"That sounds…nice," he told her, realizing that the comment was unsatisfactory but unable to think of another. "If you think of anything you want or need, just let me know."

Caleb picked up the farming quarterly, effectively ending their conversation, which Abby thought was a shame. She'd enjoyed learning more about him and his likes, and the bit of sparring they'd engaged in about the pie had been stimulating after so many days of dealing with each other by saying and doing only the appropriate thing.

A time or two, she'd thought they were making a bit of progress, but the truth was that Caleb hadn't been the same since the night she'd cut his hair and he'd kissed her. Knowing the kind of man he was, she imagined he was berating himself for the momentary lack of control, since Emily had been gone such a short time. But since he'd confessed the true circumstances of his marriage, Abby wasn't sure she understood his guilt. Common sense told her that she should be satisfied with her life, and in many ways she was, but she'd be a lot happier sparring with him from time to time rather than dealing with a polite stranger. Like Laura, Abby knew she should be happy with baby steps.

Something positive had been accomplished through their decision to stay at home for Thanksgiving, though. As much as she might have liked to spend the day with Rachel and Edward, the things she'd told Caleb were true. She did feel it would be uncomfortable for them both to spend the day with friends, even though those friends were much loved, and she would enjoy beginning a new tradition that was centered on their new family. A baby step, but a strong one.

Abby was shelling pecans for Caleb's pie in front of the kitchen fireplace when the back door was flung open and Ben poked in his head.

"Mom, come see!" he yelled, his smile so broad it looked as if his cheeks should hurt.

"Shush! You'll wake the babies," she cautioned, casting a cautious glance toward the playpen and cradle. Seeing that neither little girl was stirring, Abby set the bowls onto the table and shook out her apron in the ash bucket.

"Does all this excitement mean you got us a turkey for tomorrow?" she asked.

He nodded vigorously. "I got a big old tom. He's got a beard and everything."

Grabbing a shawl from the hook next to the back door and draping it around her shoulders, Abby followed him onto the porch. "And are you sure it was you who shot him?"

"Positive!" he cried, racing down the steps and across the yard.

In typical mother fashion, she was torn between pride and a hint of sorrow that her little boy had taken one more step toward manhood. "Where is he? I can't be gone from inside but a minute."

"Out by the woodpile. Caleb said you should see him before he chops off his head."

Abby grimaced. William had never hunted, but with the help of neighbors they'd slaughtered pigs, goats and even a calf or two. He had always been careful to shield her from the grisly side of putting food on the table, just as she had been shielded from the financial ugliness that had hit her with such brutal force when he died. Deciding that she would rather know what to expect than not, she gamely followed her son out near the henhouse, where Caleb was building a fire beneath a huge cast-iron cauldron.

He looked up when he heard them approach, an expression of satisfaction in his eyes.

"Mom's shelling pecans for your pie!" Ben announced, skittering to a halt in front of Caleb.

"That's good."

"He shot this all by himself?" Abby asked with a dubious lift of her eyebrows.

Caleb nodded. "I called him up, and Ben blasted him."

"Caleb's gonna teach me how to call them up, too," Ben boasted.

"What's the fire for?" Abby asked.

It was Caleb's turn to look disbelieving. "You've never pulled feathers from a chicken?"

"No. We always bought ours from a neighbor, already dressed."

"You're kidding."

"No."

"All right. Here's what happens, and you need to pay attention, since you'll be killing and dressing chickens often in the future."

Abby's stomach churned at the thought.

"I'm going to chop off his head and gut him, and then we're going to dip him in scalding water so the feathers will pull out easier."

"Can't we just pull off the whole skin, like you do a rabbit or a squirrel?"

"Nooo," Caleb drawled in a measured tone, clearly holding some emotion in check. "If we skin him, he'll dry out something fierce in the oven. With the skin on, he'll get nice toasty brown and juicy."

"Oh," she said with a reluctant nod. "I suppose gutting is a man's work and plucking is a woman's."

"In most cases, yes. Today, I'll be glad to do it since you're shelling pecans for my pie." She thought she saw a twinkle of pleasure in his gray eyes. "Also, it's pretty cold out here, and you have two sleeping babies that neither Ben nor I are in condition to watch since we're not fit to be inside until we clean up. Besides, you look all nice and fresh."

A gentle rush of pleasure spread throughout her. Somehow the simple statement felt like a compliment, whether or not he meant it as one. "Should I stay and watch so I'll know what to do next time?"

"Your nose is already getting red. We've got it, don't we, Ben?"

"Yes, sir." He looked at Abby, his eyes glowing with pleasure, something she hadn't seen in a long time. "Hey, Mom, do you have any cocoa?"

"Yes."

"Do you think Caleb and I could have a cup of hot chocolate when we finish here?"

"I think for a couple of men who've provided Thanksgiving turkey, anything might be possible, including sugar cookies with raisins." She was talking to Ben, but her eyes were on Caleb.

"We'll see you inside in a bit, then," he said with a slow smile.

Abby turned and crossed the yard, her heart filled with lightness. There was no mistaking the new camaraderie between Ben and Caleb. She smiled. *Thank You, God.*

The changes since she'd altered her attitude and her prayers were just short of miraculous. She wondered how many other things she might have accomplished sooner if she'd just gotten out of the way and let God do what He did best.

An hour later, the big bird had been plucked and all its pinfeathers singed off. Since the weather was so cold, Caleb had hung it in the smokehouse overnight. Since Abby liked Thanksgiving dinner to be served at exactly noon, he would fetch it for her early in the morning.

She was stirring together a slurry of cocoa powder, sugar and a bit of milk when Ben and Caleb came into the kitchen, leaving their coats and muddy boots inside the back door. Their faces were red with cold, and their eyes alight with anticipation.

Ben headed straight to the table where a platter of fresh-baked sugar cookies sat waiting. The moment Laura saw Caleb she squealed "Dada" and held out her arms to be picked up. Caleb went straight to her, and then crossed to the cradle where Betsy was waving her arms around and staring at something mesmerizing on the ceiling. Balancing Laura on one hip, he reached down and put one big hand on Betsy's tummy, asking her if she'd had a good nap, almost as if he expected her to supply an answer. She kicked harder, which drew an unexpected chuckle from Caleb. Laura, who wanted to be the center of his attention, grabbed his face and forced him to look at her.

"That situation is going to get sticky in a few years," Abby told him.

"What's that?" he asked, crossing to the stove and peering over her shoulder.

Abby drew in a shaky breath at his nearness. He smelled of wood smoke and cold and the spicy masculine soap she associated with him. "Both of the girls vying for your attention."

"Why would they do that?"

"Because that's what girls do," Abby said, looking up at him from over her shoulder. "Big or small, they all want to be Daddy's girl."

"What does Daddy do in a case like that?"

It sounded like a teasing question, but the alarm on his face and the anxiety in his voice told Abby he was concerned. And why not? The man had never been around children, which, even to her, were sometimes strange little beings. She couldn't help the laughter that spilled from her lips. "If Daddy is as smart as I believe you are, he will be very careful to treat them the same and not show any favoritism."

He gave a purely masculine sound, something between a grunt and a growl. "Sounds impossible."

"It is. My dad always said he just muddled through as best he could."

"What's that stuff?" Caleb asked.

"Cocoa powder, sugar and a little milk," she explained. "Cocoa won't mix into milk if you just dump it in. You a have to make a syrup of sorts and then pour it in the hot milk. I like to add a dash of cinnamon and a teaspoon of vanilla if I have it."

"It smells delicious. I can't wait to try it."

Abby stirred in the cocoa mixture and swirled the wooden spoon around in the pan of hot milk. "Surely you've had hot chocolate before."

"Back before my mother left, but I barely remember it."

Abby stared up at Caleb in disbelief, again struck by the unfairness of his upbringing and the sadness she felt every time she thought of all the things he'd never experienced and those he had because of his parents' actions. Caleb had a long way to go, but like him, she had never shirked a challenge. She would take one day at a time, deal with one thing at a time, and put her trust in God, who could make anything happen.

Caleb went to bed filled with a satisfaction he could not remember ever experiencing. Furnishing the family with the main part of the holiday dinner was something he wouldn't soon forget. It had been a satisfying day in many respects. Ben had listened to Caleb's instructions from the moment they'd left the house until he came back the hero. The two of them had not only gotten along, the boy had actually seemed to have… fun. Caleb smiled into the darkness. If easy companionship and pleasure at seeing someone else's eyes light up with enjoyment was the definition of fun, then he'd had fun, too. When Ben took aim and shot the turkey, Caleb had felt his heart swell with something that superseded satisfaction and felt a lot like pride.

Other than work, he couldn't remember doing anything with his own dad. Lucas had never taught him or Gabe to fish; that had been left up to Frank. Caleb wondered if his life might have been different if his mother had stuck around, but knowing his father, the best she might have done was soften the most painful moments of his childhood.

His childhood. That was a hoot. He'd never had a

childhood. But Betsy would, and so would Ben and Laura and any other children he and Abby might have. He stopped breathing momentarily. The notion of having a baby with Abby brought a feeling of contentment that warred with a sudden panic reminiscent of that which he'd felt during Emily's labor. He wasn't sure he could survive a second round of the terror he'd suffered in the hours before Betsy's birth. The thought of losing Abby in the same manner left him feeling empty inside. He couldn't deny his growing feelings for her any longer. He could tell himself he was only being drawn into her circle of caring kindness, that he was becoming attached to Laura and forging a better relationship with Ben, and he could admit he was attracted to Abby physically. He could even let himself believe that it was okay for all these things to happen, that it would only make things better for all concerned. So why didn't he embrace this new life and all its good things?

Fear.

He was afraid. Maybe the anxiety was a result of his mother's abandonment, or maybe it was just an innate part of his personality, but he always liked controlling a situation, afraid to trust anyone, especially where his feelings were concerned. On the other side of that coin, in spite of his successes, he had never felt he measured up to Emily, who he knew wanted someone more polished and outgoing than a farmer from Wolf Creek, or to his father, who always found fault, always made Caleb feel as if he came up short. He'd often wondered if he'd worked harder or pushed himself more if he might have received a few simple words of praise for a job well done.

Caleb prided himself on his honesty. He worried that if he had not been enough, done enough for his dad or Emily, those shortcomings might cause whatever tentative feelings Abby might have for him to wither and die. The bottom line was that he was afraid that if he allowed himself to care she would leave him as his mother had, and if that were to happen, he knew the pain would be more devastating than anything he'd ever experienced.

Thanksgiving dawned cold, cloudy and damp, and when Caleb brought the turkey inside before daybreak, he declared it would snow before evening.

"Snow! Isn't it early for snow?" Abby asked, placing the bird into a blue granite roasting pan with white speckles.

"It is, and we don't usually see much if any, since the winters are comparatively mild to other parts of the country, but I've seen it snow in November a couple of times. What are you doing?" he asked as she smeared her hands with butter and began rubbing it over the carcass.

"Putting butter on so it will get golden-brown."

Finished greasing the bird, she plopped on the lid, and then washed her hands in a pan of soapy water. She was reaching to open the oven when Caleb held out a restraining arm.

"I'll get that."

She watched as he lifted the bird, which must have weighed at least fourteen pounds, slid it onto the bottom rack and closed the oven door.

"What next?"

"Nothing for now. I'll get the sweet potatoes ready in a bit and peel the others to mash. Then I'll get the green beans simmering with some ham, open a jar of corn and make the fruit salad. By the way, thank you so much for getting the ingredients for me. I didn't get any last year."

"You're very welcome."

Much to her astonishment, he had come home from town two days before with ingredients for her fruit salad. There had been oranges, some canned pineapple and even some grapes that had been shipped from California along with some bananas, a dear item for folks in Wolf Creek. When Caleb had seen the joy on her face, the cost had been worth every penny.

"So you don't have anything to do for a little while. Sit." He placed a hand on her shoulder and guided her toward a chair. "You've been going strong ever since your feet hit the floor. In fact, it makes me tired just watching you."

"But I have to fix breakfast."

"No buts. The kids won't be up for at least a couple of hours. The coffee is ready. Sit down and have a cup with me."

The request was unexpected and thoughtful. The idea of sitting down and sharing a cup of coffee and a few moments without three children afoot was deliciously pleasing. And a bit scary. It was seldom they talked without children around as buffers, and when they did, they generally wound up arguing.

Or kissing.

The wayward thought sent a frisson of nervous awareness shivering through her. To hide it, Abby tucked a strand of hair up into the knot at the top of her head. She started to sit, then bolted upright, only to feel Caleb's hand on her shoulder, forcing her back down.

"What's the matter now?"

"I have to pour the coffee."

There was a considering look in his eyes. "Believe it or not, Mrs. Gentry, I can pour a cup of coffee for myself and for you, too."

"But—"

"I said no buts. I doubt my manly ego will be more than slightly bruised."

Abby didn't say anything, but she'd noticed that more and more often lately, his sarcastic comments could be construed as poking fun at himself or even teasing. Another change that had happened since her prayer.

Abby watched Caleb pour himself a mug of coffee and then reach for the pretty floral cup that had belonged to her mother. Funny that he would remember that she liked drinking her coffee from the delicate china cup instead of a thick mug. It was one of her quirks, one she was surprised he'd noticed. Surprised, but pleased.

She was also pleased with the unrelenting masculine portrait he exhibited. Work-hardened muscles rippling beneath the fabric of his shirt, strong, yet gentle hands doing the things she usually did, and doing them with care and efficiency. Abby thought his hands were one of the things she most loved about him.

With a sigh, she accepted the cup he offered and helped herself to the thick cream he'd set before her.

"I don't suppose you'd let me have a slice of that pecan pie for breakfast." It was a statement.

"What pecan pie?" she asked, unable to stop herself from casting a flirtatious glance at him.

Caleb's eyes narrowed in mock ferocity. "The pie you hid in the pie safe," he said, once again surprising her with his teasing comeback.

She rested her elbows on the table and propped her chin in her hands. "The pie I hid? I thought that's what a pie safe was for," she countered. "To put pie in to keep it…safe."

"Until you came the only thing it kept safe was extra bullets."

"I'm glad I could make proper use of it, then," she told him. She pushed away from the table with a smile. "Of course you can have pie for breakfast. You brought home a turkey and cleaned it for me. Pie for breakfast seems a pretty fair trade."

"Thank you, but sit down. I can get it. I'm not used to having a woman wait on me the way you do."

Abby sat. "And I'm not used to not waiting on a man."

Caleb took the pie from the cabinet and reached for a saucer on the shelf. "Want some?" he asked, taking a large butcher knife from a wooden container.

"No, thank you. I can't do the sweet thing this early."

"I can do the sweet thing any time," he said, cutting a slice that was almost a quarter of the pie.

"I've noticed," she said, tongue-in-cheek.

Abby was afraid to consider the easy tone of their conversation overmuch. She didn't want to dwell on what had brought it about or if it might last. All she wanted to do was enjoy it while it did.

"I want to thank you for taking Ben hunting," she said, hoping to keep the mood alive.

Caleb took a seat across from her and reached for his mug. "I thought you were against the idea."

"I was," she told him with a nod, "but I'm not the kind of person who can't admit to being wrong. I could tell from the look on his face and the way he interacted with you that he enjoyed himself, and he was really proud. I think it was a step in the right direction for the two of you."

Caleb nodded. "He did a good job. He listens and does what he's told. He'll make a good hunter eventually."

"I'm glad he's learning to be more comfortable with outdoor pursuits. William wasn't. He was better at figuring out how things worked and working with wood. He made Ben's train that last Christmas."

"All I can do with wood is cut and split it," Caleb said. He lifted a forkful of pie to his mouth.

Abby didn't miss the humorous glint in his eyes as he chewed and swallowed. "You are definitely becoming adept with the teasing...or the sarcasm, whichever you want to call it."

"I take it that's good."

"I like it." She took a swallow of coffee and decided to push a bit. The man was floundering in an uncharted sea of children and anchored down with an unwanted wife, yet he was staying afloat better than she'd expected. Maybe he needed a little assurance that he was doing okay. "You're very good with Laura."

He looked embarrassed by the praise. "All I do is pick her up when she wants me to." He flashed one of his rare, quicksilver grins. "Let me clarify that. When she *demands* it."

"She is a bit pushy, isn't she?" Abby said, smiling back. "All in all, Caleb Gentry, for a man with little to no experience, you're doing very well with your unwanted family."

Clearly surprised, he dropped his gaze to his uneaten pie. He didn't speak for long seconds. Finally he looked up at her, an unexpected intensity in his eyes. "Thank you for saying that. As for you all being an unwanted family…that might have been true at the beginning, but we are a family. I know too well that I'm not William, but I am trying."

Her heart breaking the tiniest bit, she said, "You aren't William and you never will be."

Caleb looked as if she'd slapped him.

Furious at herself for not saying the right thing, she leaped to her feet and leaned across the table. "I'm sorry. That didn't come out the way I meant it to," she said, earnest entreaty in her blue eyes. "What I meant to say is that you aren't William and I don't want you to be. I want you to be you. He was a good man, and you're a good man, too. But you're different, and that's the way it should be."

She straightened and whirled away from him. As usual when she was upset, she began to pace. "I know you're trying very hard, but I don't want us to always be the unwanted family. I don't want us to be a burden you have to bear for the rest of your life so that you spend every day trying to do what's right.

"I want you to do things with Ben that you both like to do. I want you to teach him all about farming and hunting, and the satisfaction that comes with a hard day's work. I don't want you to mimic what William and Ben had, I want you to build your own relationship with him, just as you're starting to do.

"I want you to help me in the kitchen, but only if you want to be here. I want you to keep on loving Laura and I want you to become comfortable with us in your life. I want to see you smile more, to hear you laugh."

She paused and looked at him. Her eyes filled with tears, but she didn't try to hide them. "What I want, Caleb Gentry, is for you to be h-happy." The last word was choked out on a sob.

Before she realized what he was about, Caleb had risen and crossed the room to her, blocking her path. She stopped but refused to look up. To her dismay, he lifted her chin, forcing her to meet his gaze. "Pity, Abby?"

"No!" she said with controlled vehemence. "Not pity, Caleb."

Tension vibrated from his big body as he searched her tear-drenched eyes for long, tense moments. Finally, the breath he'd been holding hissed out in a long sigh. Then without another word, he turned and strode for the doorway, nabbing his coat from the hook as he went.

Oh, why, why couldn't she learn to leave things

alone? Why must she always have to open her mouth? Now, he probably suspected that she cared and he would not like that one little bit. "Caleb, wh—"

He turned abruptly. "Shh," he commanded softly, holding up a silencing finger.

He didn't look angry, she thought. He looked perplexed, or… Oh, she didn't know how he looked! "Where are you going?"

"To do the milking. It's a holiday, so I'll give Ben the day off. I won't be long." He took the lantern and a box of matches from a nearby shelf, opened the door, and let himself out.

It was only after he'd gone that Abby noticed that he hadn't finished his pie. Reaching for his fork, she cut an oversized bite for herself and chewed on it while her tears flowed down her cheeks. She took a sip of her coffee only to find that it had grown tepid. Feeling as if she were recovering from a bad bout of influenza, she rose, refilled her cup and fed another log to the fire, praying that her impulsiveness had not ruined the progress they'd made. Praying that she had not ruined his mood or the day.

Then she sat down and finished his pie.

She had shed tears for him.

Caleb milked the goat and thought about what a difference a day could make in someone's life. His fear aside, Abby was different from any woman he'd ever known. He couldn't pretend as he had the day before that he was attracted to her or that she and the children were working their way into his life. The truth was they had worked their way into his heart, and he loved her. Loved her as he had never loved Emily, as he had never expected to love anyone. Loved her as he had never imagined he could love.

He wanted to keep her from ever hurting again, wanted to lavish her with everything his money could buy. Wanted to look up in ten or twenty or fifty years and see her sitting across the room from him, and know he was the reason for the smile on her face. He wanted Ben to look at him and feel the same love and respect he'd felt for William. He wanted Laura to look at him and see the kind of man she could use as a measuring stick when she sought her own husband. *Dear God, I want them all to love me.*

The problem was that with that love came an overwhelming responsibility. It wasn't just a feeling, it was action, and Caleb wasn't sure how to make his prayer come true.

Prayer? Had he just prayed? He didn't think so, wasn't sure. Maybe, though, he had let God know his feelings. What next? If he knew what to do to become a better husband and father, would it make a difference? Were there any guarantees that his feelings would be reciprocated?

He thought Abby felt something for him, but was her desire to see him happy just her natural longing for things to be right for everyone, or were the tears she shed for him based on something more? How could he know?

Caleb had no illusions about his past. He did not condone his mother's actions, but if Libby Gentry had sought love somewhere else, it was only because Lucas had driven her away with his inflexibility, his disagreeable attitude and his acerbic tongue. Caleb had lots of memories of his soft-spoken mother crying tears of hurt and humiliation.

This marriage was no business deal as he'd alleged when he'd proposed marriage to Abby. This was the lives of five people. It all boiled down to whether or not he was willing to risk opening himself up to change, to try to become the man Abby deserved.

What if you do something to hurt them without meaning to? What if you can't be all she wants in a husband?

There was no way of knowing how it would end, but one thing was certain. He had come a long way in a short time. He wasn't going anywhere, and neither was Abby. The best tactic was to take one day at a time and try to build on their shaky foundation. It was all he could do.

Abby was opening a particularly stubborn jar of green beans when he came back inside. One look at his rugged face told her that she needn't have worried. Whatever he thought of what she'd said, whatever he felt about it, he was in perfect control, and she saw no animosity in his demeanor or his eyes.

"No one's up yet?"

"No. Thank goodness." She grabbed a dish towel and looped it over the top of the jar for a better grip. "I'd like to get things under control before I'm inundated with little people."

"I'll get that," he said, walking over and taking the can from her and giving the top a hard twist. "I'd open another if I were you. Frank and Leo have pretty good appetites, and it isn't often they get to eat someone's cooking other than their own."

"You're right. I'm not used to cooking for three big men."

"You'll never guess what I found in the barn," Caleb said, opening the pie safe.

"Probably not," Abby agreed, dumping the beans into a pan and heading for the pantry for another.

"Traps."

She turned. "Traps?"

"Animal traps," he said, with a nod. "What happened to my pie?"

She changed the subject to hide her guilt. "Animal traps? For what?"

"For Ben. I'll teach him to trap and tan the hides and he can make himself a little money. I used to love to trap when I was a kid."

Abby looked at him with raised eyebrows.

"Yeah. I know I said I didn't do anything for fun, but I started thinking about it and I realized I did enjoy trapping, although it was primarily a way to earn some spending money, since my father was such a skinflint."

"And you think Ben will like it?"

"I think Ben likes anything outside—even milking that ornery goat."

"Okay. Hunting and trapping." Abby sighed. What next?

Caleb placed his hands on his hips. "What did you say you did with my pie?"

Abby blushed. "I'm sorry. I ate it."

The Thanksgiving meal was far different from those she'd shared with her friends and William, but it was enjoyable just the same. Abby had managed to get Betsy fed before the men came in, and thankfully she had fallen asleep. Laura's chair sat next to Abby's so that she could dole out spoons full of potatoes and fists full of green beans as the meal progressed.

Ben gave thanks for the meal, while Frank and Leo sat with bowed heads, their eagerness to get at the food almost palpable. The older men ate with gusto, and though their manners left much to be desired, their lavish compliments on Abby's culinary skills far outweighed her dismay. Still she barely suppressed a shudder when Frank reached out with his fork to stab another slice of turkey and Leo gave a loud belch after the meal. When she sneaked a glance at Caleb she saw amusement in his eyes. She also knew somehow that he would deal with the situation after the meal.

One step at a time, she thought. At least the two men were entertaining. Frank regaled her with tales from Caleb and Gabe's youth, though Abby saw the darkness gathering on her husband's face whenever his brother's name was mentioned.

As had been a practice in the past, Abby asked that everyone at the table tell one thing for which they were thankful.

Ben started. "I'm thankful for killing a turkey and for my new traps."

Abby smiled. "Leo?" she urged.

"I'm thankful for this here fine food. It was truly delicious, Missus Gentry."

"Thank you, Leo," Abby said, knowing the praise came from his heart. "Frank."

The older man sat there a moment, a thoughtful expression on his face. "I'm thankful that you've come here, Mrs. Gentry. For the first time in many a year—maybe since Miz Libby left—this old farm has a good feeling about it."

Abby wondered if she could speak for the tears she felt tightening her throat. "Thank you, Frank. That's very sweet." Blinking hard, Abby's gaze moved to the next person, who happened to be Laura. "Laura, love, what are you thankful for?" Abby asked.

The baby, who had been chattering throughout the meal, and periodically trying to tempt Caleb with various squished food, smiled broadly, held out a handful of sweet potato and said as if she understood the question perfectly, "Dada."

Everyone at the table laughed, including Caleb. Sensing she was the center of everyone's attention, Laura's grin widened, and she smacked both hands down into the food smeared on her tray. "Dada," she chortled again, as if to prolong her moment of recognition.

Caleb was next. "I'm thankful for Laura, of course," he said with a quick grin, "and for everyone else here at the table. Leo, you and Frank make my workload lighter, and Abby, you and the children have indeed made this house feel like home."

Abby swallowed and blinked hard and fast to hold back the incipient tears.

"Mom, it's your turn," Ben prompted. "What are you thankful for?"

Knowing she was the focus of everyone's attention, Abby stared at her plate and tried to gather her thoughts. She was thankful for so much she hardly knew where to begin. Finally, she said just that.

"But to be more specific," she continued, looking at each of them, "I'm thankful that God brought me here when I was at such a low point in my life, and I'm thankful for each and every one of you."

Her gaze, filled with the love she could not speak aloud, rested on Caleb. "To second Laura, I'm thankful for Caleb. I'm very blessed."

Chapter Ten

The cold two weeks following Thanksgiving raced by in a tumble of windswept leaves and dreary days of rain and fog. Considering the year had started out with such tragedy, it promised to end on a positive note. As usual, Caleb was unfailingly polite and helpful, but it seemed that he smiled more, and there was a relaxed, almost contented air about him that had not been present when she'd first come to his aid.

With things going fairly well between Abby and Caleb, and a bit fearful the lingering grief over William's and Emily's deaths would cast a pall over the day, especially for Ben, Abby had decided to change tactics and ask both the Stones and the Emersons to Christmas dinner, reasoning that Daniel's presence might make the day easier for Ben and that Bart and Mary might like spending the day with their baby granddaughter. At the very least, company might provide at least some distraction from everyone's grief.

Except for the day she and Caleb had gone to fetch

her things from her old house, Abby had not been away from the house since she'd come to the Gentry farm. She longed for an afternoon free from the demands of children to be by herself and do some Christmas shopping, since for the first time she could remember, she had money enough to buy gifts without feeling guilty, thanks to Caleb's generous household allowance. The problem was that she wasn't certain how a shopping expedition could be accomplished short of leaving the children in Caleb's care for an afternoon. He would balk, she knew, but the weather had been too miserable to get the girls out, which left no choice but to ask him.

She waited until all the children were down for the night before she broached the subject.

"I'd like to ask a favor," she said.

"If I can, certainly," he replied, but there was a wary expression in his eyes.

"Christmas will be here before we know it," she said. "If it's all right with you, I'd like to have both the Stones and the Emersons for dinner. Company might make the day less difficult for us all, and with Danny here, Ben's day might go easier."

"That sounds like a good idea," Caleb agreed. "I'll ask them the next time I'm in town."

Abby laced her fingers together. "I wanted to talk to you about that, too."

He hiked one dark eyebrow in question.

"Except to get the last of our things from the farm, I haven't been anywhere since Betsy was born." She didn't miss the stricken look on his face, as if he'd never realized that fact before.

"I'm sorry. I never thought— I mean..."

"I didn't mention it to make you feel guilty, Caleb. It's no one's fault, but I was wondering if you would mind watching the children one afternoon so that I can buy a few gifts. It's next to impossible to browse with three little ones—not to mention the surprise element. And the babies don't really need to be out in this damp cold."

"You want me to watch them? Here? Alone?" There was no mistaking the panic in his voice.

"It would only be for a few hours."

"But how will I handle the girls?"

"Laura drinks from a cup and can eat almost anything soft. I'll feed Betsy before I go, and if she begins to fret, you can give her some warm cow's milk in the bottle Mary brought. As you said, we're a family. What if something happened to me?"

All the color drained from his face. "Nothing's going to happen to you!" He bit out the words with chilling intensity, as if by doing so he could actually prevent it from happening.

Abby understood that the burst of anger stemmed from his fear that history would repeat itself with her. "I'm sure you're right, but nevertheless, you'll never learn how to deal with them all if you don't start somewhere," she told him, her voice patient, but firm.

"What if something happens to one of them while you're gone?"

"Nothing will happen."

He swallowed hard. "How can you be sure?"

"Do you want me to yell it like you did?" she asked with a ghost of a smile. "Just to make sure?"

He offered her a sheepish half smile. "I'm being foolish, aren't I?"

"Just a bit."

He blew out a deep breath. "I'm afraid I'll do something wrong and hurt one of them…or something."

"Don't you think that I'm afraid that something will happen every day?" Abby asked in a gentle voice. "Just because I care for them day after day does not mean I don't do things that are wrong, and even potentially harmful."

"But you'd never hurt one of them," he argued.

"Neither would you."

"All right. All right." The expression of panic in his eyes matched the shaky tone of his voice. "Only for a few hours. And it may as well be tomorrow, so we can get it over with."

"I'll leave as soon as we have an early lunch and be back by dark," she promised.

"I want to go!" Ben cried when he found out she was going to town.

"Not this time, Ben. I'm going to buy Christmas gifts, and I can't buy yours if you're along."

"But Caleb doesn't know what to do if the babies start crying."

"You can help him. You're very good with them both."

Knowing he was fighting a losing battle, Ben sighed. "Me and Caleb can't stand too much of that squalling. It gets on our nerves."

"Caleb and I," Abby corrected, trying her best to suppress a smile. She leaned down. "Guess what?" she whispered conspiratorially. "It gets on my nerves, too, sometimes."

"Really?"

"Really."

"It will be fine, Ben," she said, pressing a kiss to the tip of his nose. "I promise."

After the noon meal, Caleb hitched up the buggy and helped Abby climb in, and after giving last-minute instructions on what to do, she headed toward town.

Caleb watched her go with a feeling of doom closing in on him. He knew she was right, but how would he survive the next few hours with three demanding children when he had no clue what he was doing?

Thankfully, once Laura's belly was full, the heat from the fireplace soon made her eyelids droop, and she fell asleep in the pen contraption.

Caleb decided to try his luck at rocking Betsy to sleep while Ben got out his train and stacked some wooden blocks in it for freight.

Abby's quest for gifts started Caleb thinking about Christmas presents of his own. Though he'd picked up a trinket for Emily each year, there had been no thought put into it since Mary always told him what Emily wanted. He had no clue what Abby might like, and he'd never bought anything for a child before. A fresh dousing of reality rushed through him. There was more to this husband and parenting thing than he'd ever imagined—if you wanted to do it right.

That realization made him feeling a little sorry for himself. Laura slept in the pen William built and Ben was playing with the train his father had crafted. As Caleb had told Abby, he was no good with woodworking. He couldn't make a rocking horse for Laura or Betsy, or fashion a dollhouse when they grew older.

Wearing a brooding expression, he was watching Ben stack the blocks in the train cars when he recalled the day he'd "borrowed" his chessmen to haul around. Sudden inspiration struck. Toy soldiers! He could buy Ben some toy soldiers to play with. And maybe a book about trapping and tanning hides. Betsy was so little that a dress from the mercantile would suffice, and Laura would likely be tickled with a rag doll of some sort. Surely Mary would have something in stock for everyone.

But what about Abby? Other than books, he didn't know what she liked. Did she knit? Crochet? What? All he'd seen her do since she'd lived under his roof was cook and clean and wash clothes and take care of little ones.

A now-familiar rush of guilt swept through him. As much as it galled him to admit it, Abby was the one doing most of the giving around the Gentry household. He hadn't meant it to be that way, but it was, which just proved that he was no better at the husband thing than he was the father thing.

She needed something special, something just for her—but what? He had no idea what kind of clothes she liked, and had no one to ask. He doubted Mary knew anything about her likes and dislikes. Maybe Rachel…

Suddenly, he remembered her wistfully mention how nice it would be to have a slipper-shaped bathtub to relax in after a long day. Though he already owned the biggest oval-shaped trough the mercantile carried, he knew first hand that it was not long enough to stretch out in. Maybe she'd like a new tub. He thought he'd seen one at the mercantile a while back. Maybe he'd run the idea past Mary the next time he went to town.

Feeling pleased with himself, he looked down at the baby sleeping in his arms. Moving slowly, to keep from waking her, he rose and put her in her cradle, covering her with a small colorful quilt. Feeling sleepy himself, he settled into a corner of the sofa and stared at the mesmerizing dance of the flames. Betsy gave a soft snuffle, and the muffled whistling wind sent some lingering leaves clattering against the house. The crackling, hissing and pop of the burning logs sent his eyelids downward....

The sound of a log falling jerked him to wakefulness with an undignified snort. Straightening, Caleb wiped a hand over his face and stole a glance at the babies, who still slept soundly. Ben sat staring at him, amusement in the blue eyes so like his mother's.

"How long did I sleep?" he asked.

"Not long."

"Bored?"

Ben nodded.

Caleb recalled Abby telling him you had to look for the fun times, that they were where you least expected them. After a moment's thought, he disappeared into the bedroom and began rummaging around in the bureau drawers, soon finding what he was looking for.

"Come here, Ben," Caleb said, entering the parlor. Curious, Ben crossed to him. "These were Emily's," Caleb said, holding out a drawing tablet and a box of pastel crayons.

He walked over and took an autumn landscape with mountains and a lake from the wall. Done in an impressionistic style, there was little detail in the picture, and he thought Ben might be able to make a credible replica of the piece.

"I thought you might like to try your hand at drawing. Look at this and see if you can copy it."

"Drawing's for girls," Ben said with typical masculine disdain.

"Actually, most of the famous artists are men," Caleb said, searching his mind for some other activity the boy might enjoy. "But if you don't want to try, how about a game of chess?"

"I don't know how to play chess."

Well, it wasn't a no, Caleb thought. "Then it's high time you learned. Why don't I make us a cup of hot chocolate, and I'll teach you?"

"You don't know how to make hot chocolate."

"Sure I do," he said with a confidence he was far from feeling. "Your mom told me how."

"Abby! What are you doing in town?" Mary Emerson asked when Abby stepped through the door of the mercantile.

"I escaped for the afternoon," Abby said, unwinding the woolen scarf from around her neck and tugging off her gloves. The warmth from the potbelly stove in the center of the room felt wonderful against her chilled face.

"Where are the children?"

"Would you believe Caleb is watching them?"

Mary's eyes widened and she burst out laughing. "Caleb? All of them?"

Abby's smile could only be described as mischievous. "All of them. I told him he needed to learn to take care of them and that I needed to get away for a few hours to do some Christmas shopping. I left him instructions on what to do with Laura and Betsy, and here I am."

"Will wonders never cease," Mary said, her eyes still glittering with mirth. She came around the counter and gave Abby a hug. "It's so good to see you. How is Betsy?"

"Growing like a weed," Abby said, shrugging out of her coat.

"We've been meaning to drive out, but the weather has been so nasty, and it's almost dark by the time we close, that we just haven't made it. How are things with you and Caleb?"

"All of us still walk around on eggshells from time to time, but we're doing well enough, I think."

"Be patient, Abby," Mary told her. "Things will work out."

"I pray you're right."

Abby extended the invitation for Christmas dinner and was assured that, like the Stones, the Emersons would be there "with bells on." She knew she was blessed to have the Emersons' support and wondered if Bart and Mary would be so generous with their approval if they suspected that Abby had fallen love with their son-in-law, even though they knew Caleb and Emily had not loved each other.

Abby pushed away the troubling thought and wandered through the store, taking time to look at everything that caught her interest. Mary pointed out some soft yarn hats with earflaps and mittens to match, and Abby bought one each for Laura and Betsy. She also bought them each a rag doll—Laura's with blond braids, Betsy's with brown. It was a foolish purchase, since it would be spring before Betsy could even hold hers, but it still gave Abby a great deal of pleasure. She bought Ben a pair of new boots, a game of checkers and a book about horses.

Choosing a gift for Caleb was harder. She knew so little about him, and he could buy himself whatever he wanted—not that he did. In the end, she chose three dime novels, a soft flannel shirt and a pocket knife with a scrimshaw handle. She splurged on oranges and chocolate and licorice for Ben's stocking.

She was almost finished with her shopping when Mary carried a small wooden crate from the storeroom. "I want you to have this," she said, placing it on the counter.

"What is it?"

"It's a china nativity set Emily bought while she was away at school. She always put it on the mantel at Christmas. I brought it here because I thought it might make me feel closer to her at this time of year, but when I took it out, I only felt sad. I'll understand if you feel uncomfortable using it, but please take it. It should be Betsy's one day."

"Of course I'll take it," Abby said. "And I'm sure I'll use it." She smiled gently at the woman who had the power to make her life miserable, and had instead been one of her most loyal champions. "And you can be sure that Betsy will be told about it when she's old enough."

"Thank you, Abby," Mary said, enfolding her in a close embrace. "You're a blessing."

Abby hugged her back. "So are you."

After telling Mary she would load her parcels later, Abby bade the older woman goodbye and picked her way across the still-muddy street to the café, where she was meeting Rachel.

"Did you get your shopping done?" Rachel asked as they took off their coats and scarves and hung them on the pegs near the door.

"I did, and it was nice not having to worry about how much money I was spending."

"I know," Rachel said. "Not everyone in town is so fortunate."

Ellie, tall, blond and curvaceous, waved them to a table, took their order and soon set slices of caramel apple pie and mugs of fragrant coffee in front of them. To Abby, her friend looked more like she belonged in the pages of *Godey's Lady's Book* than she did running a small-town café.

"Who's having a hard time?" Ellie asked, joining them at the table.

"The Thomersons," Rachel said. The expression on her face looked as if she'd taken a bite of a green persimmon. "Elton got into the hooch last night and knocked Meg around again. Our new sheriff put him in jail for a few days to let him think about it, but he won't be there long—unfortunately."

"How badly did he hurt her?" Abby asked.

"He broke her arm, so she won't be taking in any laundry for a while. Her parents can help with the kids, but he'll tell her he's sorry and she'll go back to him, and it will be the same thing a few weeks or months from now."

"What can we do?" Abby asked.

"Not much," Rachel said with a sigh. "The truth of the matter is that nothing will change until she decides she's had enough and leaves him."

Blowing out a frustrated breath, Rachel forced a smile, picked up her fork and said with forced gaiety, "Well, enough of that! I came here to enjoy some time with my friends."

Abby savored every bite of Ellie's luscious pie and the precious time with her friends even more. As she expected it would, the talk turned to her and Caleb.

"So how is Caleb Gentry as a husband?" Ellie asked, her brown eyes sparkling with curiosity. "Brooding? Frightening? What?"

Abby laughed. "Brooding? Yes, sometimes. Frightening, never. Well," she amended, "not after I lost my temper that first time."

"You lost your temper with Caleb Gentry?" Ellie

breathed, leaning her elbows on the table and leaning forward.

"I did," Abby said. "And lived to tell about it." Seeing the horrified expression on Ellie's face, she said, "I'm only joking, Ellie. I have lost my temper with him, more than once actually, but he takes it in stride pretty well."

Abby grew thoughtful. "In fact, the last time we argued was before Thanksgiving. He wanted to give Ben a shotgun and take him hunting. As you can imagine, I was furious, and then I looked over and saw him leaning back in his chair with his arms crossed over his chest watching me rave and rant with this sort of…almost a *pleased* smile in his eyes. If it weren't crazy I'd say the wretch was enjoying every minute of it."

"That's strange," Ellie said.

"Our whole marriage is strange," Abby replied, taking a sip of her coffee. "But it's not bad," she hastened to add. "In fact, on the whole, he's been very good to me and more accommodating than I would have imagined from our first meeting."

She flashed a smile between Rachel and Ellie. "He likes to read, so we talk about that. And I see a lot of changes in him already, and he's solid and dependable…"

Lost in her thoughts, Abby didn't see the look that passed between her friends. "And he's really attractive if you like rugged-looking men."

"Oh, dear!" Ellie said, her eyes wide.

"Oh, dear what?"

"You're falling for him."

Horrified that her feelings were so obvious, Abby

flashed a flustered look from Ellie to Rachel, who was regarding her with a considering expression.

"Don't be ridiculous!" Abby bristled. She made her tone cool and impersonal. "I think Caleb is a good man, but most people don't realize it because he'd not very social and because of his father's reputation. He's treated me and my children well, that's all."

Wearing a delighted smile, Ellie got to her feet and swept up the two mugs for a refill. "Pull the other one, honey," she said, tossing a teasing smile over her shoulder. "It's got bells on it."

Thirty minutes later, Abby gave Rachel some money to help out Meg Thomerson, and said goodbye to her friends. It was almost dark when Abby pulled the buggy into the front yard. Happy at having the afternoon to herself, and filled with the joy of the season, she'd stopped on the way home and plucked an armful of pine and holly branches to make a wreath for the front door. It was only when she saw the lights of the house in the distance and allowed herself to contemplate the disaster that might be awaiting her that her happiness started to dissipate.

Laden with packages, she was halfway up the front steps when she heard what sounded like a crow of laughter from Caleb. Surprised, a bit wary, she stopped in her tracks. What on earth?

Balancing her parcels, she turned the doorknob and stepped inside, stunned at the scene before her. Caleb and Ben were seated at the game table, the chess set in front of them. Laura sat in the crook of Caleb's arm, gnawing on a crust of stale bread. The cradle sat near Caleb's elbow, and she watched as he gave it a gentle push.

Hearing the door open, Ben cried, "Hey, Caleb! Mom's home."

Abby's gaze met her husband's. He looked exhausted but oddly content and achingly appealing. His hair looked as if he'd run his hand through it several times—a gesture that was becoming endearingly familiar. A streak of some indeterminate substance that was most likely wet, mushy bread was smeared across his cheek. His end-of-day beard gave him a beguiling but dangerous look that set Abby's heart to racing. She felt her heart swell with love.

For the first time since she'd stepped into the Gentry house with Rachel, it felt like home.

The weeks leading to Christmas were the most pleasant Abby had experienced in years. With her help, Caleb had fashioned the pine boughs into a wreath and wired pine cones to it. She'd cut strips from one of his seen-better-days red flannel shirts and sewn the strips together, fashioning a bow at the bottom for a splash of color. When they'd finished, he'd smiled at her, a smile so stunning she'd dared to hope his feelings toward her were changing.

Two days before Christmas, Abby was baking star-shaped sugar cookies when a beaming Ben bounded through the back door. Laura, who was sitting in her chair munching on a cookie, waved her sweet at him and said what sounded very much like "Ben."

"Mama! Come see what we brought you," he shouted.

"Shh," she cautioned, holding a silencing finger to her lips. "You'll wake Betsy."

"Okay," he said in a loud whisper. "But you gotta come see what Caleb and I found."

Drying her hands on her apron, Abby grabbed a shawl and threw it around her shoulders. Then she settled Laura on her hip and wrapped the heavy wool around them both.

The wagon sat near the back porch, and lying in the bed was a cedar tree. Caleb stood near the rear of the wagon, an expression of anticipation on his cold-reddened face. "Ben said you liked to have a tree," he said, almost as if he were asking if he'd done the right thing.

"I love a tree, don't you?"

He lifted his shoulders in a shrug. "I don't know. I don't recall ever having one, though we might have when my mother was still here. It's really nicely shaped," he added.

"It's wonderful. Thank you for going to the trouble."

"It wasn't any trouble. I'll make a stand and Ben and I will put it in the parlor. Where do you want it?"

"Mm, somewhere away from the heat of the fireplace. Maybe in front of the window to the left of the door. I can slide the chair over a bit."

"That's where we'll put it, then."

As it turned out, the tree was much more than just nicely shaped. It was perfect. When the girls were down for the night and the Bible lesson was over, Abby popped popcorn, which both she Ben both insisted that Caleb help string for a garland.

Mumbling that he "didn't sew," Caleb nonetheless took the piece of thread Abby handed him and proceeded to work the popcorn along its length.

"Caleb Gentry, stop that!"

His gaze flew to hers and he spoke around a mouthful of popcorn. "Stop what?"

"Stop eating the popcorn. I've been watching you and Ben both, and you're eating more than you're stringing.

"Doesn't the Bible say something about a man not eating if he doesn't work?"

"Yes."

"Then since I'm working, I thought I'd earned the right to eat," he said his expression one of false sincerity.

"And I think that's what's meant by twisting the scriptures," she told him in a prim tone as she tore more narrow strips from the cast-off shirt to use as bows on the tips of the branches. Neither Caleb nor Ben missed the way she pressed her lips together to keep from smiling, and they both broke out into soft laughter.

Perfectionist that he was, Caleb made certain that the popcorn garland was draped just so, then looked the tree over and announced that it was lacking something.

"A little sparkle would be nice," Abby said after a moment. "Something to catch the lamplight. I have some silver stars William cut from the bottoms of cans, if you don't mind us using them.

"That sounds like just what we need."

Then she remembered the crate Mary had sent. "I don't know if you'll feel comfortable with it, but Mary sent some things that belonged to Emily. A nativity set and some ornaments, I think."

"I don't mind using them. What about you? This is your house to decorate as you will, Abby."

"Thank you, but if it's all the same to you, I'd like to use them. Emily will always be a part of Betsy, and I think we should do everything we can to give her a sense of who her mother was, don't you?"

Caleb looked a bit taken aback by her unselfish attitude. "Of course. You're right."

When everything was hung on the tree, they all stood back and surveyed their handiwork. "It's beautiful," Abby said.

"The best ever," Ben said, nodding.

"I agree, Ben," Caleb added, a look of almost childlike wonder on his face. It might have been a trick of the light, but Abby thought she saw a suspicious sparkle in his eyes. Once again, her heart ached for the little boy who'd never had a chance to be. She vowed that if he would let her she would try to make up for all the experiences he'd been denied by his mother's leaving and his father's heavy hand.

By Christmas Eve, Caleb felt like a child living in some faraway, make-believe land. The house was redolent with the scents and sounds of the season: pine and cedar, cinnamon and cloves, roasting chestnuts. Abby seemed determined to make this the best Christmas he'd ever experienced, which wouldn't have taken nearly as much work as she insisted on doing. She'd baked all sorts of goodies and placed boughs and berries in every nook and cranny, insisting that they sing carols and other Christmas songs as they worked, including her favorite, "Jolly Old St. Nicholas."

Caleb somewhat recalled the song and joined in with his pleasing baritone when the words came to mind.

Since he'd never had gingerbread men that he could recall, Abby baked some and gave them raisin eyes. The crispy gents rested on a platter next to crunchy crystal-dusted sugar cookies, waiting to become a bedtime snack along with a cup of hot chocolate.

Before she would let them indulge in the sweet treats, Abby took her Bible, settled Laura in her lap and began to read the story of Jesus's birth. Caleb had given up retiring to his office weeks ago, and as he did every night, he listened as she answered Ben's questions with enviable patience. When the child's curiosity was satisfied, they bowed their heads and Abby began to pray.

"Father in Heaven, we come to You with grateful hearts. We are so blessed, not only this holiday season but every day. We're thankful for the beautiful world You made and for creating us with all of our senses so that we can enjoy its riches. We ask for Your continued blessings as we end one year and move into another. May the coming days and weeks be happy and peaceful. I'm particularly thankful, Father, for all You have given me. A wonderful home, three precious children to love and a husband who has been a blessing in so many ways…"

For a second, Caleb could have sworn that his heart stopped. He never heard her end the prayer, but when she looked up at him, the warmth of her smile felt like a benediction. Without waiting for him to respond, she got to her feet and held Laura out for him to take while she went to get the pot of chocolate that had been warming on the back of the stove.

When the cookies had been passed out and their hands were wrapped around steaming mugs of cocoa, they sang Christmas carols until their voices grew hoarse. Then, just before sending Ben off to bed, she read *A Visit From St. Nicholas.* By that time, Ben's eyes were growing heavy and he was ready to go to bed and sleep so Santa could come.

Caleb followed Abby into Ben's room to tuck him in, something he'd started doing a few days before. Ben seemed to like it, and it was an easy enough thing to do. Caleb stood watching Abby brush a tender kiss to her son's forehead. He was torn between an almost overwhelming feeling of humbleness that she was actually thankful for him and wishing he could share in the love and closeness she felt for her family. What would it be like to have that every day for the rest of his life?

Wonderful.

It would be the most perfect life he could imagine, one he did not dare to hope was within his grasp. How could he ever fit into Abby's perfect world where people worked together and sang while they worked…where they made things and did things for one another just because they got joy from doing so?

Though the night was as close to perfect as Caleb ever hoped to experience, he went to bed certain he had never felt more alone in his life.

Chapter Eleven

Christmas morning dawned cold and windy. With a sigh, Caleb padded out of his room in sock feet, lit the lamp and began to stoke the fire, something he did throughout the night so the house would be warm when Abby and the children got up. Going to the kitchen, he did the same, and then filled the coffeepot, set it back on the stove and returned to the parlor and lit another lamp.

A quick glance at the mantel clock told him it was more than an hour until dawn. Since he didn't recall having a traditional Christmas, he was uncertain whether or not he should wake everyone or wait for them to get up on their own. He admitted to feeling eager—and anxious—to see how his gifts were received.

Before he could make a decision, he heard Ben's bedroom door open and saw a tousled blond head poke out. "Is it time?" he asked, his sleep-roughened voice holding suppressed excitement.

Caleb shrugged. "I don't know. Shouldn't your mother be up first?"

"She's up," Abby said, stepping into the room and

covering a wide yawn. Closing the bedroom door behind her so they wouldn't wake the babies, she crossed over to warm her hands at the fireplace. A plaid robe of red wool covered her long flannel gown and was belted around her slim waist. A long blond braid hung over her shoulder. Thick wool socks covered her feet.

She cast Caleb a hopeful look. "I don't suppose the coffee is ready yet." It was more statement than question.

"I don't think so, but I did start it."

Her eyes closed in appreciation and a soft smile curved her lips. "You're a good man, Caleb Gentry."

The heartfelt compliment filled him with inexplicable pleasure.

"Can we open our gifts now, Mama?"

Abby gave in with a sigh. "I suppose so, but we'll take turns just as we always have." She looked at Caleb and explained. "We'll each open one gift in turn. That way we can not only enjoy our gifts but take pleasure in watching everyone else." She cast Caleb a wry look. "Otherwise, Christmas would be over in about two minutes." Turning her attention to Ben, she reminded, "Stockings first."

Brought up as he had been, Caleb knew nothing about building anticipation.

Ben passed out the stockings. When he handed Caleb one of his wool socks, he shot Abby a surprised look. Her answer was a gentle smile. Caleb dumped the stocking's contents, wondering what unexpected delights it might hold. He vaguely remembered having a stocking when he was very small, no doubt before his mother left. This year, Santa had filled his sock with an orange, an apple, a tangerine, a handful of exotic-looking nuts, licorice, a new shaving brush, a box of .22 bullets, a stick of taffy and the biggest peppermint stick he'd ever seen.

He looked up to thank Abby and caught the excitement on Ben's face when he shoved his arm into his sock up to the elbow and pulled a yo-yo. Once Ben had looked over those goodies, Abby let him choose another gift to unwrap. Ben chose a small leather bag.

"Marbles!" he cried. "Wow!"

"Those are from Caleb," Abby told him. "Just be careful that you don't leave any lying around for the little ones to put in their mouths," Abby cautioned. "They might choke."

"I won't," Ben promised.

"Abby, you go next," Caleb said. "You'll have to go into the kitchen to see one of your presents."

Her blue eyes narrowed in mock consternation, but Caleb didn't miss the curiosity in their depths. "What have you done, Caleb Gentry?"

"Go look in the kitchen. Take the lamp."

Rising, Abby grabbed the lamp and gave him a sidelong look in passing. Ben, wearing a conspiratorial smile since he was in on the whole thing, was close on her heels.

Her squeal of pleasure just seconds after she entered the kitchen said without words that she was thrilled with her new slipper tub and a smile of satisfaction curved Caleb's mouth. Abby came back to the parlor, almost in a run, pleasure shining in her eyes. "I love it! I can stretch out, but oh, Caleb you shouldn't have."

"Why not?"

"It's too much."

"Not if you let us all use it."

"Oh. I see," she told him with a knowing nod. "It's my gift, but I have to share."

"Something like that. You don't have to share the French gardenia bath salts and hand cream I left in the bottom, though." He winked at Ben. "I don't think Ben and I would smell too manly if we used that."

"Deal," Abby said. "Thank you very much. I'm sure that I—we—will enjoy it very much. Now you open one."

The request took Caleb aback. The truth was that he didn't recall ever receiving a present from anyone before. He felt his throat tighten, and a strange ache squeezed his heart. He heard the quaver in his voice when he said, "You weren't supposed to get me anything."

"Why? You bought all of us gifts, didn't you?"

"Yes, but—"

"No buts," she said holding up a silencing finger.

Admittedly curious as to what the package might hold, he pushed the tissue paper aside to reveal Allan Pinkerton's latest publication. "Dime novels! Three of them."

"I thought books were a pretty safe bet, and since I haven't read any of them, I thought they'd be perfect."

"Oh," he said, taking care to keep his expression neutral. "I see how this works. You give me the present," he parodied, "but I have to share."

Abby looked shocked for an instant, and then broke into a giggle. "Touché. I do hope you'll enjoy them."

"I know I—we—will," he deadpanned.

The next half hour was one of the most enjoyable

times Caleb ever recalled. He loved seeing the happiness on Ben's and Abby's faces as they opened the gifts he'd selected in such high hopes of pleasing them. Ben was thrilled with his boots, book and checkers game Abby bought him, but when he opened the larger package from Caleb, he gasped in amazement. Exquisitely detailed tin soldiers of the North and the South, including Grant and Lee astride their horses. He lifted a glowing gaze to Caleb, speechless for once.

"You can haul them in your train," he said, "since you're now using the chessmen for their intended purpose."

"They're really, really nice, Caleb. Thank you."

Caleb was as humbled by Ben's gratitude as he was the thought that had gone into the gifts his new family had chosen for him, especially since they were his first.

Besides her tub, Abby unwrapped a new Sunday dress of sky-blue trimmed with a white collar and cuffs that Caleb knew would be a perfect match for her eyes, and an ivory-handled mirror, comb and brush set. There was an everyday skirt and blouse from "Ben, Laura and Betsy." Caleb had let Ben look over everything he'd bought and pick which outfit he wanted to give his mother from him and his sisters.

When he opened the shirt given to him by "the children," Abby smiled. "It seemed a fair trade since I ripped up one of yours to use for bows."

"I like it a lot, Ben. It looks very warm. Thank you."

When he opened the knife and saw the intricate scrimshaw working on the handle, he said, "You've done too much."

"No," she told him, her blue eyes dark with sincerity. "It really isn't enough considering all you've done for me, and besides, I could only do it because of your generosity."

Caleb cleared his throat, and uneasy with the unexpected praise, asked Ben if he was ready for breakfast yet.

Later, wearing her new dress with her mother's brooch pinned at her throat, Abby played hostess for the first time as Mrs. Caleb Gentry. Since Caleb's shirt was too short in the sleeves, he said he'd send it back with Mary and Bart and pick up another the next time he went to Wolf Creek.

Frank had accepted an invitation to eat with a family in town, and Leo was having Christmas dinner with the Widow Lambert. Caught up in her own feelings for Caleb, Abby wondered if there might be a romance brewing between the middle-aged couple.

The Emersons and Stones arrived in plenty of time for Rachel to help with the meal, while Mary kept the girls entertained. The boys played with their new toys, and Edward and Caleb discussed the almanac's predictions for the winter and whether or not the summer would be as mild as the previous one.

The Christmas meal was filled with laughter and stories of past Christmases, though Abby noticed that Caleb was more of an observer than a participant in that particular venture. A couple of times she'd caught an expression that could only be described as bewilderment in his eyes. The afternoon was spent playing chess and checkers, and once the babies were put down for afternoon naps, the three women sat at the kitchen table and had a "hen party."

Finally, in midafternoon, Edward declared he was ready for a nap, and the gathering broke up. As Abby straightened the kitchen and put the worn-out children down for naps, Caleb and Ben changed out of their holiday clothes and went to set the traps Caleb had found.

Propped against the corner of the sofa with one of Caleb's new books, and covered with an afghan, Abby let her mind drift back to past holidays with William. She thought of them lovingly, a bit longingly and with more than a hint of sorrow. Then she tucked the bittersweet memories away until the next year. Those days were gone. She had a new husband now, a new family, and so far, though they had miles to go, things were better than she had dared to hope.

To Abby, the week following Christmas was always a bit of a letdown after the building anticipation that accompanied the holiday. Nevertheless, the day after Christmas they got back to their routine. She tried to get Ben involved with learning the state capitals, but her son, in a dejected mood of his own, was being uncooperative and whiny about the slightest thing. Though he was still enthralled by his gifts, he was tired of being inside. Mostly he wanted Caleb to take him to check the traps they'd set after their company left the day before.

Abby felt in limbo herself, as if the old year was gasping out its last dying breath, and hope, in the guise of a new year, was not yet born. She felt unsettled and just a bit depressed for no reason she could put her finger on. The knock at the door promised respite from her feelings, as it must have Ben, who jumped up from his chair and raced to the window.

"It's Mrs. VanSickle, Mama," he said, wrinkling his nose in disgust. Though Abby was always careful not to talk about people in front of him, he was a smart child who had an uncanny ability to pick up on nuances of people's character.

Abby felt her heart sink and her stomach tightened with anxiety. Why on earth had Sarah VanSickle come to call? What new gossip could she possibly have that she felt might interest Abby? For a heartbeat, she considered not answering the summons, but knowing Sarah, she would start yelling for entrance next.

With dread in her heart and a false smile of welcome on her lips, Abby opened the door to the woman whose personal goal seemed to be causing misery for others.

The fiftysomething woman was dressed in an eggplant-hued morning gown trimmed with black velvet. A bulky overcoat and the stylish shelf bustle of her dress did nothing for her portly figure. Jet earrings dangled at her ears, and a jaunty hat of black velvet with two pheasant feathers and a veil sat atop a jumble of sausage-like curls, a style that would have been far more appropriate for a younger woman.

Her eyes, so dark they looked as black as the dress's trim, snapped with some sort of energy that seemed to radiate from her in waves. Struck by the notion that nothing good could possibly come from this visit, Abby tried to brace herself for whatever was to transpire.

"Aren't you going to ask me in?" Sarah said, her voice as crisp as the winter air.

"Certainly," Abby said, her manners returning along with a semblance of composure. "Please, come in."

Huffing out her displeasure, Sarah stepped inside and began to shrug out of her coat, while Abby instructed Ben to get his own jacket and go outside to help Caleb with whatever he was doing.

After glancing around the room with an air of disdain, Sarah hung her coat on the oak and brass hall tree next to the door and began pulling off her soft kid gloves, which she tucked into the reticule hanging from her wrist.

"Please sit down," Abby said, gesturing toward the sofa.

Sarah sat, smoothed her dress over her knees and stared at Abby, who perched on the edge of a wingback chair, facing her unwanted guest.

"I must say, you're very looking well. Marriage seems to agree with you."

Abby ignored the implications of her statement and offered a halfhearted smile. "Yes, well, it has been something of an adjustment for us all, but we're doing well." Not for all the tea in China would Abby let the detestable woman know that her forced marriage was anything other than perfect.

"What do you think William would say to your being widowed less than a year before taking a new husband?" Sarah asked with a scornful lift of her dark eyebrows.

Lacing her fingers together in her lap, Abby struggled to rein in her temper and choose her words with care. "I think he would understand that sometimes we are required to do things we would rather not, for the sake of the better good."

Her meaning could not have been clearer, yet Sarah didn't have the grace to even blush. Abby wondered a bit uncharitably if her guest had brains enough to realize what she'd done. Then, seeing the undeniable glimmer of satisfaction in Sarah's coal-black eyes, Abby realized she knew exactly what she was about.

"I haven't seen you at church in a long while," the busybody said after a moment.

From anyone else Abby might have taken the words as a statement of concern; from Sarah it was an indictment.

"I know," Abby said, striving to make her reply pleasant. "I miss going very much, but with this cold, wet weather setting in so early, it seemed unwise to take the baby out. We plan on getting back when she's a bit older or we get a break in the weather."

"I don't suppose I can see the child? I vow, she's all Mary and Bart can talk about."

"I'm afraid she's asleep. Perhaps another time." Abby, who was barely controlling her irritation, took perverse pleasure in the refusal, as petty as it was.

"Hmm." Sarah tapped an impatient foot. "Aren't you going to offer me any refreshment?" she asked, making Abby's purposeful lapse in protocol sound like the gravest affront to etiquette.

Abby should have known not to twist the lion's tail, but she was so furious over the woman's gall at coming under the pretense of friendship, that all she could think of was getting rid of her. Instead of answering, Abby met the older woman's gaze with a steady one of her own. Her meaning was very clear. "Was there any particular reason you stopped by, Sarah?"

In the blink of her dark eyes, Sarah's veneer of civility vanished. She regarded Abby in a considering manner. "You've heard of Caleb's newest enterprise, I suppose?"

Taken aback by the sudden shift in the conversation, Abby said, "I'm afraid my hands are a bit full with taking care of the children to take much interest in Caleb's business dealings."

"A pity."

"And why is that?"

"If you paid more attention to the kind of man you married, you'd realize that Caleb Gentry is a manipulator just like his father. Surely you're smart enough to know he only married you to get his hands on your farm."

Abby couldn't be more confused, though she did realize two things: Saran VanSickle was indeed a vicious person, and she was taking a great deal of pleasure from whatever bit of information she was about to impart.

"And why would he want my farm, Sarah? It isn't even a good farm. It's nothing but a pile of rocks, actually."

Sarah laughed. "Which is precisely why he wanted it, my dear. Lucas started a gravel business, which Caleb inherited when his father died. Viola Haversham told me last winter that Lucas had his eye on your property, and then within weeks of each other, both he and your husband died. I can only imagine that Caleb was thrilled to snatch up the property by marrying you."

Abby's heart thundered in her chest. Lucas Gentry had been the person William had said was interested in their land! But that had nothing to do with her and Caleb. Certainly not with their marriage. Did it?

"Actually, Sarah, the land has been sold. The papers were signed just over a week ago."

Sarah laughed, an unpleasant sound that held unmistakable satisfaction. "Oh, so he told you he bought it, did he? I do hope you actually saw the bank draft."

Abby's stomach tightened in sudden nausea, even as her mind struggled to digest Sarah's statement. Her meaning could not be clearer. She was saying that Caleb had not sold the land. Saying in effect that he had not even bought the land himself, but had lied about it selling at all. She was telling Abby that he had taken advantage of her self-acknowledged ignorance of business affairs to steal the farm from her.

Ridiculous! Or was it? Could there be any truth to Sarah's claim? The banker's wife would know what was going on, wouldn't she? Isn't that what pillow talk was all about?

Abby's mind whispered that Caleb wouldn't do something like that. He was too principled, and she trusted him. She had to trust him, or her whole world would fall apart…again.

"The farm did sell, but Caleb didn't buy it," she said in a firm voice, while some contrary part of her mind argued that she had no way of knowing whether he had or not since she had given him her power of attorney.

Sarah rearranged her sharp features into feigned regret. "Oh, well, forgive me for even mentioning it, then. I'm sure Vi must have misunderstood, but I'm sure you understand that I only wanted to make certain that you knew what kind of man you've married."

Getting to her feet, Abby crossed to the hall tree, took down Sarah's coat and held it out toward her, her whole body trembling with fury. "And why did I marry him, Sarah?" Abby said, her temper and her voice spiking in spite of her attempts to control them. "If it weren't for you and your need to hurt people, Caleb and I wouldn't be in a marriage we neither one wanted."

"Why I'm sure I just—"

"Not another word, you venomous biddy! Take your coat and get out of here."

Both Abby and Sarah gasped and whirled toward the door leading to the kitchen. The quiet command had come from Caleb, who was striding across the room.

Sarah's face paled, and with a little squeak of fear, she rushed to Abby and jerked the coat from her hands. In her hurry to get away from the man bearing down on her like an avenging angel, she didn't even bother putting it on, but grabbed the doorknob and hauled open the door.

"Sarah."

Caleb's voice was deceptively quiet.

She turned, her eyes wide with alarm.

"I'm sure you'll understand if I tell you that I never want to see you on this place again. And be assured that if I ever hear of you saying anything hurtful about me or my wife, I will go to your husband and see to it that he knows what kind of person he's married to. Assuming there's a remote possibility he has any doubts."

Without granting him an answer, Sarah rushed through the open door and slammed it behind her. The sound of her shoes clattering down the steps was loud in the stillness of the room.

Caleb and Abby stared at each other across the expanse of the room, across a sea of uncertainty and doubt. Caleb felt his whole world crumbling for the second time, but all Abby saw in his eyes was a wary stiffness.

"Hey, Caleb!" Ben came running into the room by way of the kitchen. "Are you ready to go?"

Caleb's gaze never left Abby's. "Not now, Ben."

"But you said we could—"

"Not now, Ben!" Caleb said in a tone so harsh that Ben visibly flinched.

From the corner of her eye, Abby saw her son turn and run from the room, but her gaze never faltered from her husband's.

"It's true, isn't it?"

Caleb's mouth twisted into a humorless smile. "What? That I married you to get your land? I think you know why we entered this marriage we neither one want to be in."

Hearing him repeat almost verbatim the words she'd spoken to Sarah, sent a searing pain through Abby's heart. It was clear that they'd wounded Caleb, too. While it was true that she hadn't wanted the marriage, it was also true that now she did. Very much.

"Was your father interested in the farm back before William died?" she asked, a wary challenge in her voice.

"Yes, though I didn't know anything about it until I talked to Nate about selling it for you. He told me that my father was considering offering for the place and suggested I do just what Sarah said. I was marrying you, so why not just consider it mine once we tied the knot? I told him I couldn't do that. I wouldn't." Breaking eye contact, he strode to the fireplace and stood staring at the flames.

"So you really did sell it," she said, moving to stand behind him.

He scraped a hand through his tousled hair. "Yes."

"To whom?" she demanded, wanting, no, *needing* to know the truth, to prove Sarah a liar.

Placing a booted foot on the hearth, he rested his forearm on the mantel and shot her an insolent look over his shoulder. "Me. All the gravel on it makes it worth a great deal of money, and I am in the gravel business." His tone was mocking, bitter.

"I see."

He whirled suddenly. "Do you?"

"I see that you kept something very important from me," she cried. "Something that affects my children's future."

He actually jerked his head back as if she'd struck him. She saw his eyes go from silver to stormy gray as distress and uncertainty mutated to cold anger. Too late, she realized she'd made an unforgivable lapse in judgment.

In a voice as frigid as the winter day, he said, "Let me be very clear, madam. Your children's future is well provided for. I did not marry you for your farm. We both know the reasons we married. I said I would find a buyer for you, and I did. I told you that I would set aside the money for your children's future. I did."

Abby had never seen him so angry. She hardly knew the man looking at her with such harsh arrogance. She sucked in a breath, realizing with a dreadful certainty that she was losing him—probably had lost him—and all because for a few tormented minutes, she had bought into Sarah VanSickle's lies.

"Why didn't you tell me you were the buyer?" she asked pleadingly, wanting to understand, hoping to appease his anger. "Why didn't you at least discuss it with me?"

Caleb threw back his head and stared at the ceiling for a moment before pinning her with a contemptuous look. "Ah, yes, you are an intelligent woman who is accustomed to having her say, therefore I should have talked it over with you. After all, that's what you and William would have done."

"Yes, we—"

"I am *not* William Carter, Abby," he told her with a quietness that was far more devastating than yelling would be. "I am not used to asking for anyone's opinion when I enter a business arrangement. I'm certainly not used to consulting my wife!"

No, he was not William, and though Caleb had done remarkably well adapting to their marriage, he would never be like the easygoing William—in any way. Caleb was a proud, difficult man whose integrity she had cast doubt on. She wasn't sure he could ever forgive her for that. Her remorseful, aching heart broke a bit more.

"Couldn't you have at least *told* me?" she asked, her voice a soft tremble.

"I suppose I could have," he said, his tone softer now, too, "but I didn't because you're going at a dead run from daylight until dark, and because you told me you had no understanding of such matters. When you gave me your power of attorney, I assumed you trusted me. I didn't think it mattered who bought the farm, as long as I kept my end of the bargain."

Though Sarah's poison might have caused Abby to question Caleb for a brief moment, she knew beyond doubt he was telling the truth. He would never lie to her about something like this. He would never lie about anything. She felt the hot scald of threatening tears and wondered if he could ever forgive her.

"If there is any question in your mind about my cheating you," he added, "rest assured, I did not. I paid you far above market value. If you don't believe me, feel free to ask Nate."

"I don't need to ask Nate," she whispered brokenly. "I do believe you."

He didn't bother to answer. Turning, he left her standing beside the fireplace, her heart and her hopes for the future shattered like the china figurine of his mother's. All by one moment's carelessness.

Chapter Twelve

Abby hadn't wept this deeply since the first weeks following William's death, but she did after Caleb left her alone in the parlor with nothing but the ticking clock for company. Drawing a shuddering breath, she berated herself for her suspicions. How could she have doubted him even for even a second when he had proved over and over that he was honorable?

He had come so far the past few weeks in the way he related to all of them. There were moments she'd felt they were starting to build something that held the potential for a lifetime of love. Now she had ruined everything by questioning his integrity. He'd been angry when he left. Furious. Fresh tears streamed down her cheeks. Could he ever forgive her? Would he?

Caleb stormed out of the house, his long strides eating up the distance to the barn while despair gnawed at his heart and sickness clawed at his stomach. He scraped back his hair with both hands and gave a throaty snarl of fury.

He should have known better than to let any woman work her way beneath his guard and his skin! Hadn't his mother's desertion taught him that much? He must have been a fool to feel guilty about his growing feelings for Abby, when it was clear now that nothing he'd done or tried to do to make things better between them had made a nickel's worth of difference. In retrospect, there was a lot to be said for loveless marriages, like the one he had shared with Emily.

The thought had no sooner entered his mind than he knew he was lying to himself. As devastated as he was by Abby's distrust, he knew his life with Emily had been a shadow life compared to the past few weeks. The problem with feeling too much was that it opened you up not just to the good things, but the bad. Mutual caring was part and parcel with the ability to inflict not just joy, but pain, intentional or not.

On some level he'd known that, but experiencing it firsthand was far different. He'd also known his growing feelings for Abby were dangerous, but he had no more been able to stop them than he'd been able to stop the sun from rising each morning. Now he was paying the price.

He relived the scene with Abby, hearing again her accusing voice demanding to know the details about the sale of her farm, demanding to know why he had not talked to her, had not told her about his plans. He felt the prickle of tears beneath his eyelids. It hurt. Dear sweet Heaven, it hurt.

But no more. The price of loving was just too high.

He was mucking out the horse's stall thirty minutes later when he heard Abby calling for Ben. He hardened his heart against the sound of her voice and the mental image that accompanied it, and kept scattering fresh hay around the cubicle. After a while, she called again.

He was just closing the door to the stall when the barn door was flung against the wall and Abby rushed in. He couldn't ignore her. They were married. He braced himself and turned to face her.

Her hair was coming loose and the expression in her eyes bordered on panic. His heart tightened in pain and he fought the urge to go to her and pull her into his arms. Instead, he stood there leaning against the pitchfork, regarding her with what he hoped was a neutral expression.

"Caleb," she said, breathing hard, the heat of her breath creating a fog in the cold air. "Is Ben with you?"

"No."

"I've looked the house over, and he's nowhere inside. I've called and I've called, but he doesn't come and doesn't answer. That isn't like him."

A memory flashed through Caleb's mind. Ben coming into the parlor wanting to go check his traps as Caleb had promised him they would. A promise he'd made before he'd known that Sarah VanSickle's spite was about to send his whole world crashing down.

"Not now, Ben."

He'd told him no twice. And not kindly.

"Go back to the house, Abby," Caleb told her. "I'll find him."

She made a little whimpering sound and looked as if she might burst into tears. "How can you possibly know where he's gone?"

"He wanted to go check his traps and I told him no, so I imagine he took off to do it by himself."

Caleb didn't tell her how dangerous that seemingly easy task could be. Who knew what might be caught in the traps? Critters like coyotes and bobcats and the like had to be shot in the head before you could remove them from the traps. Caleb's blood ran cold. Ben didn't have a gun—did he?

Leaning the pitchfork against the wall, Caleb grasped Abby's elbow and guided her toward the door, pulling her outside into the overcast, foggy day. "I need to get my .22," he told her, "and see if Ben took the shotgun."

Abby gasped. "He knows he's not supposed to have it unless you're along."

"I know, but he's a boy, and boys are not noted for doing what they're supposed to." The words were accompanied by a grim smile. "He'll be somewhere along the creek."

"How do you know?" she asked, trotting along beside him.

"Because everything has to have water, so you look for different animal trails along the creek and set your traps accordingly."

Caleb hauled her up the back porch steps and they stepped into the warmth of the kitchen. Abby stayed near the door, her arms crossed as if to ward off a chill, while he went to fetch his gun.

"The shotgun's where it should be," he said, grabbing a felt hat from the rack to protect his bare head from the rain.

"Thank God," Abby murmured.

Resting the rifle on his shoulder, he reached for the doorknob, troubled by a growing sense of alarm. The temperature was dropping every hour, and with the light drizzle, Ben might lose his way. Unfamiliar panic rushed through Caleb's body. Panic and that too-familiar guilt.

"Caleb."

He turned. Abby stood before him, her face pale, blue eyes awash with tears she somehow held at bay. She reached out, as if to lay her palm against his chest, and then caught herself, clenched her hand into a fist and let her arm fall to her side.

"I'm sorry."

There was no need for her to say more.

Face grim, eyes as hard as steel, he said, "So am I."

It took every ounce of willpower to turn and walk away from her when all he wanted was to cradle her close and tell her that he would make things right somehow, if only he knew how.

Caleb made his way across the barren, fallow fields to the tree line, his booted feet squelching through the mud as he headed toward the big pine that marked the spot where they usually went into the woods. Entering the copse of trees was like stepping into another world. The fog was denser beneath the shelter of the trees, as if their overarching branches held it close to the earth. Seeing beyond a few yards was all but impossible. Silence ruled the gray day; all the forest critters must be snug in their nests. The misty rain had become a light drizzle that dripped from pine needles, bare tree limbs and the brim of his hat, the only sound to be heard besides his ragged breathing and the soft soughing of the rising wind.

Caleb picked up his already-hurried pace, refusing to let himself think of what might happen if Ben was not found soon. Picking his way through the sodden ground cover, stepping around muscadine vines and over moss-covered trees and lichen-scaled rocks, Caleb moved closer to the spot along the creek where he and Ben had placed their first trap the day before. The creek was bordered by banks so steep they were almost vertical in some places, dangerous on a good day. Now, slick with rain and fallen leaves, the softened edges prone to crumble, they were downright treacherous. Swollen from all the rain they'd received recently, the water of the usually placid brook rushed headlong to the Little Missouri. Thank goodness all the traps were set on high ground.

Caleb located the animal trail and the trap, saw that it was empty and scanned the area for sign of Ben's blue plaid coat. Nothing. He did see leaves that had looked as if they'd been scuffled through and followed the trail to the next spot.

No sign of a trapped animal, no sign of Ben.

Caleb trudged on, filled with a sense of urgency and that nagging, growing guilt.

Ben opened his eyes slowly and blinked against the rain falling into his face. He was cold. Freezing. And his leg hurt like the very dickens. He'd lost his cap somewhere. Rain plastered his hair to his head and ran in icy rivulets down his neck. With his teeth chattering like the Morse code the telegraph man sent through the lines, he lifted his upper body to his elbows to see what was wrong with his leg. His stomach roiled, and he lost his breakfast. Broken, he reckoned, from the look and feel of it.

When the queasiness passed, he lifted his head again to look around. He lay at the bottom of the gorge where he'd tumbled after slipping on a pile of slick leaves. Water raced pell-mell over rocks and boulders just feet from where he lay. He realized his shoulder ached, and his head. He reached up to check his forehead and found a big goose egg. Drawing back his hand, he saw that his fingers were covered with blood.

He had to get home. His mom would be worried sick, as she always said. He could stand the pain…Caleb said men had to be tough, and blood had never bothered Ben, so he had to try to get home. Gritting his teeth, he tried to get up, but realized pretty fast that even if got to his feet, which he didn't think he could do, there was no way he could climb up the steep bank.

A wave of worry and self-pity settled over him. No one knew where he was. The realization was soon followed by a reassuring thought. As soon as his mother realized he was gone, she'd send Caleb to find him. He was good at tracking. He was good at a lot of things. Course his father had been good at a lot of things, too, Ben thought loyally. Just different things.

Though he'd tried not to, Ben liked Caleb more all

the time. He'd felt ashamed at first, but Caleb had been right. Even though his father would always be his father, he and Caleb could be friends. He thought his mama was starting to like Caleb, too, but something had set her off today. Probably something Mrs. VanSickle said. Caleb hadn't looked too happy, either. He hated when his parents argued, hated that his mom and Caleb were at odds.

Ben gave a violent shiver. He was so cold, and it was raining right into his face. He tried to turn onto his side and cried out in pain, but managed to turn just a bit. His hands felt like ice. He blew on them and then tucked them beneath his armpits, the only halfway dry place on his coat.

A new worry surfaced. What if his mother didn't tell Caleb? What if they were too mad to talk to each other? What if no one came looking for him? How long until dark? A rush of panic sent him scrambling backward, and loosed a scream of agony. Grinding his teeth together, he tried to curl into a ball, and the tears started up again. He didn't think he was brave enough to stay here all night by himself.

Only two more places to check. If there was no sign of Ben, he'd gotten off the trail in the fog and was lost. Caleb's jaw tightened. Trudging through the woods, he'd called out for Ben periodically, but heard no answer. Once, he caught himself mumbling beneath his breath, and when he'd realized what he was doing, he'd stopped dead in his tracks. Praying? Had he really been praying to find Ben? Well, why not? There was no doubt that Abby was calling on God for help and strength. And it couldn't hurt.

A sound, the first he'd heard since stepping into the foggy emptiness of the forest, stopped Caleb midstride. What was that? An animal of some sort? Ben calling out? Caleb cocked his head, listening for the slightest sound.

An agonized cry sent his head up, like a hound catching scent of its prey.

"Ben!" he cried, running farther along the ridge of the creek. "Ben! Where are you?"

"Caleb!" a muffled voice shouted. "Over here!"

Holding the .22 rifle at his side, Caleb slogged over the mushy leaf-strewn ground toward the sound of Ben's voice. "Ben!" he called again.

"I'm down here, at the bottom of the gully. I slipped and fell."

Caleb located Ben a minute later. He was lying flat of his back no more than five feet from the rushing waters of the creek, and it was clear from the pain lingering in his eyes that he was hurt. The expression of joy that flashed on Ben's face when he saw Caleb almost broke his heart. "Where are you hurt?" he asked, scanning the sheer embankment for the safest, fastest way to descend.

"I'm pretty sure I broke my leg."

Caleb didn't miss the slight catch in the boy's voice.

"Hang on. I'll be right there." He leaned the rifle against a nearby tree and edged sideways down the sharp incline, grabbing small saplings and bushes for handholds. He was soon squatting next to Ben, who reached up and flung his arms around Caleb's neck. A feeling of love so intense he could barely breathe surged through him. He closed his eyes and hugged Ben close. "What happened, bud?" he asked, hearing a catch in his own voice.

Ben pulled back to look into Caleb's eyes. "I was checking the traps and slipped. You told me we could come and check them and then you and Mama were arguing, and..." His voice trailed away, and his eyes grew wide with apprehension. "Is she mad?"

"No," Caleb said, pushing a lock of wet hair from Ben's eyes. "She's not mad. She's worried. You shouldn't have come out here alone. Not in this weather."

"I know." He looked toward the top of the ravine. "How are we gonna get back to the top?"

"I'm going to carry you."

"Is it gonna hurt?"

"I'm not going to lie to you, Ben. I'll try to be easy, but when I pick you up, it will probably hurt pretty bad. If you feeling like yelling, yell."

He did. Loudly.

A baby in each arm, Abby looked at the clock. Almost two hours since Caleb had disappeared into the darkness of the woods beyond the cornfield. She pressed her lips together and blinked fast to hold back the tears. Where could they be? To make matters worse, both babies seemed acutely attuned to her mood. She fed Betsy, who was usually content once her tummy was full, but not today, and sunny Laura refused to play in her pen and wanted every bit of Abby's attention, which was impossible with Betsy in her arms.

She felt another tear slide down her cheek when she heard someone at the back door. Setting Laura into her playpen despite her angry protests, and laying Betsy in her cradle, Abby ran to the kitchen.

Caleb stood in the doorway, rain dripping off the brim of his felt hat, holding Ben in his arms. Both were sopping wet and shivering. Ben's eyes were closed; Caleb's were haunted.

"What's wrong?" Abby wailed. "Is he all right?"

"He'll be fine. I think he fainted, which is probably the best thing he could have done."

"Fainted? What happened?"

"He slipped down the creek embankment and broke his leg," Caleb told her. "He's got a giant bump and a cut on his head, but he isn't talking crazy. Right now he's chilled to the bone."

"Bring him to his room. I'll get him stripped down and under the covers, so he'll warm up."

"While you're doing that, I'll ride into town for Rachel."

"Change into something dry before you go," Abby told him, wifely concern in her voice. "I don't need you sick, too."

She hurried ahead of him down the hall to turn back the blankets on Ben's bed. "Your rain gear is on a peg in the pantry," she said over her shoulder.

She rushed into the room ahead of Caleb. "Just put him on top of the quilts until I can get him out of these wet things. That way, he won't get the sheets wet."

Caleb did as she instructed, and Abby made fast work of cutting Ben out of his pants and his other wet clothes and then Caleb eased Ben beneath the blankets and left the room while Abby was still fussing over him.

Assured by Rachel that Ben would most likely sleep through the night, Abby had been persuaded to go to bed in her room to be near the girls if they needed her.

Tormented by the day's events, more specifically his part in them, Caleb was unable to sleep. The house was silent except for the chiming of the clock in the next room and the hiss and *clunk* of the wood burning in the fireplace. He sat in the rocking chair next to Ben's bed, his elbows resting on his knees, his clasped hands dangling between his thighs, his weary gaze focused blindly on the rag rug beneath his feet.

Rachel had come and gone, working her healing power with bandages and splints and pain medication. Ben had cried out once, probably when she'd set the leg. Caleb wasn't sure there was a medicine on earth that would help his pain; as far as he knew, there was no cure for guilt.

He'd made a mess of everything—his marriage to Abby, his feeble attempts at learning to be a father… all of it. Ben's accident was his fault. Caleb should not have let the boy see the anger directed at his mother, and Ben should not have been sent away as he had been. Not when Caleb had made a promise.

Beyond that, he never should have let Sarah Van-Sickle coerce him and Abby into marriage. He should never have become entangled in Abby's and her children's lives. He'd had no experience with children to fall back on, and even though he and Emily were married for six years, he had scant knowledge of how marriages worked. He was not good husband material. He was definitely not father material. He'd let Ben down, let himself down. Caleb dug the heels of his hands into his eye sockets, pressing hard to try to drive away the pain. He didn't remember being so miserable in his entire life.

"I'm sorry, Ben," he choked out in a low, emotion-clogged voice. "I never meant to hurt you or for you to get hurt. I never meant to hurt anyone."

He rested his forehead on the edge of the bed, and sobbed, huge gulping sobs…the first time he remembered crying since the afternoon he and Gabe had come home from school and were told their mother had gone to live in Boston, that she hadn't cared enough for either of them to take them with her.

The first thing Abby did when she woke up was check on Ben. He was sleeping deeply, no doubt due to the pain medication Rachel had given him. After laying the back of her hand against his forehead to check for fever, Abby headed for the kitchen. She rubbed at her gritty eyes and prayed Caleb had made the coffee as he usually did before she woke up.

She smiled when she saw the coffeepot sitting at the back of the stove. Her gaze drifted to the door. His coat was gone. He was probably doing not only his chores, but Ben's this morning.

Abby poured herself a cup of coffee and sat down at the table, resting her chin in her hands. How could she approach Caleb about their argument the day before? What could she ever say to make him realize that she must have temporarily taken leave of her senses?

Even knowing the horrible woman had come to stir up some kind of trouble, Abby had fallen for her lies—hook, line and sinker. Well, it hadn't exactly been a lie, but she had manipulated the truth enough to make it sound plausible...like saying that Lucas wanted the property, a statement that meshed perfectly with Abby's knowledge that someone had been interested in it before William died. Adding that Viola Haversham had been told the truth by her husband seemed likely, too; otherwise how could Sarah have found out?

Stating that she should have checked on the sale also made sense—most people would—except that as Caleb reminded her, she had given him her power of attorney and therefore she'd felt no need to check on the sale. Which brought her back to the certainty that Caleb would never have cheated her in any way. Yet she'd all but come out and accused him of just that.

Even her argument that he should have talked it over with her held no real weight, because she had trusted him with the task. Once again, she'd let her quick temper put her in an awful spot. All the time Caleb had been looking for Ben she had prayed that he would be found, that he would be all right, and for God to give her the right words to fix the mess she'd made of things. But morning had arrived and her mind was still a blank. She wasn't sure she could talk herself out of this one, but she had to try.

How would Caleb act this morning? Would he still be

angry? Cold and distant? Or, like her, would he feel remorse and a soul-deep need to make things right again?

As if thinking of him conjured him up, she heard his step on the porch. She sat very still, her gaze focused on the doorway, barely breathing. He strode into the room, bringing in cold air and vitality and a quiet strength. Blinking back tears, she wondered why she had fought her feelings for him for so long and knew that she had never loved him more than she did at that moment. She watched as he hung his coat on the hook and then turned to look at her, his gray eyes devoid of emotion. "How's Ben?"

So, she thought, his attitude was to be the polite cordiality he'd displayed during the first days of their marriage. Fine. She could deal with that until she had the opportunity to change it.

"He's resting well and doesn't seem to have any fever. Would you like a cup of coffee?"

"I'll get it."

She watched the play of muscles across his shoulders as he reached for the cup he must have used earlier. She noticed that his hair was already brushing his collar. She sighed. He would need another haircut soon. Filling his mug, he sat down across from her.

"Caleb, I don't know how to say this, but—"

"Then don't." He words were hard. Harsh. Like the expression in his eyes.

"But I said things to hurt you, and I didn't—"

"You said what you felt," he said. "There's no need to apologize for your feelings. Ever. It probably happened for the best."

"How can you say that?" she asked, frowning. "I know you would never do the terrible things I all but accused you of, but Sarah made it all sound so…so logical, and I…" She stopped, drew a breath and took another tack. "And you're perfectly within your rights to refuse to discuss your business with me. I had no right to expect you to, just because William did."

"It won't work, Abby."

"What?" She blinked in surprise. Was he going to refuse to accept her apology then?

"This marriage."

"What?" she said again, unable—or unwilling—to believe what she thought he was saying. Their marriage wouldn't work? But it *was* working.

He shook his head. "It won't work, and we knew it wouldn't, but we let Sarah VanSickle manipulate the situation. Face it, Abby. I'm not husband material, and God knows I'm not father material, as I'm sure Ben will tell you."

Was he saying what she thought he was? Abby felt as if her whole existence were in jeopardy, as if her world were about to collapse and there was nothing she could do about it.

"Actually, I think you're adapting to fatherhood very well." Her voice shook as she tried to make her argument. "You and Ben have been getting along so well and Laura…"

"Loves me. I know." He gave a bitter laugh. "And what about me as a husband? If I'm adapting so well, why is it that we quarrel so much?"

"But we don't. Not really. Not any more than any husband and wife."

"I like peace and quiet," he said brusquely. "I'm not used to being in the midst of chaos."

She felt the blood drain from her face. He was saying that he didn't like the confusion and disorder that was their family dynamic. Had all the changes she thought she'd seen in him been an act, then?

"What are you trying to tell me, Caleb?" she asked, her troubled gaze probing his, as if she could find the answers she sought there. "Just spit it out," she commanded, not realizing she had stolen one of his favorite phrases.

"I've been planning on making a trip to Fort Worth to see about buying some new equipment. I'd planned on leaving after the first of the year, but I've decided to leave this afternoon."

Abby opened her mouth to tell him that he'd never mentioned that he was planning to go anywhere, that she had no idea he was even thinking of buying more equipment, but then she remembered that he was not William, that he felt no need to confide in her, or talk over his plans…or his dreams. Her mouth snapped shut and she pressed her lips together to keep them from trembling. She imagined she saw a sardonic smile in the calm depths of his eyes. Something in that look told her that the conversation was over, that there was nothing more to be said, nothing to gain by saying anything.

"I see," she said in a low voice. She pushed away from the table and stood, hoping he did not see the shaking of her hands. "I'll get your clothes ready. Will you need your suit?"

"Don't bother."

The coldness of the two words snatched away her breath.

"I can get my things together," he said. "I've been doing for myself for a long time."

Yes, she knew he had. Knowing how much of himself he put into his work and those who worked for him, it had given her much pleasure to do for him for a change.

"How long will you be gone?"

His gaze shifted from hers and he spoke to the doorway behind her. "Possibly a week."

He drew in a deep breath, and Abby had the distinct impression that he was trying to fortify himself for something. Finally, he brought his gaze back to her. "I want you and the children to be gone when I get back. It shouldn't be too painful for Ben to travel in a few days."

A pain so sharp that she actually felt as if she'd been struck in the solar plexus knocked the air from Abby's lungs. The room began to spin. She swayed and pressed her palms hard against the tabletop. She would not faint. She had never fainted in her life.

If he noticed her distress, he never let on. "I'll buy your train tickets to anywhere you like. Don't you have a brother in Springfield?"

She nodded. She wanted to tell him she would buy her own tickets but it was hard to talk when you couldn't even breathe.

"When you get settled, you can let Nate know where

you are, and he can transfer the money from the sale of your farm and what I've put into savings for the children to a bank of your choice."

There were so many questions churning around in her head that Abby could not seem to grab hold of any coherent thought.

"Betsy?" she managed to squeak out.

Caleb rose and set his coffee cup on the counter. He leaned back against it, crossing his arms over his chest in a gesture of finality. "I'll have Mary come and get her. She'll just have to get used to the bottle."

"I see you've thought of everything," she said.

The words hung in the air between them, the same words she'd spoken the day Rachel had explained why taking Betsy to her place would not work. She could see that he remembered by the stiffening of his shoulders.

"I hope so."

She drew herself up straighter and lifted her chin. "What about the children? What about Ben?"

For the first time, Abby thought she saw a softening in his attitude. Imagined she saw a glimmer of pain in his eyes.

When he spoke, his voice was huskier than it had been. "Tell him the truth. That I would not make him a good father. He got over losing William, and he'll forget me soon enough. It isn't as if we were close."

But you were! Abby wanted to scream. She could *see* the closeness growing between them every day. Despite her breaking heart and an aching sense of loss, Abby felt the first stirring of anger.

"I won't do it."

"I beg your pardon."

The tears she'd kept at bay spilled over her lashes and down her cheeks. "I will not do your dirty work for you, Caleb Gentry," she spat out, swiping at the tears with her fingertips.

"What?"

"You heard me! I've thought you many things these past weeks—stubborn, hard, fair, even kind and gentle, but I never thought you were a coward. I will not have you do to Ben what your mother did to you. You will tell him goodbye, and why you're forcing us to leave here."

There was no compromise in her voice, or the gem-like hardness in her blue eyes. "I mean it, Caleb. Either tell him yourself, or be man enough to stay."

He left on the afternoon train as planned, but as per Abby's demands, he had told Ben himself that he was going. Caleb had not known what to expect from Ben, but the boy had listened to what Caleb had to say, and then nodded and turned his head away. There had been no reproach in his eyes, no discernible emotion. Unlike his mother, Ben had not argued that they were growing closer, and he had not cried or begged him to stay, as Caleb expected. Hoped? Feeling a bit let down by Ben's lack of emotion, Caleb considered the possibility that the medicine Rachel was giving Ben for the pain must have dulled his senses.

Caleb left the room feeling as if he had just lost something irreplaceable. When he'd carried his bags to the wagon where Frank waited to drive him to town, he'd had to pass through the parlor. Laura was in her pen. Abby was holding Betsy at her shoulder, her face buried against his daughter's soft dark hair. She didn't look up as he passed, but Laura called to him. He didn't stop. Didn't even look at her. Couldn't. He had to let them go. For their sake and for his.

"You're a dad-blamed fool, is what you are, Caleb Gentry," Frank said.

"I didn't ask your opinion, Frank."

"Well, you're gettin' it, anyway!"

Caleb cast him a sideways look. "You might remember who you're talking to, old man," he growled.

"You don't scare me none. And maybe you should remember that I tanned your hide many a time when you were a snot-nosed whippersnapper and did something stupid." He slowed the wagon a bit to go around a pothole. "And tellin' Abby and the kids to leave is about the most dim-witted thing you've ever done."

Caleb had had no choice but to tell Frank and Leo what was going on, since he would be leaving Abby's and the children's departure in their capable hands.

"Frank..." Caleb warned.

Frank was wound up. "You need that woman and those kids like roses need sunshine. Lord knows I thought the world of Emily, strange as she was, and I was more'n sorry she died. But she did, and ain't nothin' we can do about that. Sarah VanSickle aside, Abby Carter and her younguns are the best thing that ever happened to you."

Frank wasn't telling Caleb anything he didn't know, but that didn't mean he wanted to hear it.

"You're crazy about Laura, and you and Ben have got about as close as dirt to a fence post since you started teachin' him about the woods and all." Frank cut a sly look at Caleb. "And unless these old eyes are worse off than I think they are, you're sweet on that wife of yours, too."

"I do care for them," Caleb said on a sigh, giving his longtime friend that much. "But all that aside, it's better for everyone this way. Better to send Abby away now before she gets fed up with me the way my mother got sick of Lucas. I don't want to come home one day five or six years from now and see that she's packed up and took off to—to Springfield. I don't think I could stand that, Frank. I don't want Betsy to have to go through what Gabe and I went through."

Frank scowled. "And why would she do that?"

"Because I'm just like my father."

Frank croaked a hoarse laugh. "You're *nothing* like Lucas Gentry," he said, "but at least we're gettin' somewhere—I think." He looked at Caleb across his shoulder. "Let me see if I got this straight. You sent her away, even though it's tearin' you apart, just so you won't fall for her any harder and have it tear you apart later?"

Caleb nodded.

"Like I said, son, this is one of the most brainless things I've ever known you to do. And what did you mean about not wanting Betsy to go through what you and Gabe did?"

"No child should come home and be told that their mother didn't care enough for them to take them with her when she walked away."

A frown furrowed Frank's wrinkled forehead. "And where did you hear that load of nonsense?"

"From my father," Caleb said bitterly.

"I always knew Libby's leavin' hurt Lucas to the bone, and I always knew he was a ruthless son of a gun. Never knew him to be a liar until now, though."

"What are you talking about?"

"Libby got a hankerin' to go back east for a few months," Frank said thoughtfully, "seein' as it had been years since she'd gone for a visit. Said she wanted to take you boys to visit your grandparents, since they'd never set eyes on either one of you. Lucas said no. Maybe he was scared that if she took you boys with her, she'd never come back."

"So she left without us."

"Nope. She didn't go." Frank took off his hat and scratched his grizzled head. "That next spring, her brother, Tad, and his wife, Ada, came and brought Ada's brother with them. Do you remember your mama, Caleb?"

Caleb shook his head. "Not much."

"She was a looker, Libby Gentry was, and I knew she was really unhappy, but even so, I never knew her to look twice at another man, least not until then. Long story short, your daddy claimed he caught them together in what they call a 'compromising situation.'"

"Go on," Caleb said in a voice that sounded like he was talking around ground glass.

"Lucas beat Ada's brother, Sam, to within an inch of his life. Edward Stone can vouch for that. Lucas told her to pack up and go back east. Said he'd handle the divorce."

"Divorce?"

"Yep. Pike County scandal of the year. Libby denied everything and tried to talk him around, but you know how ornery yer daddy could be. She and Gabe were up front, and the wagon was loaded, ready to head out—we were supposed to pick you up at school, Caleb, and then put you on the train—and your daddy, he walks out of the house as calm as you please, smokin' one of them cheroots he was so fond of and tells me and Micah—" he shot Caleb a questioning glance "—you remember Micah?"

Caleb nodded.

"Well Lucas tells Micah to unload the trunks with your and Gabe's stuff in 'em, and told me to get Gabe down 'cause she ain't takin either one of you nowhere."

"What!"

"It was a dad-blamed mess, let me tell you. Your mama is a-cryin' and screamin' and Lucas just takes Gabe and turns around and starts back to the house, lookin' all pleased with hisself. Your mama jumps down and starts trying to get me and Micah to reload the trunks, but Lucas says that if we do he'll see that we never work in these parts again, so we did what he said.

"Then she goes and grabs your daddy's arm and starts screamin' at him that she can't leave you boys—she won't. He just takes hold of her hand, moves it off his arm, all the while he's callin' her a few choice names. Then he sets Gabe down, slings Libby over his shoulder, dumps her back in the wagon and tells her to never show her face back here again, or he'll see to it that her family loses everything they have."

"Could he do that?" Caleb asked, shocked to his soul by what he'd just heard.

"Probably."

Abby spent the next four days packing the bare minimum of what she and the children would need in Springfield. Let Caleb do what he would with what she left behind. Her emotions ranged from fury to a sadness that eclipsed what she'd felt when William died. Was it because she and William shared a loving relationship, and even after his death she'd been sustained by memories and the children they'd had together? Did her suffering seem more acute because she felt as if she'd failed Caleb and this marriage somehow?

Prayer brought no answers or peace. Convinced always that God was in control, she had no idea why He would bring her and Caleb together only to rip them apart.

She couldn't eat, couldn't sleep. The only decent rest she'd had since the afternoon he'd left was the day she'd climbed into his bed and breathed in his familiar, beloved scent. Ben was surly; Laura was whiny and seemed to watch the back door for Caleb's return. The essence of him haunted the house, bombarding her with dozens of recollections of him throughout the day. Cutting his hair. Him kissing her. Seeing his dry sarcasm slowly become teasing. When she forced the memories away, tangible reminders of him tormented her: his rain gear hanging in the pantry. His coat hanging near the back door. The smell of his woodsy soap that clung to the clothes and sheets.

On the second day of his absence, she decided that she was going crazy worrying. There had been no compromise in Caleb, and unable to bear the idea of never seeing him again, of never having the hope of him loving her and feeling his arms around her, she knew there was no sense putting off the inevitable. She'd packed in a frenzy. There were still three days until Caleb's week was up and he came home, but they would be long gone when he did. They were leaving this afternoon, with Abby praying she could run far enough away to forget. Knowing it was impossible.

"Are we going back to our old house?"

Ben was propped up in bed where he'd been reading his new horse book. Abby was scurrying around the room, stacking his clothes so she could pack them in the trunk Frank and Leo had brought down from the attic.

"No. Someone else…owns it now. We're going to see Uncle Phillip and Aunt Zoe in Springfield. You'll like it there."

"Can I hunt and trap there?"

"Oh, no," Abby said, keeping her voice deliberately light. "Uncle Phil lives in the city. There are other things to do there. Theater, and museums, and libraries, and parks with lots of trees where you can run and play."

"If I can't hunt, I don't want to go." His voice was firm and his lower lip stuck out in an all-too-familiar pout, something she'd not seen much of the past couple of months but that had made regular appearances since Caleb had left.

Abby saw one of his stubborn spells on the horizon. “We have to go, Ben.”

“Why?”

“Remember when you were so unhappy about living here and I told you it was only until Caleb could find someone else to take care of Betsy, or she got a little older?”

Ben nodded.

“Well, Betsy’s grandmother and another lady in Wolf Creek will be taking care of Betsy from now on, so there’s no reason for us to stay.” She could not tell him that Caleb had demanded that they be gone when he returned. It would break his heart.

“Why would he do that when he said…”

Hearing his hesitation, Abby paused and turned to look at him. “What did he say, Ben?”

“That he loves us.”

Abby kept her silence. Where on earth had Ben gotten such an idea? If Caleb loved them, he had a strange way of showing it.

“Benjamin Aaron, you know what happens when you tell a lie.”

“Yes, ma’am.”

“Tell me the truth now. Did Caleb really tell you he loved us?”

Ben’s fair eyebrows drew together in a frown. “Not in those words, but that’s what he meant.”

“And when did you have this conversation with him?”

"The night I got hurt. I woke up and he was sitting beside my bed."

Abby's heart stumbled. She'd had no idea that after sending her to bed, Caleb had sat up with Ben in case he needed something. "Exactly what did he say?" she asked, her voice a thread of sound.

"That he was sorry. That he didn't mean to hurt us, or for me to get hurt."

No surprise there. Abby knew Caleb was not a monster. "That's all?"

Ben looked as if he were about to burst into tears. "He said he couldn't stand it if we left him, but he had to let us go because it was the best thing to do."

Abby felt the prickle of tears beneath her own eyelids. "And what did you say?"

"Nothing. He didn't know I was awake."

"I see."

"He was crying, Mama," Ben said, and burst into tears himself.

Abby went to the bed and gathered him close. If what Ben said was true, Caleb no more wanted them to go than she wanted to leave him. She recalled him telling her that he wasn't good husband or father material. By some twisted reasoning that only a man like her husband could concoct, he'd convinced himself that he was undeserving, that it would be better to end things before… What? His inexperience hurt one of them? Or was it because he was falling in love with all of them and feared that he would somehow lose them?

Trying to control another sob, Abby wiped at the

tears running down her cheeks. Oh, what a muddle they were in!

Ben drew a shuddering breath and sobbed, "We can't leave, Mama. We can't."

Abby placed her hands on his cheeks and tipped his head back to look into his eyes. "Darling, we have to. It's what Caleb wants."

"It's *not* what he wants, and besides, when you guys got married, you said it was until death do you part. You promised. Both of you promised in front of God."

Being reminded of that sacred vow by a six-year-old drew Abby up short. Out of the mouths of babes…

Abby kissed away his tears and gave him a brief, hard hug.

"You're right, Ben," she said offering him a shaky smile. "We did."

It was just getting light the following day when Caleb guided the rig he'd rented in Gurdon down the lane toward home. He'd gone to Fort Worth and bought his equipment, but his heart and mind were in Wolf Creek. He'd spent the four days he'd been gone thinking about what Frank had told him. When he'd asked the older man why he'd never said anything before, Frank told him that Lucas had forbidden anyone to talk about it and that Caleb had never asked.

Caleb had no reason to doubt the story, and Frank was right, he had not asked, and he had not talked about his mother because Lucas had forbidden him and Gabe to even mention her name. With no one to offer the other side of the story, it had been easy for Lucas to poison their malleable minds against the woman he and Gabe had both adored.

Having misjudged his mother set Caleb to thinking about some of the things Abby said about God and letting Him become a part of life. His thoughts drifted back to his sixteenth summer when he'd gone to town for a night of revelry with his friends and found that Wolf Creek Church was holding a revival.

Caught up by the size of the crowd, he'd wandered over in time to hear the preacher talk about Jesus's sacrifice on the cross. Caleb realized his life wasn't what it should be, and along with many others had been immersed in the nearby creek. He remembered how good he'd felt when he'd come up out of the water, how clean.

Then he'd gone home and told Lucas what he'd done. It hadn't taken his father's ridicule long to shatter Caleb's newfound peace and joy. He'd tried to stay faithful for a while, but gradually, he'd slipped back into his old ways.

Now, thinking about the parable of the seeds and Abby's explanation of them, he knew he'd received the message with gladness, but his new and fragile faith had no time to take root before Lucas's taunts had ripped it away.

Caleb had thought a lot about his life and God as he'd driven through the night, and he'd decided that with Abby and God on his side, there was hope that he could become a better man.

Unable to wait until morning to catch the next train to Wolf Creek, he'd paid an exorbitant price to rent the buggy and had driven all night.

The nearer he got to the house the better he could see. No one was outside doing chores. The house was dark and uninviting. There was no smoke coming from the chimneys, and there would be no mouthwatering scent of bacon frying when he stepped through the back door. No Abby bustling around. No Ben waiting patiently to start eating. No Betsy sleeping in her cradle and no Laura waiting with a wide smile.

He was too late.

Pulling the wagon to a stop near the back porch, he jumped down, looped the reins over the hitching post and trudged up the back steps, his jaw set and his heart like a stone in his chest.

He'd see how things were with Frank and Leo, and then he'd go back into town, check on Betsy and then go and buy a ticket to Springfield. When he found Abby, he'd tell her that he was a fool, that he loved her, that he'd try harder to be what she and the children needed. He'd get down on his knees and beg her to come back, if that's what it took. After all, he was the one who'd said he believed in the sanctity of marriage.

When he opened the door, the first thing he saw was Laura's empty chair. He could picture her smile with her little nose wrinkled up as she held up her arms for him to hold her. Caleb blinked hard and let his gaze roam the cold, spotless room. He should have known Abby would leave things clean and tidy.

There was no fire in the fireplace, and with a sigh, he reached for the shovel and bucket to clean out the ashes. The first scoop revealed red-hot coals. They hadn't been gone all that long then. Late yesterday, maybe. He was reaching for some slivers of pine knot when he heard a sound behind him and bolted to his feet.

Abby stood in the doorway wearing the ratty red plaid robe and a pair of his wool socks. Wavy blond hair had escaped her braid and straggled around her pale face. There were purple smudges beneath her eyes from lack of sleep.

She was the most beautiful thing he had ever seen.

"You're still here." An absurd thing to say, but a ridiculous joy was filling his heart.

"And where else would I be?" she asked, launching herself across the room. For an instant, Caleb thought she was running into his arms. Then he realized that it was not welcome he saw in her eyes. It was fury.

Before he could more than register that fact, she flung herself at him.

"Don't you ever, *ever* send me away again!" she cried, anger bracing her voice while her small fists beat feebly at his chest, punctuating every word.

Of all the things he'd expected, this was not it. He circled her wrists with his fingers in an instinctive gesture of self-protection.

"Calm down, Abby," he said, holding her at arm's length and frowning down at her.

"I won't calm down!" she choked out, tears streaming down her cheeks as she struggled to free herself. "I won't leave, and I won't let you leave, either. If you do, I'll hunt you down."

A curious peace began to steal through him as she spoke. All the pain from the previous days evaporated like a mist burned away by the sun.

"Why would you do that, Abby?" he asked softly, gentling his hold.

She glared at him and even stomped her foot. Laughter of pure joy welled up inside him and spilled into the room. She was really something when she was mad.

"Because I love you, you big thickheaded lout! And don't you dare laugh at me! We promised before God that we would stay together until we die and I promised to love you but I didn't and I felt guilty because I was lying to God but the children loved you and then suddenly I did, too, and you promised to love me, Caleb, you promised, and you *will* love me, I'll make you love me if it's the last thing I do!"

The words came out in a rush, one long meandering statement that could be summed up in six words. He was a very lucky man.

"You'd do that?" he asked, releasing his hold on her and reaching out to push a wayward lock of hair out of her eyes. She trembled at his touch. "You'd really hunt me down?"

Suddenly all the starch went out of her and she collapsed against him, burying her face against his chest. "If I had to I would." She looked up at him with troubled eyes. "Will I have to?"

He smiled then, and knew his world was all right once again, maybe for the first time in his life. "No, Abby. You won't have to hunt me down, and you can't make me love you, because I already do."

With a little cry, she wound her arms around his neck and pressed her lips to his.

Finally, he pulled away, a smile on his lips. "I forgot to tell you that I've finally found something fun. Something I like."

Wearing a bemused expression, Abby ran a fingertip over one of his dark eyebrows. "You did? What?"

"Seeing you mad. It's fantastic."

"Seeing me..." she began heatedly, and then stopped when she realized he was teasing her. "And why do you like making me mad?"

"Because your eyes light up with fire, and...I don't know, you're just amazing when you're angry."

"You are a strange man, Caleb Gentry," she said with a shake of her head.

"But you love me."

"I do."

He kissed her again, kissed her the way he'd wanted to for weeks, the way he would kiss her for the rest of their lives.

Chapter Thirteen

One year later

"Whas that, Mama?" almost two-year-old Laura asked, pointing out the window.

Abby rose from the rocking chair near the fire, where she'd been sewing a patch on Ben's denim overalls, and went to look out the window.

"That's snow. Isn't it pretty?" she said, her heart filling with wonder at how the pristine blanket of white covered the dreary winter landscape, capping the barn roof and fence tops with white and leaving a glittering layer on the pine boughs and bare branches of the trees. It looked as if they'd been dressed up especially for Christmas, which was just two days away. The timing couldn't be better.

"See the snow, Betsy?" Abby said, pulling the little girl close and pointing to the flurry of flakes falling outside the window.

"See," one-year-old Betsy chimed in, copying her mother.

"It's pretty," Laura repeated with a smile.

"If there's enough on the ground, by morning, you and Ben can go outside and make a snowman," Abby told her.

"Snowman?"

Abby laughed and drew her other daughter close. "I'll just have to show you. And if it's deep enough to be clean, I'll make snow ice cream."

Laura's eyes, the same brilliant blue as her mother's, lit with delight. She knew all about ice cream. "Mmm. Like ice cream."

"Speaking of *mmm,* would you like me to make you some hot chocolate while we're waiting for your dad and brother to get back?"

"Hot choc'late!" Laura cried, turning to skip toward the kitchen. Betsy, who had been walking for only a month, fell in her haste to follow her sister. With a laugh, Abby picked her up, though with the size of her tummy, it was getting harder and harder to carry her for very long.

As she went about settling the little ones in their high chairs, adding a couple of logs to the fire blazing in the fireplace and making the hot cocoa, Abby couldn't help comparing this Christmas with the previous one. A year ago, she'd been in a hopeless situation, newly married to a man she didn't even know, just to provide a home for her two children and a wet nurse for his child.

This year everything had changed. She was Betsy's only mother, just as Caleb was Laura's only father.

Though Ben and Caleb would always butt heads from time to time, probably because Ben was as argumentative as his outspoken mother, they had grown as close as any father and son. Ben was teaching Caleb how to enjoy boyish pursuits, and Caleb was leading Ben toward manhood one step at a time.

Abby grew to love Caleb more every day. She could not bear to think what her life might have been like if she hadn't listened to Ben's insistence that they stay despite what Caleb had ordered her to do. She was expecting his son or daughter any time now.

The day she'd told him she was having his baby he'd turned as pale as a ghost, turned away without a word and disappeared for hours. Worried that he was unhappy about adding another child to the three they already shared, Abby found him down by the creek Ben had almost fallen into the day he went missing. Caleb was sitting on a big rock near the edge of the creek, staring at the rain-swollen water, as if he might find answers there.

She'd approached him with more trepidation than she'd felt with him for months. When he heard her footsteps, he'd looked up for just a second and then turned away. In that moment, no more than a heartbeat, she'd seen the torment in his eyes. Of all the things she'd imagined him feeling, she had not expected his reaction to be anguish.

Sudden understanding snatched away her breath.

Kneeling behind him, she slid her arms around his waist, resting her cheek against the work-hardened muscles of his back. He stiffened at her touch, and then she felt the tension holding him ease a bit. She let their breathing and their heartbeats meld into one while she struggled to find the words to ease his torment.

"It will be all right, Caleb," she said at last. "Nothing will happen to me."

"Can you promise me that, Abby?" He jerked free and stood so suddenly that she had to catch herself with her palms. Contrition replaced the despair in his eyes. He bent and helped her to her feet, but released her as soon as she was steady.

"I thought you might want us to have a child together."

His answer was to throw back his head and laugh, a bitter, hopeless sort of laugh. When he lowered his gaze to hers, his silver eyes were glazed with tears. Finally, he reached for her, pulling her so close she thought he would crush her. Instead of pulling away, she pressed even closer, willing her strength and certainty to permeate every atom of his being so that he could face his wrenching fear.

"Heaven only knows there's nothing I'd like more, but not at the risk of losing you." He whispered the words into her hair.

"You won't lose me," she said again.

"How can you be so sure?" he asked, gripping her shoulders and holding her at arm's length. "Why should God give me anything when I've done so little for Him? I try to pray, and I go to church with you, and I try to be a decent person, but I wake up every day wondering if this is the day He'll decide I've had enough happiness and take it all away."

"Oh, Caleb," she said, lifting a hand to cradle it against his stubble on his cheek. "What a terrible way to live! We're supposed to wake up each day and rejoice in it. Good or bad may come, but even if it does, He'll help us through it the same way He did when He brought us together last fall."

"God working in His mysterious ways?" he said with a dubious lift of his dark eyebrows.

She nodded and watched his eyes, imagining she saw a lessening of the desolation reflected there. Hoping to lighten his mood even more, she gave a slight lift of her shoulders. "We can't undo it, you know. And even if we could, I don't want to."

"You're happy, then?"

She spoke with no hesitation. "Happier than I can say."

"But you'll have three babies to care for."

She gave him a stern look and raised her eyebrows. "I intend for you to help, Mr. Gentry."

He shook his head. "A year ago, I had one child I didn't know what to do with. Soon I'll have four."

"But you do know what to do with them," she'd told him.

"I do?"

She'd nodded. "Give them a firm, steady hand and do it with love."

"That simple, huh?" he'd said, finally smiling a bit.

"Well, no. But it's a good starting place." She'd grasped his hands with hers and tugged gently. "Come home, Caleb," she'd urged. "It's almost dinnertime, and I left Frank and Leo watching the children."

He did smile then, and slipped his arm around her shoulders. "Now that's a scary thought."

The sound of feet stomping off snow sounded on the back porch and brought Abby's thoughts back to the present. Caleb and Ben burst through the door, accompanied by a blast of frigid air.

"I smell hot chocolate!" Ben cried.

"Me, too," Caleb said. "I hope you made enough for us men." Abby didn't fail to notice the way Ben's chest swelled with importance at being called a man.

"As a matter of fact, I did. I thought we could warm it up later."

"We didn't tarry in town. Just got our supplies and—" he winked at Ben, and swung Laura up in one arm, Betsy in the other "—did our Christmas shopping and got on our way. It's really getting cold out there. I'd guess the snow's already four or five inches deep. By the way, Mary and Bart sent their gifts, just in case they can't make it on Christmas."

Quite a speech for a man who had trouble expressing his feelings just over a year ago, Abby thought. "Surely it won't get that bad," she said, "but if it does, I suppose it's a good thing we're ready."

"Dad says you can never tell about this Arkansas weather," Ben said, taking the cup she offered him. With a soft smile, Abby handed a second cup to her husband. This time it was Caleb's turn to puff out his chest a bit.

Seeing the growing closeness between the two men in her life was as perfect an ending as Abby could want for a cold snowy day.

The mantel clock chimed 3:00 a.m. Abby had risen an hour earlier to pace the parlor floor. The evening had gone downhill ever since dinner, when her lower back had begun to ache. The baby, who'd been doing somersaults the past day or so, lay heavy inside her. Symptoms she knew well. She hoped she could hold off sending Caleb for Rachel until daylight. From what she could tell, the snow was still falling.

Without warning, a pain struck, robbing her of breath and sending her to her knees. When it passed, she clung to the wing chair and heaved herself to her feet. Like her others, this baby looked to be anxious to be born.

"Abby?"

The sound of Caleb's voice sent her gaze flying to the bedroom doorway.

"What are you doing up?" she asked as he crossed the space separating them and took her in his arms.

"I heard you cry out," he said. "The baby?"

She nodded against his chest. "I wanted to wait until morning to send you for Rachel, but my babies come fast, and something tells me this one is impatient to get here."

"Go back to bed. I'll get ready and—" His horrified voice came to a sudden halt as Abby doubled over in his arms.

When the pain passed, she grabbed double handfuls of his shirt and gave him an angry shake. "Listen to me, Caleb! You won't have *time* to go for Rachel!" she almost snarled. "I've had two very strong pains in a matter of minutes."

He paled before her eyes. "Surely you aren't implying that you want *me* to help with the delivery."

Realizing that she was not behaving in a rational manner, she released her hold on his shirt and smoothed it with gentle, deliberate hands. It was hard to act reasonable when you felt as if you were being torn apart, but there was no time to plead her case. Things had to be done, and soon.

Trying to maintain her composure, she looked up at him and said in a serene tone, "I'm trying to be sensible, Caleb, but if you do not want me to have a conniption fit, you will stop wallowing in self-pity and do what needs to be done."

Even though her demeanor was tranquil, the fury in her eyes would have left a lesser man quaking. His eyes narrowed in response. "Now is not the time for one of your tantrums, woman."

Abby remembered her mother telling her that when men encountered a situation that scared the living daylights out of them, they resorted to temper. She smiled, her own anger gone as quickly as it had come.

"I'm glad you finally realize that," she said in a voice dripping sarcasm just before she doubled over with another pain.

Caleb held her until it passed and spoke against her hair. "I adore the ground you walk on, Abby, but I don't think I can do this."

He sounded broken. Panting, she straightened and looked at him. Panic had gathered like storm clouds in his gray eyes. At least he'd gone from not being able to do it to not *thinking* he could. Everything with Caleb was baby steps, but this time there was no time to take things slow.

"I don't have any idea what to do," he told her in a shaking voice.

"The main thing to remember is that this is not about you. It's about our son or daughter. Just do what I tell you to, and everything will be fine. I have faith in you."

"I don't know why," he muttered.

"Because you've never let me down, and you never will." Caleb was done arguing. He leaned over, planted a hard kiss to her lips, swung her up into his arms and carried her to the bedroom.

With trembling hands, he stoked the stove and started water to boiling. Abby was gathering cloths and getting the bed ready. Occasionally, the sound of a stifled cry filtered through the dark house to the kitchen, and Caleb's heart tightened in a painful spasm. The soft cries resurrected memories he thought he'd forgotten. Pictures and sounds echoed through his mind. Emily's endless screams and moans. The soft soothing sound of Rachel's voice.

This wasn't about him. It wasn't about Emily, he thought as he sterilized the knife and scissors and washed his hands thoroughly. When he carried everything into the bedroom, Abby was there, propped up in bed, sweat beading her brow, a soft smile of encouragement on her face, her eyes alight with love.

"I love you, Caleb."

He gave her a sour look. "Don't try to butter me up."

Surprisingly, she laughed. "Everything will be fine,"

she said, clutching his hand as another pain snatched at her breath.

When it passed, she said, "Where is your faith? Do you truly believe God brought us through all the trials of these past months to not give us a healthy baby?"

"I don't know what He intends. You're the expert on that. All I know is that I'm worried about you, and with good reason."

"There's no time to worry anymore," she said, gritting her teeth against an onslaught of pain. "Your son or daughter is eager to make an appearance."

Within minutes of her announcement, Elijah David Gentry made his entrance into the world screaming his little lungs out. Caleb stared down into the face of his son and felt like crying himself.

"Give him to me," Abby said. She took the precious gift and saw the look of awe on her husband's face. "Isn't it amazing?" she said, pulling a flannel blanket over the baby, who calmed almost as soon as she took him.

Swaying a bit, he nodded.

"You aren't going to faint, are you?" she asked, her eyes growing wide.

The perceived slur to his manhood stiffened his spine and brought a hint of irritation to his eyes. "Is it so terrible that I was worried about you to the point of total terror?"

"Come here, Caleb."

Obediently, he sat down on the edge of the bed, and she reached up and caressed his bristly cheek. "It isn't terrible at all. Knowing how much you love me is the most wonderful thing I've ever experienced, and I thank God every day for bringing you into my life. I'm very grateful."

"I'm the one who's grateful," he told her.

And he was. He was doubly grateful to God for sending him a woman as wonderful as Abby. He knew he had much to learn about wives and children and God and that it would be a lifetime of learning. He did know that God indeed worked in mysterious ways. Without Emily's death and the problems it brought him, he might never have known real love, might never have known true forgiveness.

The past year had taught him that God truly was in control, that He had a plan and that love did indeed cover a multitude of sins. Caleb knew that if he held on to those truths, that even if there were moments of pain and doubt in the days, weeks and years ahead, life would still be full, complete and sweet.

* * * * *

COMING NEXT MONTH FROM
Love Inspired® Historical

Available December 3, 2013

MAIL-ORDER MISTLETOE BRIDES
by Jillian Hart & Janet Tronstad

When two brides journey to the Montana Territory, will they find a love—and family—amid the Rocky Mountains?

THE WIFE CAMPAIGN
The Master Matchmakers
by Regina Scott

The Earl of Danning is quite certain a house party is *not* the place he'll find his future bride. Especially not one arranged by his valet! But the lovely Ruby Hollingsford could change his mind....

A HERO FOR CHRISTMAS
Sanctuary Bay
by Jo Ann Brown

Amid the bustle of her sister's wedding plans, Jonathan Bradley's sense of humor is Lady Catherine Meriweather's only respite. But will secrets from Jonathan's past thwart any chance they have of a holiday happily ever after?

RETURN OF THE COWBOY DOCTOR
Wyoming Legacy
by Lacy Williams

Hattie Powell won't let anything hinder her dream of becoming a doctor—especially not the handsome new medical assistant. When an epidemic strikes, can they work together to save their small town?

LOOK FOR THESE AND OTHER LOVE INSPIRED BOOKS WHEREVER BOOKS ARE SOLD, INCLUDING MOST BOOKSTORES, SUPERMARKETS, DISCOUNT STORES AND DRUGSTORES.

LIHCNM1113

SPECIAL EXCERPT FROM

Love Inspired

Bygones's intrepid reporter is on the trail of the town's mysterious benefactor. Will she succeed in her mission?

Read on for a preview of
COZY CHRISTMAS
by Valerie Hansen, the conclusion to
THE HEART OF MAIN STREET *series.*

Whitney Leigh rolled her eyes. "Romance! It's getting to be an epidemic."

Because she was alone in the car, she didn't try to temper her frustration. Fortunately, this time, the editor of the *Bygones Gazette* had assigned her to write a new series about the Save Our Streets project's six-month anniversary. If he had asked her for one more fluff piece on recent engagements, she would have screamed.

Parking in front of the Cozy Cup Café, she shivered and slid out.

As a lifelong citizen of Bygones, she was supposed to have been perfect for the job of ferreting out the hidden facts concerning the town's windfall. Too bad she had failed. Instead of an exposé, she'd ended up filling her column with news of people's love lives. But she was not going to quit investigating. No, sir. Not until she'd uncovered the real facts. Especially the name of their secret benefactor.

She stepped inside the Cozy Cup.

"What can I do for you?" Josh Smith asked.

Whitney was tempted to launch right into her real reason for being there. Instead, she merely said, "Fix me something warm?"

"Like what?"

"Surprise me."

She settled herself at one of the tables. There was something unique about this place. And, truth to tell, the same went for the other new businesses on Main. Each one had filled a need and become an integral part of Bygones in a mere five or six months.

Josh Smith was a prime example. He was what she considered young, yet he had quickly won over the older generations as well as the younger ones.

He stepped out from behind the counter with a steaming cup in one hand and a taller, whipped-cream-topped tumbler in the other.

"Your choice," he said pleasantly, placing both drinks on the table and joining her as if he already knew this was not a social call.

"I see you're not too busy this afternoon. Do you have time to talk?"

"I always have time for my favorite reporter," he said.

"How many reporters do you know?"

"Hmm, let's see." A widening grin made his eyes sparkle. "One."

Will Whitney get her story and find love in the process?

Pick up COZY CHRISTMAS to find out.
Available December 2013
wherever Love Inspired® Books are sold.

LIEXP1113

Love Inspired